Layla's Gale

Nicole Pouchet

Layla's Gale
A Paranormal Romance

Book 2 of the Elemental Myths Series

by Nicole Pouchet

Art Direction and Cover Design: Ann Alger

Editing: The Editor Fairy

Advance Praise

Publishers Weekly says Nicole Pouchet "provides an intriguing blend of the earthly and supernatural worlds with emotional telepathy, reincarnation, superhero-like powers, and explosive carnal energy... Lively, flirtatious characters make this an appealing romance."

To Matt

Prologue

1532, "Lost City of the Incas," Machu Picchu

Ceiba hurried to complete the ritual before the demons fighting among the Spanish outsiders could find her or the secret location. Heart hammering inside her blood-spattered vest, she grabbed vials of herbs off the shelves, dumping their contents onto the only bare table in the cavern temple. Glass bottles, full of potions she had painstakingly mixed weeks ago, smashed onto the floor in her haste. A pang shuddered through her at the thought that no one would be there to put the sacred room back in order. Goddesses and gods willing, she would complete her task and no one would ever see this place again.

She fought long with her sword and spells, but it was now clear the ultimate plan did not include her civilization's survival. When she watched the first of her children fall across the field, she knew all was lost. Each of them needed to be alive and properly mated in order for her to complete her destiny.

It was the first time in all of existence when all nine souls, including her own, resided together in one time and one place. Together, they managed to achieve feats only previously imagined. Now, the mangled bodies of her daughters and sons-in-law lay on slabs of earth at each right angle of the temple. Ceiba tried not to look at them as she worked. There was no time to smooth their hair or straighten a fold as she'd done previously in life. Now she must save their souls. She tossed her silver-streaked braid over her shoulder and pounded at the herbs, her measurements calculated only by practiced eye and feel.

Shouts rang from above. Ceiba's kinsmen were losing this final war. Her brew complete, she closed her eyes, pressed the palms of her hands together at her heart, and knelt.

"Goddesses and gods of Earth," she prayed aloud. "Pachamama, I beseech you to protect your guardians and cardinals." Raising her arms over her head, she clasped her hands together and stood up in one fluid motion. "I come to you as your mortal vessel. Take their souls and cloak them in their next lives, so they might have a chance to learn and grow before being found again. Care for them as I could not. Protect them as I did not. Love them as I dared not." Her melodic voice reverberated throughout the underground temple's stone walls, calling forth wind to whip scrolls into the air.

Sounds of death grew louder. Clangs of metal swords on shields rang closer. Ceiba recognized individual cries of agony from cousins and friends. She thanked the heavens her granddaughters had been spirited away with the rest of the city's children as soon as the fighting began.

Tears streaking down battle-worn cheeks, she strode to each body and whispered the last incantation before smearing each forehead with the herbal concoction. "Free from sight, free from harm, full of light, full of charm."

Her magic was powerful. Not only would the souls of her children be safe, but even the sounds of war quieted outside as those spirits became protected as well. She managed to cloak the entire city with her spell.

With a final caress of the soft brown curls of her first-born daughter, Ceiba turned away from her charges. She retrieved her jewel-encrusted sword from where it was discarded by the underground temple's sole entrance, and hacked at the stone wall, which formed the doorway.

"Goddess, give me strength," she whispered. The Incan woman's sword fell mightily as the opening collapsed on her, sealing in the nine warriors and all of their sacred knowledge.

Chapter One

Spring 2014, Washington, D.C.

His big, calloused hand wrapped around her fingers, pulling her into the tall grasses. The sensation of his lips on the nape of her neck as he swung her around to face him drove out all thoughts of the work awaiting them. When she grasped his back, he wasted no time hiking up her long skirts before lowering her onto the clover-covered ground.

His full lips smiling at her, the sharpness of his jaw was offset by the softness in his eyes. She felt his heart reaching out to her as plainly as his thickness poised at her entrance below. Her heart answered with a warm, welcoming response as he nipped at her earlobe and pushed inside her, inch by maddening inch. His deep chuckle sounded in her ear as she thrust her hips forward to close the final distance between them. She kissed his shoulder, caught in the headiness of their lovemaking.

Her senses blossomed as his fingers reached down to her bottom, urging her body to meet each forceful exertion. She let her hands wander down his back, across the thick, bunching muscles as he plunged into her, a steady sensation growing in her center. Nonsensical mutterings of unbridled rapture escaped her mouth when she came.

Still riding the crest of bliss, she opened her eyes to find sandy brown hair curled over a suntanned chest of the same golden hue. She gasped when he coaxed her back over the edge. Pleasure inundated her brain.

She stared into glowing, green eyes.

"Kiss me."

The alarm replied.

Layla woke up with a start and found herself clutching her pillow while coming down from one of her best orgasms of recent memory. She was alone. But she'd die happy if every night she spent alone was followed by a wake-up like that. After a minute of stretching, she hopped out of bed, like one of those psychopathic morning people she habitually hated, ready to take on the day.

Her audition last week with Sylph Theater Company had gone rather well. Today, she dared hope for the lead role during her call-back audition. There was fierce competition for good theater roles in Washington, D.C., and not enough professional, paid opportunities outside of New York City. The actress wasn't completely sure her acting chops measured up.

She pulled her curly, dark brown tresses into a messy bun at the nape of her neck. Her hair was nearly impossible to tame so she learned early in life to let it go naturally. It worked for her in a bohemian-chic kind of way.

Her charcoal gray pants-suit was fresh from the cleaners. Days ago, she made sure to wash and iron the matching blouse, but couldn't find it anywhere now. Running around the apartment in her bra and slacks, she spotted Anne sitting at the glass kitchen table, eating Cheerios.

Anne sat with wire-rimmed glasses perched on her nose, wearing Victoria's Secret's latest flannel pajama ensemble while thumbing the BlackBerry in her hand.

"Do you know where my light green blouse is?" Layla asked.

"Yeah, I wore it yesterday," Anne mumbled around a mouthful.

"You did?" Layla resisted the urge to scream—or cry. This was included as part of the arrangement for living rent-free at her best friend's place. Anne could borrow whatever she wanted, whenever she wanted. "Well, where is it?"

"I took it to the cleaners for you. Thought I'd be nice. Where are you off to?"

It just figured. What can go wrong will go wrong. "I have a call-back audition for the play."

Anne responded with a sleepy, blank face.

"The paying one," Layla reminded her. "Remember? It's the story about Machu Picchu, circa 1500s. It's kind of interesting, though. This Incan woman in her forties has… are you listening?"

"Yes, absolutely," Anne replied while typing a message.

"I remember. It's a play about ruins and destiny and other cheesy stuff. Sorry, sweetie. I've got to run or I'll be late." She stood up to put her empty bowl into the sink. "Good luck!" she called out before dashing off to her bedroom.

The play *was* kind of cheesy, but it was the Syfy type of cheese that Layla loved. And landing the main role would be a good line on her résumé, if she were talented enough to get it. It might even pay a few bills.

She put her suit jacket on over her bra – sans blouse – and checked the mirror. Decent enough. She jumped up and down a few times as a test; the boobs stayed in place. More importantly, if she wasted any time ironing one of the wrinkled blouses in her closet, she would be late. Although displaying a little more cleavage than usual, this would have to do. Throwing the audition script into a messenger bag, she grabbed a light jacket to ward off the early spring chill before heading out of the apartment.

Walking to the Metro, she passed rows of thin townhouses. Historic old homes, sporting fresh coats of paint, also lined the street, while sturdy cars slowly made their way through rush-hour traffic. Executives, politicians, children, and parents flooded the sidewalks.

"Hola chica, chica!" A car horn tooted as a young guy in an oversized sweatshirt leaned out toward her.

"Hola chico!" Pulling her five-foot-two frame as tall as she could, Layla tossed back a friendly greeting and carried on. She hoped her mother's Puerto Rican heritage shined through in her own darker skin and curly hair, considering the role for which she auditioned. Then again, maybe her ample chest drew the young guys' attention, which, at the moment, was peeking out of her suit blazer.

Hopefully, her hasty clothing choice wouldn't scream "whore for the taking" to the director of the play. It was too late to turn back and change now.

A glance in the side mirror of a parallel-parked car reassured her she looked professional. Maybe the subtle hint of sex could work to her advantage. Either way, Layla was fully ready for her monologue, after going to great pains to nail the part. The director had already displayed his appreciation of her ability. Instead of scribbling away on a notepad, or shuffling through other actors' headshots, he actually paid attention when she performed during the first audition. She couldn't see his expression because of the lighting in the theater, but his silhouette was clearly leaning forward. That was a good sign. Now, she would just have to get him past the cute, round face that made her appear younger than her twenty-eight years, and convince him she could play the role of a forty-year-old woman.

She reviewed her lines again during the Metro trip, although the words on the script kept blurring into scenes from her nocturnal fantasy. Closing her eyes, she imagined her dream guy moving over her. Sandy tufts covering his chest; his hard, little nipples pressed against her breasts as he rocked them back and forth… Green eyes staring into hers. Were they glowing?

"Dupont Circle! This is Dupont Circle!" The scratchy, intrusive voice of the Metro conductor jerked Layla instantly out of her fantasy. Grabbing her bag, she jumped off the train just as the doors began to close.

* * *

"… and as foretold, so shall we perish!" Layla let the final tear roll down her face before looking toward the shadowy figure of the director in the dark audience. She was expecting a lot more people to be present. Stage manager? Assistant? Only the director was out there. Perhaps it was a good thing they were missing. No one to distract him. His silhouette perched on the edge of the seat, again paying close attention to her performance.

"Well done," the director called out as he approached the stage. "Thank you, Ms. Cohen. Let's have a chat." He crossed the small, black-box theater as Layla peered into the spotlights.

The theater was a wonderful space, one in which she ached to work. All of the walls, the floor, and rehearsal blocks were painted black. A traditional design, it was completely blank so that any set could easily be created onto it. The crimson, plush bleachers were mobile; the stage sunken in the center of the room; while the acoustics created by the high ceiling made Layla's voice sing throughout the room with little effort on her part. She felt quite at home in Sylph Theater already. "Thank you. Mr. Tawanti," she replied as he stepped into the spotlight. "Call me L-Layla." She stumbled over her own name when she noticed his sharp green eyes.

"All right, Layla," he replied. "As long as you call me Sebastian."

What. The. Hell? He was the man of her dreams – literally. His honey-colored skin, full nose, high cheekbones, and kissable lips filled in the forgotten details of the face looming over her in her fantasy. How could this happen? Maybe she saw a picture of him online when she was researching the theater company. Yes, that must be it. But no. She specifically remembered her disappointment that there were no images of him available. She had absolutely never seen this man before. He should *not* be prancing around naked in her dreams. What kind of messed-up subconscious did she have? How could it even be possible for her to dream of doing the carnal cuddle with a real person whom she'd never met?

And, oh, but the reality was even better than the dream! Sebastian was one of those drop-dead beautiful men. With perfect features, he looked like the masterpiece of an ancient artist, carved in some faraway land. His exquisite flawlessness was further set off by a broad, muscular body, not fully concealed under the form-fitted, white t-shirt and khaki pants he wore. The pecs on his chest were distinctly outlined under his shirt. Taut thigh muscles appeared when he moved closer to her. The man was almost sin incarnate. No wonder her over-active brain greedily scooped him up as dream fodder even before she ever saw him.

Dammit all! Leave it to her to have sex dreams about her delicious, potential boss. She cursed her skin as a furious blush crept into her cheeks. Sebastian was pulling a rehearsal bench over to where she stood.

She plastered a smile on her face. She needed this part. As she stepped over to the bench, she thought his eyes fell to her cleavage. *Well, I guess that was bound to happen,* she thought. She never anticipated having her own physical reaction to the director as well, though. Another look at him caught his eyes boring into hers again. Maybe she only imagined his glance.

"So, Sebastian," Layla choked out, trying to forget the feel of his dream hands on her bottom. "What's the next step? How many other women did you call back?"

"There's just one other actress. She already had her call-back yesterday. Have you gotten a chance to read the full play?"

"Yes, it's an interesting take on Machu Picchu and the fall of the Incan Empire. But, there's so much detail regarding the Incan culture. You wrote this, right?"

"I did."

"Where did you learn so much about the Incan people? It must have taken years to find all the material in this play. Do you have a degree in anthropology or history?"

Sebastian offered her a radiant smile. "My, you're full of questions. Most actors just want to know when rehearsals start."

"Yeah, sorry. I've been interested in Incan culture for a while, but I've never found so much research from one source. I'm assuming the play is fiction?"

"I wouldn't exactly call it fiction." He gave her another heart-stopping smile, and she stifled a gasp. The man was gorgeous. "I have to admit I haven't done much actual research and I have no degrees – at least not in history or anthropology. It's not historically accurate. The whole thing is based on stories my mother used to tell us about her family. She's fully Incan, born in what is now Peru."

So that was the source of his dark skin, green eyes, and curly hair. Gorgeous, and the man was magnetic as well. The side of his leg slightly brushed against hers while he spoke and was still resting there. She wondered if he could feel the sparks stemming from the tiny contact.

"That's marvelous," Layla replied, finding herself staring at him. "How wonderful to have so much family history passed through the generations. You say it's not factually accurate. Does that mean you don't believe any of it?"

"Well, it's a story about spells, cloaking souls, and guardians saving the world. The world would be in a lot of trouble if it depended on my crazy family to save it." His leg rubbed against hers as he laughed.

She looked down at the leg, embracing its warmth, which sent heat waves straight up her thigh and directly into her center. The man was like a turbine of sexual energy. He ran his hand through his hair, fixing the curly lock that dropped onto his forehead.

"I'm sure the world would be fine." Biting her bottom lip, Layla forced herself to focus on his words.

"Maybe. Well, I know I've already made up my mind. You'll be terrific as Huayra. She plays a pivotal role in the story; and it's a dynamic part if done correctly."

"That's great! Thank you! *Way-ra*. I was wondering how to pronounce her name." She smiled.

"Yep, Huayra. Rhymes with Layla. I know you were hoping for the lead, but my producers managed to get Allora Delaney for that."

Her jaw dropped open. "Allora? *Delaney*?" Allora Delaney was an icon men slobbered over and women strove to emulate. Back in high school, Layla cut her hair into the actress' signature bob, along with every other girl in her class. She still had posters of the actress stored away in boxes from college when she studied Allora's character acting methods. "Wow!"

"It was unexpected, but she chose not to do the remake of Casablanca. She wants to get into theater, and we're absolutely thrilled to have her."

"I'll say! You really got Allora Delaney? That's wonderful!" A broad smile took over Layla's face.

"Yes." Sebastian lifted an eyebrow. "It *is* wonderful. I'm glad you're not upset."

"Upset? No, she's an amazing actress." She clasped her hands together, nearly bouncing on the bench.

"I agree. But, y'know, so many actresses would become bitter if their roles were suddenly given to someone else, no matter how appropriate the other person." He watched her excitement grow. "Yeah, you're going to be a great addition to my theater group."

"I get to work with Allora Delaney! Oh my God! Thank you so much." She reached over and embraced him in a heartfelt hug.

Once her arms were wrapped around his back, the images from last night's dream surged into her mind. She should probably let go and leave the theater while she still had a smidgen of dignity. But Sebastian seemed in no rush to stop the hug either. He held her just as tightly as she embraced him.

With her breasts pressed against his firm chest, Layla reached up to touch one of his sandy curls. His hand fell onto the small of her back, pulling her closer. His big, green eyes softened as he moistened his lips. Her eyelids fluttered closed.

And then... nothing.

Opening her eyes, she found Sebastian recoiling from her, his eyes wide in shock.

"Um," she started.

"Layla, I'm so sorry. That was awful!" Backing away a bit, his hands went up, along with his nose, as if he'd just sniffed a rat's ass.

"Awful? Oh." She looked down, refusing to meet his gaze. It would have been no less startling than if he'd just slapped her. Was he disgusted?

"No, that's not what I mean. Layla, I'm sorry that—whatever that was—happened. I don't know why I..." He stood and moved across the stage, putting more distance between them. His voice became firmer as the space between them got wider. "It can't happen again."

"Right, of course," she managed with a smile. Picking up her messenger bag, Layla walked out of the perfect, black-box theater, using the back door. What a mess. She couldn't believe how her working environment could already have its own drama even before she had the job a full hour! One thing was certain: her overactive imagination would not get the best of her again. It was purely business with her new boss from now on.

Chapter Two

Sebastian half-listened to the voice on the other end of his Bluetooth headset. He grasped the stem of the wineglass in one hand while shuffling pages of his script with the other. Early for a lunch meeting with Philip, the show's producer, he sat alone in one of D.C.'s biggest tourist traps, Old Ebbit Grill.

The spot was one of a chain of trendy restaurants. Located within steps of the White House, it was frequently filled with camera-toting, shorts-wearing, vacationing families. More than one wife/mother stared at Sebastian. In his impeccably tailored suit, he resembled a snarky, young politician. It wasn't the look he normally went for, but these producer types showed him more respect when he dressed the role of a big-shot theater director. They also appreciated the indulgence of a sprawling, over-priced restaurant like Old Ebbit Grill. He would have been much happier wearing jeans at one of the Latin dive eateries in his own neighborhood.

His new actress seemed as laid back as he was. Instead of complaining that she didn't get the lead role, Layla instantly grasped the advantages of placing the more famous actress in the production. Even better, the young actress' timing was spot-on, her movements graceful, and her ready command of the material superior to any of the others he auditioned. The foundations for a great working relationship were undeniably there.

Why did I go and ruin it? That impromptu hug had morphed from innocent to sexual so quickly, he didn't even realize it was happening. He knew he should have explained his abrupt rejection of her embrace, but he couldn't trust himself not to grab her again if she seemed the least bit willing.

The old adage, "Actors are cattle" always served him well after his graduation, and ever since he left New York University's theater program six years ago to direct. He tried to treat actors with the same affection he showered on the cat he temporarily inherited when his ex moved out two years ago. Humor them, nurture their spirits, and make sure they had the basic necessities. But, just as he regarded the cat, he resisted the urge to get emotionally attached.

Damn. His visceral reaction to the woman annoyed Sebastian. Sure, she was a pretty package with a great intellect to boot, but plenty of actresses could boast those characteristics. Allora Delaney was one. He met the bonafide movie star yesterday morning, yet didn't find it the least bit challenging to keep his cool around the woman who once graced the covers of *Vanity Fair*, *People*, *Cosmopolitan*, and *Vogue* in the same month. Those appearances were fifteen years ago, but Allora was still stunningly beautiful, and a woman no man in his right mind would kick out of bed.

Allora gave Sebastian a look that might have had less controlled men groveling at her feet. But he managed to keep their interaction professional. And then, just hours later, he pounced on Layla! He shook his head, remembering the feel of her in his arms.

Maybe if he hadn't been bombarded with her emotions, he could have had a chance. For the past couple of days—actually, since auditions started—he'd been experiencing… weird empathetic symptoms. He called them "episodes" when he could swear he felt the emotions of people around him. It was usually just a whiff, almost like a happy cologne or impatient perfume. He tried to convince himself he was imagining it. But this morning, Sebastian nearly drowned in Layla's *eau de lust*. Her passion instantly fueled his attraction toward her and he couldn't stop himself from pulling her closer. Maybe he should see a doctor…

"Are you listening to me?" the voice trilled into his ear.

"Yes, Mom," Sebastian answered, his ardor fading at the urgency of his mother's voice. He forgot he was right in the middle of their weekly chat. "I just missed that last part. The phone must have cut out. Would you repeat that, please?"

"I said, you have no idea what you are doing with that play!"

"What do you mean? This is the fifteenth play I've directed. I know what I'm doing."

"*Ch'inyay!* You have not been listening to me," she

admonished in her lilting, Peruvian accent. "It is not a question of whether or not you are capable of directing the play, dear. It is the choice you have made to direct it at all. I wish you had told me what you were planning."

"I thought you'd be happy, Mom. You *should* be happy. You're the one who complains that Americans know nothing about real Incan culture. The Incan Empire is more than a crumbling building, right?" Sebastian took a sip of his pinot noir as his mother sighed her response. It signaled the beginning of a long lecture, but fortunately, Sebastian spotted Philip sauntering over to the table.

"Listen, I've got to run now," he said before his mother could begin.

"We will continue this conversation, Sebastian. This play—"

"Yes, ma'am," he interrupted. "Goodbye now." He pushed a button on the iPhone resting on the table, pulled off his earpiece, and flashed a smile. Philip was not alone. A younger version of the producer trailed him, even wearing the same Armani suit.

"Hi, Philip. Good to see you." Sebastian rose from his seat to shake the man's hand.

"Sebastian." The older black man gestured for his companion to step in front of him. "This is Alex, my nephew. I thought it would be good if you two met today."

The three men sat at the table and a waitress hurried over, carrying an extra set of silverware and a cloth napkin. Sebastian watched Alex straining to catch a look down the woman's shirt. Concealing his disdain with a proper, emotionless expression, he began the theatrical politics dance. Maybe the snarky appearance he adopted for this meeting wasn't far off.

"Nice to meet you, Alex. Do you live in the area, or are you just visiting? Y'know, I must say, you look just like your uncle."

Alex smiled and rubbed a hand against his kinky, dyed-blond hair. "Well, it's not the hair, so it must be the suit," he replied. "We did a little shopping over the weekend and managed to both wear our new suits today. Trust me. We don't usually walk around looking like this."

All three men laughed.

"To answer your question," Philip broke in, "Alex is visiting. That's also why I wanted to chat with you today."

"Oh?"

The waitress came back and took their orders. Sebastian didn't like the gleam that flared in Alex's eyes as he watched her move. Her subsequent discomfort permeated the air, and she stood as far away from Alex as the tight surroundings allowed.

"Alex just graduated from NYU's film school. That's your alma mater, isn't it?"

"It is."

Philip leaned back in his chair. "I may as well spit it out. I never was one to beat around the bush. Alex is here to play the part of Kon in your play."

"Oh?" Sebastian held onto his smile as a twitch began in his left eye.

"I think he has talent and would do well as Kon. You just have to see him perform and I'm sure you'll agree." Philip leaned forward, watching Sebastian's reaction. As though their discussion had nothing to do with him, Alex picked up the bread basket and selected a small piece of pumpernickel.

"You've been absolutely wonderful financing this production. It's become huge, bigger than I ever dreamed—" Sebastian started.

"Yes, I *am* financing it." Philip opened his mouth in a toothy grin.

"—and to get Allora Delaney on the project is a boon. It was sudden, but it's great. As for Kon, I've already cast that part."

"Yeah, I saw the guy." Philip waved a hand. "He was good, but he's no Kon. Tell you what. I'm not trying to throw my weight around. It's your play. You know what's best. Just audition Alex for the part. You may be surprised by how good he is."

Sebastian choked down another sip of his wine. "Okay, then. He can audition tomorrow."

He left New York City so he wouldn't have to put up with this kind of tampering. He'd been fine producing his own shows in D.C. for the last three years. But the lure of fame and wealth enticed him to accept Philip's involvement when the prominent producer became interested in his play early on. Philip offered him the chance to focus entirely on directing for once - no worries about getting the set, lighting, stage management, and everything else required for a quality show. Philip's production company would handle those loose ends. It was an artistic freedom Sebastian couldn't refuse.

The producer also supplied public relations on a scale that Sebastian hadn't previously even considered. The city was already buzzing with talk of his new theatrical production about the Incan Empire.

Furthermore, Philip's name drew major talent. The casting of Allora was truly a most welcome surprise. There was no doubt the producer was excellent at his job. But *this*? Being forced to cast his nephew was a major slight. Alex clearly wasn't much if he had to rely on nepotism and take advantage of a situation like this.

Then again, Sebastian couldn't feel anything from Alex. Weird as it was, he was getting used to sensing some traces of emotion from those around him. Philip was confident and amused. The waitress didn't trust any of them. And the man at the next table was more attracted to him than to his wife. Yet, there was nothing coming from Alex. Odd. Sebastian popped his head back to the table where the conversation continued without him. He stared at the young man.

"…could bang her," Alex finished.

"What was that?" Sebastian asked.

"Allora, man," Alex explained. "Even for an old broad, she's hot enough to bang, don't you think?"

Sebastian watched the young man puff up his chest in an attempt to appear more manly and older than his few years. Immaturity was not a quality he valued in his theater troupe. Sexist comments were even less welcome.

"Alex," he began. "You need to start thinking of and speaking about Allora with the deference you would show your own mother. Beautiful as she is, that's the relationship you two have in my play."

"This is true," Philip chided his nephew with a smile. "You'll be cozied up to her bosom as her bouncing baby boy."

"And a lovely bosom it is." Alex laughed.

Sebastian tamped down a glare and changed the subject. "Philip, I was grabbing a cup of tea this morning when I overheard talk of Allora and my play. She just signed yesterday. Boy, your PR team is fast."

"They're a machine, aren't they? Press releases, calls to editors, whispers to the hippest bloggers. Publicity wins the war, my young director. Even if this show stinks, we're filling the house every night."

Sebastian clenched his hands under the table. "The show will not stink."

"Yes, yes, I've got plenty of faith in you, Sebastian. Just a joke, kid. So, anyway, is that Layla Cohen actress any good?"

"Yes." Sebastian flexed his fingers. "Yeah, I just cast her as Huayra."

"Opposite Alex, right?"

"Yes, if Alex's audition goes well enough."

"So, there you go, Alex." Philip smirked. "You can have your love scenes with Layla. Stare at her and leave Mommy Allora alone."

"Is Layla hot?" Alex asked, his eyes wide and imploring as he leaned forward in his seat. Sebastian wanted to punch him right on his Clearasil-treated cheek.

"Her headshots were gorgeous," Philip answered. "Big brown eyes, dark curly hair, an olive-like complexion that will work well enough for this role. Nice little body too, by the looks of—"

"That's enough." Sebastian spoke quietly, but the hint of veiled fury in his voice caused the other two men's smiles to instantly vanish. They looked at him as if seeing him for the first time.

He held their gazes. It was a silent pissing contest he knew he was careless for starting. Philip looked away first, suddenly very interested in arranging the avocado on his salad. Sebastian was surprised to find himself staring into Alex's eyes. Alex cocked his head and allowed the corners of his mouth to turn up ever so slightly. Sebastian blinked. As if nothing happened, Alex looked down and dipped his spoon into his soup, dribbling a bit onto his starched, gray shirt as he brought the utensil to his mouth. The contest was over, but Sebastian didn't know who won.

"You've got to lighten up." The older man sipped his martini. "Actors are cattle, right? You said that during our first *budget* meeting."

Sebastian did not miss the reminder that the producer had invested a huge amount of money into his theater production. Philip was the boss for the duration of this play. "Yes, you're right. I did say that. But I never said to disrespect the cattle." He plastered the political smile back on his face to soften his comment.

"Well, I've got to have some passion for Layla if she's my wife in this play, right?" Alex shrugged his shoulders as he looked back and forth between his uncle and Sebastian. "I mean, I'll be kissing her and everything."

Wishing he could get one of those emotional reads, he tried to gauge the young actor's expression. The kid seemed earnest and genuine at the moment, no innuendo or knowing smirks. "Maybe. I'll see you in auditions tomorrow. Ten o'clock sharp." Sebastian grudgingly turned to the producer. "Listen, Philip. Thanks for lunch. I've really got to run." He pushed his chair away from the table and stood.

"So soon?"

"Yeah, sorry, but I've got a bit of a family issue to handle."

"It was nice meeting you." Alex offered his hand. The two shook cordially and made eye contact. Again, Sebastian thought he saw a glimmer of something in Alex. But it disappeared as Alex smiled the innocent grin of a kid fresh out of college. "I'll see you in the morning. You won't be disappointed with my performance."

"I'm sure you'll be great. Nice meeting you, too. Bye, Philip." Turning, Sebastian nearly trotted out of the restaurant. This financial arrangement was becoming harder to handle. Philip's production company was accomplishing great feats for the play, but at what cost? Sebastian didn't like the enormous concession he'd have to make by casting Alex in a major role. And he dreaded having to watch - and direct - that guy in the proper groping of Layla.

Chapter Three

Layla's palms sweated and she resisted the urge to wipe them onto her skirt. The white, heavy silk would probably show the stain and announce to everyone she was in awe of her co-stars. Besides, it was Anne's skirt and she hadn't asked to borrow it.

"…and Allora, this is Layla Cohen. She's playing your daughter, Huayra. Layla, meet Allora," Sebastian concluded. Fourteen more actors and a stage manager milled about the small theater. The atmosphere had a new chaotic infusion that Layla didn't feel the week before, during her final audition. It only served to ratchet up her anxiety.

Attempting to dry her hands, she waved them inconspicuously behind her back. It was no use. She took the hand Allora held out and returned her firm shake. Forcing herself to look the woman in her eyes, she bit back the nervous laughter threatening to escape. A new reason to panic presented itself. Allora Delaney was breathtaking. With her chestnut hair drawn into a messy ponytail - the kind that takes a professional an hour to achieve - she was more beautiful in person than on the screen. Layla couldn't detect a single pore in her skin. No one would believe Layla was pretty enough to be her daughter.

"What is the matter, darling?" She had a beautiful Peruvian accent, too. Allora clasped Layla's hand with both of her own. "We have only just met, so I know I could not have put my foot in my mouth already."

"No!" She felt her face burning with embarrassment. "Of course not. You're perfect. I can't—" She hesitated before making a bigger spectacle of herself. Half the cast was watching her fawn over the superstar.

"Can't what?"

"I, um, I can't believe I get to work with you. This is such an honor." Squaring her shoulders, she looked up into the taller woman's eyes and beamed her best can-do smile. If she didn't believe she belonged on the stage with Allora Delaney, no one else would either.

"Ha! Let's see if you still think it's an honor when I can't remember stage-left from stage-right and bump into you for the millionth time."

"Oh, right. This is your first play, isn't it? A new medium?" That was better. She was relating to her as a fellow professional. Should she take her hand out of Allora's grasp?

"Yes, my first one since high school. And that was a long, long time ago." Allora released her hand and patted her on the back. "Can I count on you to keep me out of trouble?"

"That's my job," Sebastian winked as he interrupted. He steered Allora away and over to a long table in the center of the stage. "Okay, people, today is what I like to call the 'meet and greet' rehearsal. Everyone puts a face to the cast name, we understand the arc of the play, and we do a quick table-read of the script..."

Layla's mind wandered as he rattled on about the rehearsal procedure. His long explanation of the theatrical process was only for Allora's benefit and he didn't bother addressing anyone else as he spoke. Which of the two women did he wink at earlier? Maybe he already had something going with Allora. That was reasonable; they'd make a beautiful couple. And that was all the more incentive to purge those naughty dreams out of her head. Sebastian didn't look at her once the whole day.

As she watched his lips move, she felt the tickle of someone else's gaze lingering on her. Allora caught her staring at Sebastian. Her head cocked to one side and cat-like hazel eyes focused, Allora appeared all-knowing. And once more, a blush furiously claimed Layla's face. The older woman smiled before returning her attention to the director. Layla was emotionally naked, her glass face revealing her thoughts. It was a gift in acting, but a curse in normal life. She had to get herself under control. *Think baseball.* Hey, it worked for men in sensitive situations.

"On to the read-through," Sebastian continued. "I don't expect a Tony-award-winning performance, but I'd like to hear a little more than rote words from the page, if you get my drift. Please sit with your 'mate,' if the play calls for you to have one, so I can get a feel for the chemistry." He moved to have more of a quiet chat with

Allora as the rest of the actors meandered to the long table in the center of the stage.

"A little intimidating, isn't it?" A young black actor with bleached blond hair appeared behind her. "I'm Alex."

"Yeah, I remember. I'm Layla. I was just thinking the same thing."

"Oh? Did your uncle get you an audition, too?"

"No…" She wrinkled her forehead in response.

"Well, then, you don't have half as much to prove as I do."

"You must have done well in the audition to actually get the part, right?"

"Exactly. And so did you."

Layla smiled. "Well said. Am I that obvious?"

"The wide-eyed, doe-in-the-headlights look kind of gives you away. But, that's okay. It's cute on you." Alex gave her a boyish grin and pulled out a chair for her before settling his long, lean body into the chair beside her.

"Ha! Hitting on me already?"

"We're supposed to be madly in love for this play. It can't hurt to get the chemistry going right away."

"Just for the play, right?"

"For the play. It's our duty. Director's orders, even."

She couldn't help but laugh. Her new acting partner didn't help his cause by bringing up Sebastian, though. The director was a chiseled work of art, while Alex reminded her of the fraternity boys from college. Being overly aware that he was attractive and stylish, his confidence and arrogance were through the roof. Come to think of it, he didn't look much older than a college guy. She asked his age.

"I'm young enough to show you a fun time, and old enough that you don't have to be embarrassed."

She raised an eyebrow.

"Twenty-four. You can't be more than thirty, right?"

"Ouch! Way to insult a girl. I'm twenty-eight. Thirty? Do I look thirty?" Ignoring the fact that she'd been praying to appear forty just a week ago, Layla stuck out her bottom lip in a pout. The panicked expression on Alex's face was worth the effort.

She chuckled. "Relax, I'm kidding. I'll take that as a compliment."

"Good." Smiling, he whispered the last word as the other actors finished mingling and settled into their seats, to begin the read-through.

Layla took in all of her co-stars at the table. Lost in her stupor over Allora, she didn't notice everyone else was a celebrity as well. Since she'd been called back for the lead role, she assumed the play was only one or two steps above her usual community theater gigs. This play was a bigger deal than she thought. Three Hollywood starlets were playing her sisters. One was currently the leading star on a television hospital drama. Another had been on a soap opera since childhood. And the third was a model/actress (as opposed to Layla's waitress/actress title). All three wore oversized sunglasses perched in their hair. Layla missed that memo.

The men were just as well known. Everyone had recognizable prior roles —or a powerful uncle, in Alex's case. Starlets or not, the actors brought the play's words to life. Voices filled the empty theater, and Layla's pulse quickened with the thrill of starting a new project.

Sneaking a glance at the head of the table, she found herself locked in Sebastian's green gaze. Eerily reminiscent of her dream, the director licked his lips, then lowered his lashes back to his script. Really? Was that a business-like thing to do? Her traitorous tummy flip-flopped at the memory of their embrace. He was deliberately teasing her! Her temper and indignation flared until Sebastian reached down into a bag at his feet and pulled out a tube of ChapStick.

She almost laughed out loud. *Get it together, girl.* No more ogling the director. He could bonk the superstar on the table if it pleased him. Her career was better served if she developed chemistry with the fraternity boy sitting next to her.

Their scene began and Layla was pulled into the part. Alex reached forward to touch her knee during some of the emotional moments. Establishing eye contact, she sensed he'd be a good acting partner. He spoke his lines with depth and sincerity. Even though his uncle had gotten him the audition, he was clearly talented.

"Great job, everyone!" Rolling his script in his hands, Sebastian looked down the table. "I hope you're all as excited to work on this as I am. Next rehearsal is tomorrow, ten o'clock sharp. Please see Jennifer with any questions." He pointed to the stage manager in an attempt to deflect inquiries. It didn't work. Most of the actors rushed out of their seats to his side.

Allora's voice rang out above the others. "Sebastian, darling, I do have a few questions about my character's motivation at the beginning. What tasks will her children be assigned to do exactly?"

Sebastian smiled at the rest of the cast as he took Allora aside. Layla couldn't hear the answer. It was just as well. He'd probably think she had motives that were irrelevant to the play if she asked for the private time she usually begged of her directors. This would be an interesting rehearsal period if she couldn't get her wandering mind under control.

"Wait up!" Alex called out as she headed toward the door. "We had some chemistry there. Don't you think?" He flashed a million-watt smile.

"Sure, Alex." Layla laughed and stopped in the doorway. Looking up, she noticed a dimple in his left cheek.

"We should get together this week. Not like that—" Alex raised his hands before she could object. "I really want to nail this part and I think it would be helpful to rehearse a bit together. Would you mind?"

If she couldn't get help from her director, she surely couldn't afford to turn down extra rehearsal time. "That sounds great."

"Cool, it's a date. I'll call you tomorrow."

"No, it's not a—"

"Bye, Layla." Alex bent down and kissed her cheek before sailing out of the theater. She glanced back in time to see Sebastian looking at her over Allora's shoulder. He shot an angry glare their way before smiling back at his main star. It happened so quickly, she wondered if she imagined it.

* * *

"No, Cocha, you must mix in the borreria first." Layla placed the delicate white flowers of the plant aside as she crushed its tiny leaves in her earthen bowl. The bangles on her strong, brown wrist echoed in the cavern.

"But why does the order matter?" Her younger sister scrunched up her face as she prepared to rebel.

"Because this is the way, Cocha! Careful! These mixtures can be dangerous if you do not respect them." Layla stood back, grabbing for the thirteen-year-old girl before her bushy eyebrows could be singed off yet again.

A part of Layla's mind wondered how she was so sure of the borreria's power. She was an actress. No, in this dream she was the high priestess of the goddess of air. And as priestess, she had access to this cavern, a sacred temple guarding her family's accumulated knowledge. It was a splendor to behold, a perfect square with intricate paintings in reds and golds on most of the surfaces.

One of the four walls held a massive bookcase filled with books on herbal medicines, incantations, the history of her people, and the names of stars. Another wall served as a giant map of the heavens with stones to pinpoint the major stars and planets. The lifework of her grandfather and generations of grandfathers lay on tables in front of this wall. Calendars of yesteryear, today, and far into the future were etched onto scrolls as well as into the floor. Renderings of the sky lay scattered about. The priestess' grandfather had often said the future was written in the sky; one just had to open one's eyes and mind to the message.

The third and fourth walls were Mother's domain, and displayed her skill of calling upon the powers of Earth's plants and elements to heal. The third wall held her pots of herbs and bottles of potions. Pottery fired by the city's best craftsmen occupied the shelves lining the wall. Most were full, but some remained empty, waiting for Layla and her sister's concoctions.

The priestess' seventeen years had been spent dutifully studying the art of potions. Layla understood the nature of these herbs better than she did her new husband. Prepared properly, the borreria could heal the neighbor girl's stomach ailments. And if they worked quickly, they might be able to store enough for the entire village. This illness was sure to spread.

Cocha pulled something out of her clutch, and a glob of the inky liquid bubbled up, splattering her tunic. "Goddesses and gods!" The girl stomped her foot. "I despise potion schooling. When will we get to sift space like Mother?" She wiped the blotch of borreria off with her hands, wringing them together in an attempt to eliminate the mess.

"Cocha, you know you must find your true mate and bond before you attain your powers. And even then, there is a chance you will not sift like Mother." Layla picked up the tossed-aside herbs and began taking note of the ones she'd need to gather later.

"I know." The young apprentice hung her head. "I apologize, Sister."

"Why?"

"You have already mated, yet you do not sift. I didn't mean to bring up your inadequacies."

Layla laughed. "Kon and I are hardly inadequate. We've only been bonded two months. There's time."

"No, Layla Cohen." Cocha ceased her fidgeting and faced her sister as a sudden wind blew through the temple. "You have run out of time. You must access your powers now and stop the evil force." Cocha's eyes brightened as she reached up and smacked her palm against Layla's forehead. "Wake up, chica!"

Layla sat up in her threadbare t-shirt and focused on the green digits of her old clock radio. *3:48.* She rubbed her eyes, wiping away the residual images of the dream. Bangles clanged as they slid down her arm. She didn't own any bracelets.

Chapter Four

Sebastian reclined in his red velvet seat, midway to the back of the theater's audience. At least he was comfortable while watching Mira butcher the words he revised nine times.

"*China*! Go back to the temple—"

"Mira, darling." On stage, Allora interrupted her scene partner with a hand to the shoulder. "The word is *Ch'inyay. Ch'inyay*, like Charlie SHEEN, then EYE. *Ch'inyay!*"

Dressed in knee-high leather boots, tight brown pants, and a cropped jacket, Allora looked more prepared for horseback riding than the light yoga they practiced before rehearsals began.

"China, *ch'inyay*? What's the difference?" The younger actress stomped her foot so hard, Sebastian thought the stiletto heel would snap off. "What does *ch'inyay* even mean?"

"Shut up," Jennifer interjected from the back of the stage, her expression never changing. His stage manager hefted a rehearsal block and carried it to the acting pair.

"Shut up?" Mira's lips pinched into a tight line while her little nostrils flared. Hopefully, steam would come out of her ears, too. A fist flew up to her hip as she glared at the stage manager. "You can't talk to me like that!"

Jennifer rolled her eyes and Allora burst into laughter.

The director shook his head as he stood to intervene. He projected his voice above the movie star's giggles. "If you read the mini-glossary at the back of the script notebook, you would know that *ch'inyay* means 'shut up.' You have to pronounce these words carefully. There's a pronunciation guide in there, too."

Mira hugged her arms below her chest, nearly ejecting her cleavage from her tiny dress as she shook her head with a pout. "Well, you didn't say we needed to read through *everything*."

The young actress was only about eighteen years old, and already trying to use sex appeal to win over the director. It was going to be a very long rehearsal period.

Sebastian rubbed his temple. The high profile play had attracted the celebrities, and now he had to deal with their attitudes and expectations. "Young Miss Gonzales, I expect you to read through every word in that notebook. It's there to help you understand the ancient world of the Incan woman you're playing."

Dropping her hands to her sides, Mira gave up the seductress role and stomped her foot again. "That's a lot of stuff to read, Sebastian. Isn't there someone to review it for me?" She stuck out her bottom lip, and the director lost his patience with the game.

"No, it's your job to understand the damn character. If

you can't do that, you can find another director to drive insane."

"I'll go over the glossary and history sections with her," Jennifer interrupted. She placed the last of the blocks down and walked to the edge of the stage. "After rehearsals. On your time, Mira." The short woman hopped down to the audience floor and glanced at her watch. "There are only five minutes left in this session, so maybe we should move on?"

"Yes." The director smiled as his stage manager plopped into the seat next to him and opened her notebook. "Thanks for volunteering," he whispered.

"Oh, you'll pay for the hours," she whispered back.

Groaning, he addressed the waiting actresses standing on stage. "Jennifer has placed rehearsal blocks around you to take the place of the set. Nothing's been decided, so feel free to move them wherever you need."

"You want me to carry furniture, too?" Mira gasped.

"Oh, child." Allora lifted the end of one block. "It is not heavy at all. He is not asking us to become burly moving men. Can you not cooperate just a little?"

"Never mind!" Sebastian yelled. "Sit on the floor instead!" He looked at his script along with all of his notes about the young starlet's attitude. Perhaps casting a bitchy actress to portray the spoiled daughter was not his best idea. He needed to find some way to break through her awful exterior and pull out the authentic performance she'd given in her last play. Directing her was a challenge he could handle, but not in the next four minutes. He raised his eyebrows at the stage manager before sitting down to take more notes.

"Okay, this rehearsal is over." Jennifer closed her binder and walked back to the stage, jeans swishing with every step. "Thank you, Mira. Email me to schedule our review. Allora, you're in the next rehearsal as well, so please sit tight."

Hugging the younger actress closely to her, Allora spoke softly into her ear. Mira turned a scarlet red as she buttoned up her shirt-dress to cover her exposed breasts. Giving a small wave in Sebastian's direction, she grabbed her designer bag and hurried out of the theater.

Sebastian wished his hearing had improved with his perception of others' emotions. Whatever Allora said made an impact, and he would have loved to know what she whispered.

"What now, brilliant leader?" The actress sat down on the stage, bringing her knees to her chin. "Are we all to perform our scenes from the floor?"

He chuckled as Layla entered the rear of the theater. Gods in heaven, the woman was breathtaking. In a white t-shirt, khaki pants, and a heavy sweater-coat, she looked like a miniature model. Her hair was held in a ponytail, stray curls falling around her face, and her cheeks flushed red from the chilly spring air. Layla glanced around, her shoulders thrown back in stark contrast as trepidation and insecurity emanated with each step.

"We're doing a floor scene?" The actress pulled her script from the bag slung across her chest and thumbed through.

He'd already caused enough confusion in one day. "No, we're not. This is Scene Two, your first scene with your mother. How are you, by the way?"

"Hi, Sebastian." She smiled as she shoved the thick script back into her bag. "I'm doing well, thanks. You? Hi, Allora!"

"Great," he said.

Allora called, "Hello!"

Anxiety wafted in his direction as Layla climbed onto the stage. Well, it wasn't everyday a small-time actress got to share the stage with Allora Delaney. He would have been nervous too if he'd taken the time to properly consider the situation. But these days, he had enough trouble trying to ignore other people's emotions while living his own life. Besides, Allora was sending out waves of insecurity whenever he got close enough to feel them.

Come to think of it, Sebastian could already feel the star's emotions all the way on the stage. No longer apprehensive, her smile was genuine, reflecting the thoroughly amused air that drifted down.

She stood, opening her arms to Layla for a hug. "Hello, my lovely daughter. It is wonderful to see you again."

A bit of Layla's fear dissolved as she embraced the woman. "Thank you. It's good to see you, too." She stripped off her coat, placing it to the side of the stage before retrieving her script again. "Scene Two?"

"Act One, Scene Two," Jennifer called. "You're entering from stage left."

Layla smiled at the director and walked offstage.

Huayra ran into the temple. "Eme said you were looking for me."

Allora was back on her feet, a look of calm on her face as she immersed herself into the role. His pen poised,

Sebastian settled in to watch the magic of theater.

"Yes, child. It is time for you to learn why you are on this earth. Hand me that pot."

Pulling an imaginary pot from an imaginary shelf, Layla walked to the center of the stage to join her scene partner. *"I am hardly a child. I have three children of my own."* She handed the pot to her mother.

Ceiba sank her hands into a bowl of dough without glancing up. "You are a woman in the eyes of the village, yes. But, now you must learn your destiny and you will be child-like again in this manner. I must resume my role as your guide until you learn to walk again."

"Mother, you're not making sense."

Ceiba took the pot from her daughter. "Sit. This story is long."

Layla retrieved a rehearsal block, dragging it back to center stage. With an arched eyebrow, Allora looked out to the director, flashing the briefest smile before resuming the scene. The pair continued while he contemplated the actresses.

Thank God Layla wasn't like Mira. He was right. Layla was a down-to-earth woman, perfect for the role and his theater troupe. The anxiety that was pouring off her vanished as she lost herself in her craft. An errant curl fell onto her cheek, and she tucked it behind her ear as her full lips pronounced each word carefully. The director jumped with a start when fresh terror spiked from the actress.

She clutched Allora's arm with a strained face as she said her next line. He realized she was projecting the character's fear. Layla was experiencing Huayra's emotions instead of mimicking them. No wonder she was such a great performer.

Huayra looked to her mother. *"But what will happen to the children? We cannot agree to such a burden. I cannot agree to this burden. I am merely a wife and mother."*

"Oh, you have never been 'merely' anything, child, and you know it. Do not lie to yourself." Ceiba tried to soften her words with a pat on her daughter's head. *"You are training to be high priestess—"*

"Yes, Mother, a priestess. Not a guardian! Not the living vessel of a goddess!" Her voice rose, taking on a hysterical edge. *"I'm not up to this task. Take it back!"* She stood, staring down at her mother with pleading eyes.

Ceiba drew in a deep breath and spoke her next words slowly. *"The goddess is already within you, my girl. Now that you have found your proper mate, it is time you both accepted your fate. The balance of the physical world lies in our hands. You, my girls, are the elementals in charge of maintaining balance. And your mates must guide and shield your immense powers. Together, we can help mankind achieve wonders."*

Huayra shook her head, hair tumbling with the violent movement. *"Kon is a farmer. It was hard enough for him to accept my role as priestess. He will never be able to handle this."* She brought her hands to her face. *"What have I turned him into?"*

"Ch'inyay!" Ceiba stood, one hand on a hip as she pressed the bowl into her middle with the other. *"Enough, child. You have not turned the man into anything he was not already. You were all chosen at birth. You have been a guardian since you were born. And he has been a cardinal just as long. You've found each other because it was destined. Just as it is my destiny to teach you and your sisters to develop your powers."* She carried the dough to another shelf, giving it the air and space it needed to rise.

"I don't understand how it's possible that all four of us are guardians, and each of us happened to mate with one of the four

cardinals. That's too much of a coincidence."

"It's not a coincidence at all. We are finally together because it's time for us to help the earth heal herself. Wind, fire, earth, water. My girls will command the elements. North, south, east, and west. Your mates will guide you in the right directions." She wrapped her arms around her oldest daughter, pulling her into a hug.

Huayra rested her head on her mother's shoulder. "But, Mama, I don't think Kon will want to guide me anywhere, except to his bed."

Ceiba chuckled as she held the younger woman out in front of her, looking into her eyes. "Then your first task is to convince him of his duty. You cannot fulfill your destiny without him. None of us can."

"Would that be so bad?" She bit her lip and stared down at her hands.

"I have told you we must restore balance, child. Our enemy seeks to create chaos and destruction everywhere they go. Like us, it can be reincarnated into any human. But it retains its memories from life to life, while you are merely a vessel and must relearn the goddess' knowledge. The evil can be born to an unsuspecting mother or will possess an open soul, and then it reaches out to other evil, feeding on the mayhem."

Ceiba sighed as she continued. "I have spent lifetimes fighting alone. Sometimes I've been lucky enough to have just one of you close enough to help. Now, for the first time we are all together. Huayra, I don't care if Kon is merely a farmer. He will fight, as will you. We will all stand together to achieve balance!"

Allora's voice rang out through the theater with her last line.

"And scene." Jennifer hopped up to make her way back to the stage. "Reset!" she called to her assistants, and the trio set the stage for the beginning of the act again.

Layla pitched in, moving blocks where the stage manager instructed while Allora stared off into the audience. The movie star's hands remained balled in little fists at her sides, anger and annoyance rolling from her body. She must have been fully submerged into her role as well.

"Great job, ladies," the director called. He finished scribbling a final note and stood. "Let's do it again from the top. This time—"

"Sebastian," Jennifer interrupted. "Allora's rehearsal is over now. She has a previously scheduled appointment today."

"Oh." He cocked his head. "Okay, I guess that's it for Allora." He focused his attention on the still-seething actress. "You did an amazing job."

She yanked up her handbag as she stalked from the stage, forcing a smile. "Thank you. This is an interesting scene. I'd love to understand the background a bit more. And I've already read through the history notes."

Hostility oozed from Allora as she neared his spot in the audience. Perhaps she was one of those artists that lost themselves in their work. Would she think she was Mother Earth for the duration of the play? Either way, his job was to help her understand and reflect her motivation.

"Sure thing," he responded. "What's bothering you?"

"Nothing is bothering me. Why would you say that?"

Because I'm a weirdo who can sense your feelings, he thought. "Never mind. What's up?"

"Ceiba wants to protect the world from this evil, yes?"

"Correct."

"But, why are the 'evil ones' attacking?"

"Pardon?"

"Your whole story is about Ceiba's great fight against this evil force. But you give no reasons for the evil to attack these people. Why are they wreaking havoc?"

"Evil is evil. Is there a reason Christianity's Satan is evil?"

Layla piped up from her seat on the stage. "Some people say Satan is jealous because God loves humans more than angels. We have free will, while angels have to do whatever God says without question. So the angel, Lucifer, left heaven and screws with humans just because he's envious."

Allora whirled around and made a show of pointing to the stage. "Thank you, Layla! See? There is a reason. There is always a motive for evil. Otherwise, you are fighting a nameless blob. And it is hard to find any passion in that."

The woman had a point. Unfortunately, Sebastian's mother managed to leave that part out of her stories.

"Let me think about that, Allora." He made a note on his script and underlined it three times.

The actress narrowed her eyes as she studied him. "You reveal much in your play. Some might say it is too much. But do you even know the full tale?"

Her last words were little more than a whisper. Sebastian leaned in, reading her lips to understand. Why did famous people have to be so melodramatic? The fact that he didn't know the answer made her question more annoying.

"So, is rehearsal over?" Layla called out from the stage.

"You've still got—" Jennifer said, checking her watch "—twenty-five minutes left." She looked at the director. "Your call, Boss."

Relieved, he took the opportunity to break Allora's challenging gaze. Glad he could read her emotions instead of the actress reading his, Sebastian flashed a radiant smile. He didn't want her to know how unsettling her comments were to him.

Allora returned the smile. "Let's chat sometime." She flipped her hair over her shoulder as she resumed her walk to the back door of the theater.

The director ignored her prima donna exit, focusing his attention on his new problem. Layla stood alone on the stage. There was no logical reason to dismiss her. One-on-one time with an actress was always a boon to the performance. They could work out any lingering issues about her character, hone her delivery, and develop her stage presence.

"No," he projected his voice. "Rehearsal isn't over. This is a good chance to work together." The wave of apprehension bursting from the actress could have knocked him over if he hadn't been sitting already. Her emotions were always so powerful.

Again, he felt guilty for allowing himself to embrace her at her final audition. He was the cause of her anxiety. Pushing guilt aside, he made his way to the stage. A typical one-on-one rehearsal called for him to be near.

She sat on a work block, casually leafing through her script. Any other observer would find her perfectly at ease. She smiled down at him, and he made up his mind to ignore his sixth sense so they could both get through the session. Good thing he started out as an actor. Those skills were certainly being put to use today.

Choosing a block out of arm's reach, Sebastian hunkered down on stage with the actress. "Normally, we'd rehearse that scene between you and Allora a lot more. But I think we've captured something already. Each run-through, a little more of the mother-daughter relationship emerged. Did you feel that?"

She straightened her back as she responded. "Yes, I did. I found myself wanting to challenge her, the way I did with my own mom when I was twenty-two."

"That came across and worked well."

She held up a hand to stop his further praise. "But then I think of how Huayra has been married long enough to have three kids. She's training to be a priestess. She's a hell of a lot more responsible that I was at twenty-two... Or now, for that matter!"

Sebastian laughed.

She continued. "Should she still be 'challenging' her mother? Wouldn't she be past that by now?"

"My take on it is that these people are still *people*. She's still a twenty-two-year-old girl with the traits and tendencies of one. Yes, she'll soon be a high priestess, but she's got the same mentality that you would have."

"If I were married for four years and Incan in the 1500s."

"Exactly. Make some choices about how you would feel, what you would want. Right now, you know you simply want to be Kon's wife and the mother to your kids."

"Being priestess is bad enough, right? I'm worried Kon

will be pissed."

"And this is all your mother's fault."

"Ah, I'm with you. So, I blame her for this turn of events." A light bulb went off in the actress' head. She leaned back with a contented smile as the apprehension released its hold on her. "How did you so accurately write the feelings and wishes of a twenty-two-year-old woman?"

He felt himself smiling back. "My mom used to paint such vivid pictures of these people with her stories. I've heard them so many times, it feels like I was there. Plus, people are people. Whether Huayra is a young woman or man, she's going to have trouble stepping out of her comfort zone."

She tilted her head and the light shone onto her face, making her brown eyes sparkle. A warmth poured from her. "Yeah, that makes sense. There's always fear in facing the unknown, in taking the next step, even if you've been working all your life to get there." She wrinkled her forehead as she pondered, staring into the empty audience.

Sebastian watched the actress, unable to resist inching closer. Did she intentionally open her heart and mind to him? Even without his sixth sense, he would have understood that she was referring to her role in the play.

"A little anxiety is natural. But you have to realize you're just as talented and attention-worthy as all the celebrities and movie stars out there. Otherwise, I wouldn't have hired you."

Her jaw dropped open as she directed her gaze at him. "I—" Shutting her mouth, she smiled and ducked her head in embarrassed shock. "Thank you."

The woman was beyond adorable, and her self-consciousness lent a humble quality to her that he missed in all the preening starlets.

She straightened her back and shoulders, and the damsel-in-distress look vanished as her guard snapped back into place. Reaching out, she patted his hand and thanked him again. "I appreciate that."

Three little taps of her palm against the top of his hand. He should have let it go at that respectable gesture. But he turned his hand over so that her last pat landed in his grasp. And now he was holding her hand. A current passed between them at the contact, and neither of them spoke as they stared into each other's eyes.

Desire coursed through his body, and any guilt he may have felt died when hers fired lust-filled vibes right back. Her body called to him, and he leaned in to respond.

With a shake of her head, Layla snatched her hand away. "I appreciate your kind words. You're a great boss." Without a backward glance, she sprang from the rehearsal block, grabbed her messenger bag, and left the theater.

Sebastian stared after her, wondering whether he should believe her words or her emotions. Either way, he *was* her boss. And, that was enough reason to stop this stupid obsession.

Chapter Five

"Behind you!" Layla yelled above the raucous din as she passed behind the bartender. With a tray of drinks balanced on her left palm, she held her right in front of herself to block the elbows and other careless limbs of the Irish pub's patrons.

"Three Harps and a Guinness." She placed the beers on a table in front of four baby-faced men in suits. Hill staffers, possibly interns. Their IDs proclaimed them all to be twenty-three years old. She smiled as she overheard their conversation about clueless senators and incompetent bosses.

"Six more, Layla!" The deep Irish accent rang out above the chatter, and the actress/waitress shoved her notepad into her back pocket, making her way back to the bar.

Six light brown beers awaited her. "Table twelve?"

"Yep."

"Which is the Killians, Tom?"

"Figure it out, miss. I havena time to g'over it again,"

the owner of the pub—doing double-duty as bartender—called over his shoulder as he pushed through the swinging doors to his back office.

Layla wanted to yell back that she was an actress, not an aficionado of imported alcohol. But, the truth was that she *did* know which beer was which. Killians was a smidge redder than the others. After being a waitress at O'Malley's for such a long time, it only made sense this stuff was finally sinking in.

O'Malley's had become her second home in the two years since she'd been searching for overnight success in D.C. theater. Tom O'Malley was the crotchety, dirty, old uncle she never wanted. More often than not drunker than his patrons, he operated on the belief that the customer was never right, and "piss on 'em" for asking. His attitude scared off any out-of-towners wandering in, which usually worked in his favor. Residents of Capitol Hill and Eastern Market adored the pomp-free hole-in-the-wall.

The bar stocked twelve beers on tap and served savory Irish meals like shepherd's pie and fish & chips. Layla was one of four waitresses employed to dish up Tom's grandmother's recipes. And, as much as she loved Tom and the bar, she was once rather proud she couldn't recognize his precious beer on sight. Lacking that skill proved her real job—her true career—was acting.

If not for her current role in the Incan play, she probably would have drowned her sorrows over the undesired beer talent in a pint of Cherry Garcia and a bottle of Yuengling when she got home. Instead, she planned to use the time to study her script. Life was good.

Dropping off the six drinks, Layla smiled to herself as she replayed her perfect response to Sebastian's weirdness at rehearsal. This time, she was able to control her body's reaction and avoid another stupid, humiliating situation. The craft always comes first. And there would be no funny business with her director.

Not even when he rubbed her hands the way a lover might caress a breast. Not even when his green eyes bore into hers with an unspoken desire plainer than the memory heating her now. And definitely not when he licked his perfect lips and made her want to kiss him, the way they previously kissed in her dreams.

That was what had snapped her out of the spell of Sebastian Tawanti. Reality overlapped dreams. Her body had started to lean in and her mind screamed, "What the hell is this?" He's not some dream god in a field of tall grass. There's no kissing the director, especially not in the middle of rehearsal with stage managers, lighting technicians, and who knew what else lurking about.

Her brain was a mess and her hormones were on overdrive. But, why was Sebastian acting so inappropriately? He was the one who demanded professionalism. Well, she passed his stupid test this time. Layla beamed as she walked up to the next table.

"You look like the cat who screwed the canary. What's that secret smile about?" The patron flashed a set of perfect pearly whites as he stood up.

"Alex!" She stepped into his open arms for a quick hug. "I was just thinking about rehearsal. Why are you here?"

"'Why are you here?'" he repeated. "Is that how you

greet all your customers? You must get horrible tips." He plunked back down onto the wooden chair and hid his laughter behind a menu. "What's good here?"

"Everything." It was her standard answer, but it was true. "My favorite is the bacon-wrapped chicken in mushroom sauce over mashed potatoes. Hits the spot, if you've got an appetite."

This time he let his amusement show. "You eat bacon-wrapped anything? Not too worried about staying a size two, are you?" He noted the scowl on her face. "I like you."

Asinine comments aside, he wasn't so bad himself. Alex wore a tight, white t-shirt that showed off his lean, defined chest. His dark skin contrasted nicely with the platinum blond curls atop his head.

"Yeah, you like me 'cause I've got the power to bring you a beer. What'll you have?"

"How about a date with the prettiest girl in this dump?" He gave a wink with his pick-up line.

"Claire's not on the menu." She nodded toward the gorgeous, young waitress across the room and walked away.

The guy was cute, but he insulted her bar. Besides, if Layla was going to keep her relationship with Sebastian professional, there was no logical reason to go down the wrong path with Alex.

"Another admirer, Layla?" Tom reappeared behind the bar by the time she returned to retrieve the Hill staffers' second round. "I swear, ya bring in as many customers as the beer. This one looks a bit cheeky. 'S he causing you trouble?"

Stifling a laugh, the actress shook her head. "Down, Tom. He's my acting partner from my new play." She patted his arm in reassurance as she walked by.

With a grunt, Tom shifted his attention to a new customer.

Layla dropped off the drinks and headed back to Alex. "All right, you can't sit there all day staring at me. My boss'll throw you out. Can I get you a beer or something?"

He sighed. "Sure. Do you have Yuengling?"

"Yeah. You drink Yuengling?"

"I do. It's a Pennsylvania beer," he answered with a shrug. "I grew up drinking Yuengling. Or, not exactly 'grew up' drinking beer, but…"

"I get it," she interrupted, ending his embarrassed, yet cute, rambling. "I didn't know you were from PA. So am I! Yuengling is like a little piece of home to me."

Alex's chocolate eyes widened. "You're from PA? I'm from Erie. What about you?"

"Ambler. It's near Philly. You're from Erie, PA, huh? I'll have to be quick with you."

"Yeah…" He raised an eyebrow, obviously not understanding her reference to an old Tom Hanks movie.

Layla mentally kicked herself for failing to rein in her encyclopedic knowledge of film and television. Oh well. She reminded herself that she wasn't into the guy, so it didn't matter if he thought she was weird. Besides, there were other tables to mind. "One Yuengling coming up." She excused herself with a smile.

Fourteen trays of assorted drinks, twenty-three plates of Irish home-cooking, and one spot of tea later, the waitress climbed up onto a bar stool and lifted her foot to massage its aching heel. It was five after ten o'clock, and the kitchen was closed, her shift finally over. Waiting tables wasn't acting, but there was a certain satisfaction involved that never resulted from any of the office temp jobs she'd had over the years. People came to O'Malley's hungry or thirsty, and Layla gave them food or drink promptly. She did her job and they tipped her well.

"What's going on in that pretty head of yours?" Alex suddenly appeared at her side.

"Hey! I thought you left already. You paid your tab an hour ago."

"I've been nursing this last Yuengling, waiting for you to notice me." His shy demeanor almost appeared genuine.

"Ha! I think I stopped paying attention when you nabbed the second girl's phone number."

"Oh, so you *were* watching me?" A giant smile spread over the young actor's face. "Are you jealous, Huayra?"

She couldn't help smiling back. "Why would I be jealous? You know our marriage isn't real, right? I'm not your wife and my name is not Huayra."

"Close enough," he muttered.

"Not really. Hi, I'm Layla Cohen, an *actress*, and you're an actor who can do whomever you want."

"I know who you are, Ms. Cohen. Forgive me." He gave a mock bow. "I find I give a better performance if I think of my partners in the way my character would."

"Oh. Then that makes you a cheating scumbag." She swatted his shoulder. "Ass!"

He laughed. "That's more like it. The problem is that

this also makes Allora Delaney my mother-in-law. And I'm not sure I can pull that off."

"What do you mean?"

"She's too hot!" He snapped his mouth shut and sank onto the stool next to hers. "I mean…"

"No, I understand," she said as she laughed. "Allora is… nothing short of breathtaking. I'm still worried no one will believe I'm worthy of playing her daughter."

Alex raised his eyebrows. "Interesting."

"What?"

"You don't know how beautiful you are."

"Thank you." The blush started its familiar creep into her face until she remembered Alex was playing a role. "Thank you, dear husband. Anyway, I got over it during rehearsals. Allora is just an actress trying to wrap her head around her character, same as us. She's a great scene partner. You'll fall into your role with her once you're on the stage."

"Or maybe I can use the attraction. There's no rule that Kon can't secretly want to bang his mother-in-law." He winked.

"No! That's not right!" Layla fought the sudden urge to push him off his stool. "Kon's not like that at all. He's deeply in love with me—"

"'Me'? I knew it! You identify with your character as much as I do with mine. Don't worry, Huayra. I only have eyes for you, my one true mate." He lifted her hand and placed a kiss on her palm.

That chaste move was more tantalizing than if he'd shoved his tongue down her throat. She stared into the eyes now boring into hers and got the feeling that he wanted to love her in real life. Her eyelids grew heavy as she anticipated the press of his lips against hers.

"Yuengling!" Tom's deep voice shattered the strange moment. He plunked down the glass and glared at the young man. "Anything fer you?"

"No, thank you." Alex turned his penetrating gaze on the bartender. "We don't need anything else. You can go."

Without a backward glance, Tom returned to his other patrons.

Layla blinked. How odd of Tom not to balk at being dismissed in such a manner. More importantly, she almost kissed her acting partner at her day job. What was wrong with her?

"Alex, I'm having a weird day. I think it's time for me to go home." She kept her eyes downcast on her beer.

"Can I walk you? We need to practice our scenes, Huayra." He smiled.

Her head began to ache along with her foot. "Not tonight."

* * *

"You cannot trust him!" Green eyes flared as the big man stabbed at the earth with his shovel.

She was back in the other world, her fantasy man decidedly less fun. Anger seeped from the dusty tunic whipping around his torso with every thrust into the ground. Leave it to Layla to drag drama into her sleep as well.

"He's a man just as you." She reached out a brown hand to still his attack on the crops. Somehow, she knew they would both regret his manhandling if he did not cease his careless actions.

"No, Huayra!" Dropping his shovel to the upturned dirt, he heeded her wordless warning. "He is not like me. Not like my brothers. He may have a wife and children wherever he calls home. But he has no respect for the land or what we must do to live."

"So he's an outsider. We're not adopting him as family, merely trading with him and the other travelers." The dream world was so detailed, she even had memories of the market where she first met the man her husband despised.

"There is something wrong with him. Have you not asked yourself how Carlos Ramirez of the white man's land speaks our language?"

"Of course. He says he is a master of tongues. He's included on these voyages because of that very gift."

The Sebastian of her dreams stared down at her, his golden face darkened by hours toiling in the sun. The hard lines in his forehead began to ease, and he smoothed the battered earth with his foot. "Yes, that does sound reasonable," he grudgingly admitted. "But, I do not like this man, nor the way he looks at you, Huayra."

"The way he looks at me? Ha! Now we have found the root of your distrust. You are a jealous man!" She poked a finger on the muscled chest she found at eye level.

"I am not! I am a careful man. A wise man. A talented man—"

"A vain man!" She laughed.

"A deeply-in-love-with-you man." He pulled her close to his body and cupped her face with one hand. "I have my own gifts. Believe me when I say you cannot trust this man, Layla."

She started when she heard her modern name spoken by her fantasy man. "Did you just call me Layla?"

"It has to be you," he whispered. "Regardless of this brown skin, your wider nose." He kissed her forehead as his fingers trailed her cheekbones. "This is a dream world, but please tell me the love I feel for you is real, Layla."

Her next words died on her lips as he bent down to cover her mouth with his. This field, this version of Sebastian, this world was real. If only in her dreams, she belonged to this man whose green eyes were glowing again. She sighed in bliss as his fingers worked their way up her shift, tumbling her onto the earth in a wanton tangle of limbs.

Chapter Six

"Ding dong, the witch is dead. Well, not dead of course. She's finally gone, though. Moved out. Yeah, so my allergic roommate moved out and I can take Mr. Snugglepants home with me. Isn't that great?" Sebastian's ex-wife rambled. She always rambled when she got flustered. He didn't need to feel the waves of uncertainty splashing over to him to know how at odds she was.

"That's… great, Ariel. You came to get the cat?" He stood at his front door, looking out at the familiar face. It had already been a year, but she still had the face of an angel - a cherub with fat cheeks, a tiny button nose, and big blue eyes, who had managed to disturb one of the best dreams of his life. He could still feel fantasy-Layla in his arms in the world of his play.

"Yep, the cat. So, can I come in? I'm sorry to show up unannounced. I should have called, I know. It's only that I wasn't really sure how you'd feel about seeing me; and I didn't want you to go to any trouble with a meal or some fancy breakfast if you'd known in advance. You were always a great cook. Can't find a guy who cooks these days. But, yeah, I want the cat."

"Okay…" He stepped aside to let her through the doorway of the townhouse they once shared. She looked good. Then again, the last time he'd seen her was at their divorce hearing, when neither of them was at their best. Once inside, she made a beeline up the stairs to his bedroom. Dropping to her knees, she peered under the bed. "Here, Mr. Snugglepants! Come here, Mr. Snugglepants! Snuggie! Where is he? He's not under the bed?" Her butt wiggled in the air as she moved Sebastian's crumpled t-shirt out of her way.

Her bottom was just as tight as ever, but his attraction fizzled out along with his love at least a year before their day in court. The thought popping into Sebastian's mind was that her slacks were the same dark gray as Layla's during her call-back audition. How would Layla's butt look waving around like that? He glanced away when Ariel turned and stared up at him, waiting for his response.

"What? Um, no, he's not under the bed," he answered. "He rarely hides anymore."

"Oh. Where is he? In the bay window? Mr. Snugglepants!" She flipped her reddish blond hair out of her eyes and got to her feet. The many shades of its natural color were once a source of fascination for him. Her blue eyes were an obsession. The body bouncing down to his dining room was his alter of worship. He was relieved to discover all that had changed. He was no longer prisoner to her wild moods either.

That was good because Sebastian was having a hard time trying to bar other people's emotions from intruding on his own. The other day, after bumping against a sulky teenager, he suddenly wanted to punch his father. Layla was still throwing off sexy vibes, making it difficult to concentrate. Hell, he still kicked himself for touching her after the first rehearsal. A little pat on the hand nearly led to a full-blown make-out session on his stage. The chemistry was undeniable, but he had to get himself in check. He shook off the memories and refused to think about that dream again.

Ariel's frantic energy bounced off her, reaching out to him in tentacles of mania. Each time she came near, he felt as if he'd just downed a double shot of espresso. He tried to keep his distance, perching on the arm of his couch as she searched the cat's old spots.

"Ariel, he liked those places a long time ago. Now he sleeps in the curtains next to the door. And I call him Mister." He rubbed his temple and whistled. "Mister, come!" A fat, black cat with white paws emerged from the windowsill and sauntered over to Sebastian.

"But he's not allowed in the curtains." She put her hands on her hips as she moved to intercept the cat. "He gets black hair all over the sheer white— Oh. The curtains aren't white anymore. Well, I guess they're different curtains, huh? They're nice. Mr. Snugglepants, how are you? It's time to go with Mommy. I missed you so much! So, Sebastian, I heard you're doing a new play with Allora Delaney. Congrats. It sounds huge. Incan mythology?" She sank into the over-stuffed, black leather couch, never taking her eyes from the cat now in her lap. Mister arched his back, pulling away and trying to extricate himself from her smothering arms. "Did you check with your mother first? I'm not sure she'd like you writing about that stuff."

Sebastian shook his head at the abrupt change in conversation. "Why do you think my mother wouldn't like my play?" When they were married, he was relieved his mother and wife shared a close relationship. Now his ex's palpable concern for his mother bordered on annoying. "Why are you worried?"

"Worried? I didn't say I was worried. It's only …" She caressed the cat's tail as he made his escape back to the floor. "Your mom was always a bit secretive about the intricacies of her family's traditions. She said there was a lot that wasn't meant to be public knowledge. I always felt somewhat privileged when she told me things. It's the one thing I regret losing when our marriage started falling apart. I lost your mom." She watched the cat hop up to Sebastian's lap and nuzzle his cheek. Her eyes widened when she noticed his amused face. "Oh, I miss you, too. You know I loved you—"

"Don't worry." He stroked Mister's ears. "I've been over us for a while. Back to my mom. She *was* upset on the phone last week. You think she really meant for all of this to be a secret?"

"Didn't she ever say so? She swore me to secrecy."

"Well, she said it was 'family business.' But she also said my aunt's drinking problem was 'family business' and she had no issues with the play I wrote about alcoholism a few years ago."

"Not the same thing."

"Why not?"

"Because anyone can be an alcoholic. You didn't name your play 'Aunt Tiffany and her Tequila Troubles' or some such. But you're completely spilling the beans with this play." The cat hopped down and sashayed into the kitchen. "Okay, what did you do to Mr. Snugglepants? He doesn't like me anymore."

"Maybe he's mad because you keep calling him Snugglepants. His name is Mister and you don't even want him." Sebastian felt no sense of longing from her. Though he'd only had his sixth sense a short time, he was positive Ariel had no more love for the cat than she did for the couch. In fact, she was clearly happier with the old couch. What he mostly felt from her was worried concern. "What's the deal, Ariel? Why are you here?"

"To get my cat."

"Ariel, you don't even have a cat box with you. You have no plans of taking this cat with you."

"Fine." She exhaled with a hint of relief. "I ran into your mother yesterday. She told me to talk to you about changing the play's more private scenes."

"What? How? Why would she do that?" Sebastian sputtered. "Why didn't she talk to me?"

"She said she tried." Ariel pursed her lips and stood. "I'm here as a favor to her, but I know enough not to come between you two. You need to sit down with your mom and figure out what you can and cannot write in that play. It's most important to her."

"I don't believe this." He rolled his eyes. "We're not even married anymore."

"I know. It's a little awkward, huh? Be a good boy and listen to your mother, okay?"

"Why did you bother asking for the cat?"

Ariel shrugged. "Honestly, I thought I could get you to

change the play without bringing up your mom. Just needed a reason to come here."

"Okay then." Sebastian shook his head to clear the waves of trepidation coming from her. "Well, thanks for doing my mother a favor, I guess. But the play has already been written and distributed to actors, crew, everybody. I can't change it."

"Talk to your mom about it. That's all I'll say." Looking back into the kitchen where Mister lay on the cool, tile floor, Ariel inched her way to the front door. "I *was* planning to get Mr. Snugglepants at some point. But he seems happy here. You want to keep him?"

Sebastian smiled for the first time since seeing her through his peephole. "Yes, I think I do."

Ariel stepped over the threshold, turned back, and hugged him. "It was good seeing you."

"Good seeing you, too." He spent many lonely nights wishing to have this woman in his life again. Now he was happy to be rid of her and keep the cat. She walked down the street toward the Metro. Mister brushed his fat body against his legs in a decidedly happier gesture. *Me too*, Sebastian thought.

* * *

"Did you enjoy your visit with Ariel?" Sebastian's mother did not try to mask the amusement in her voice.

"Mom, some people don't think it's fun to have an ex-spouse suddenly appear on their doorstep. I hadn't seen Ariel in over a year, and I was fine with that."

"Oh? I would be delighted if your father showed up

unexpectedly."

He sighed. "I know, Mom. But the circumstances are a bit different. Dad died. Ariel and I are divorced."

"True. Well, Ariel got your attention, no?"

Sebastian rubbed his temple. He couldn't argue her last point, and he knew that trying was futile. Her circuitous logic always won. "Yes, she got my attention. You want me to change my play?"

"It is imperative that you do so at this moment. I will accept whatever damage has already been done. But, you can mitigate some of the danger if you remove any references to the elementals' mates. I saw nothing in the press about them. Still, I assume you've included them in your tale?"

"Back up. What damage has been done already?"

"I knew you were not listening last week." She hissed her displeasure. "Sebastian, I told you that you would expose our family. We are the descendants of the elementals. Now anyone looking knows where the elemental lineage resides. This is a secret we had successfully guarded for five hundred years and which you have managed to publicly announce in less than one month!"

"Mom, these are fairy tales. Who cares if I brought Incan stories into the limelight?" He picked up his laptop, ready to multitask as he mentally crossed 'Placate crazy mother' off his weekly to-do list. "Besides, it took a lot longer than one month to attract the producer, and even longer for the PR team to build that kind of buzz."

"*Ch'inyay!* Will you not listen to me? The elementals are not fairy tales! All your life I have told you the old stories to prepare you for your destiny. You know about the elementals, women charged with the protection of life's building blocks—wind, water, fire, and earth. You know they each have a mate to strengthen and guide their power."

"Like yin and yang. They're unstoppable together." He already heard these stories thousands of times. Hearing it again would not turn him into a believer, but it might get his mother off his back.

"No, not unstoppable. We were stopped five hundred years ago. The Spaniards of your play nearly destroyed everything we fought so hard to protect."

"Right. The elementals left the Incans and the empire was all but obliterated. Very little remains of our history. So, including the magical bits thrown in, my play is going to be an historic representation of how the Incan people lived and worshipped." He pulled up a schematic of the planned theatrical set from the computer's files.

She scoffed. "'Magical bits?' This is not some obscure literary article, Sebastian Tawanti. We—the elementals gave their lives to protect the knowledge recorded at Machu Picchu. With their mates, they created a glimmer to shield the entire city for four hundred years."

He nearly dropped his laptop. "Wait, you're telling me the elementals hid Machu Picchu?" He couldn't believe his mother was laying it on so thick.

"Yes, and when that magic wore off, a spell was woven to disguise it as the summer home of an old king. But now you have recklessly revealed it as the religious sanctuary that it is."

"No one will believe the magical parts of my play

anyway." He didn't.

"I wish that were true. Your play gets too many details right. The four daughters as priestesses, the battles on and off the field... Our enemies will take notice if they haven't already. They will scour Machu Picchu for the hidden tomes."

"The Incan people didn't have a written language."

"Right. We mastered irrigation, but could not put ink to paper. Think, child. I told you we hid the records." She clearly had heard enough of his recitation of book-learned knowledge.

"Okay, then the damage has already been done. How does removing the mates from the play help?"

"The Supay followers, our enemies, never knew the elementals needed mates as well. They would use that knowledge against us. If they claim an elemental before she has joined with her mate—"

"All right, Mom." He didn't want to go down the 'mating' avenue of her imagination. No tales of women getting 'claimed' from his mother.

"You do not believe me." Her voice sounded tired and deflated.

"It's a lot to take in." He tapped his mouse.

"Why would I lie?" As usual, she was not hurt by his disbelief, only curious.

"You've always liked making up stories. The Houdini Machu Picchu is brilliant. Can I use that?"

"No! And you must promise to remove the mating from your play."

"If it makes you happy, I will butcher my play as you ask. I wrote this for you anyway."

"Ha! The gift that will bite me on the foot."

"Your ass," he corrected.

"The proper figure of speech is not my current concern! You keep this promise. And, Sebastian, call me again when your mind is open to the truth. There is more for you to learn, child."

He rolled his eyes. His mother's sanity would be in question if she wasn't such a master of storytelling. "Yes, Mom." She'd probably call back in a day or two, if only to laugh at her little joke.

In the meantime, he had work to do.

* * *

Sitting in rehearsal, staring at the actors who would bring his "dangerous" words to life, Sebastian again wondered if his mother was becoming insane. How could he explain that he needed to change the script because his mother actually believed her tales? Either way, this was an important session, and he would focus on the actors for now.

This was the female bonding rehearsal. For each play, he tried to foster a sense of family to develop their fictional relationships. He usually cast actors that would naturally work well together, to avoid forcing the bonding, which never worked. He simply threw them in a room together and let them find common interests for fifteen minutes before delving into the script. This time, the play's higher profile attracted C-list celebrity starlets in addition to his usual theater troupe. He watched the actresses separate with no more than a polite greeting.

The three starlets occupying the stage wore sundresses more suited to the weather in Los Angeles than the slightly chilly temperatures in the D.C. spring. Tori, the hospital drama star, stood clutching her script in her hands like a security blankie. She kept glancing at it as though it provided directions for life.

Blythe, the soap opera princess, sat on a bench with her hands folded in her lap and her ankles crossed. He imagined her stage mother must have drilled that pose into her for so many years, it was second nature now. She feigned extreme interest in the crew notices tacked to the side wall.

Mira leaned against a rehearsal block, coolly watching the other two. Her waif-like torso was draped in a nearly sheer silver dress. Impossibly long, bare legs perched on stilettos. She looked cold.

All three were small-boned, delicate looking women with dark hair. Tori was Puerto Rican; the other two white, but with darker skin coloring. Though they had little to say to each other, they looked like they could all be sisters.

The fourth sister sat in the bleachers next to the mother. Layla and Allora were on the opposite side of the theater from Sebastian. Three of Hollywood's prettiest young women illuminated the stage between the seats. And yet, all male eyes were on those two. He hoped the other men—crew members measuring for the set—were looking at Allora. His attention was riveted on Layla.

She wore a crimson sweatsuit, perfectly matched to the crimson cushions of the seats. The velvet-like material even seemed the same. Her hair was unbound, curls free to bounce in every direction. Most of the tendrils cascaded down the middle of her back; while a few framed her face. Her hair was wild, and his fingers itched to touch it again.

His active imagination placed that mane on the woman of his dream. Besides the hair, she looked nothing like Layla. But her essence was the same. In that dream world, in that other life, Sebastian was free to love Layla in a way he never imagined possible. The feeling was intoxicating. But it was just a silly dream brought on by his play, and he had work to do.

Actors are cattle, he reminded himself to ignore his fantasies. Making his way across the theater, he watched the pair. Layla was as elegant as Allora, even in a sweatsuit. Allora wore a frilly, white blouse and dark jeans, with very little makeup and her hair pulled back. She was curvier than the women playing her daughters. The coloring was the same, though. Her face tilted toward Layla as the two women laughed.

Layla glanced up and the slight anxiety emanating from her—understandable as she bantered with the A-list star—magnified. Her brown eyes locked onto Sebastian's, widening as he approached, and the pile of script pages in her hand slipped and fluttered to the floor. Scrambling to pick them up, she bonked her head on the seat in front of her. Sebastian reached them, bent to help, and struck his hip on the railing. Allora raised an eyebrow.

He thought about turning around to flee. This woman made him clumsy and unprofessional. It was completely unacceptable during the biggest play of his career. Maybe he should try a different tactic. They had to develop a normal working relationship so they could move past whatever feelings they experienced. He handed her the pages he collected and smiled at both women.

"Here you go. Y'know, Layla, right now you remind me of a scene on *Arrested Development*. There's a guy who blends into his surroundings. His shirt is the same pattern as the wallpaper. You look like you draped yourself in the seat cushions." Just as he realized he might have insulted her, she burst into laughter.

"Yes! Buster was hilarious. I loved that show! Too bad it was cancelled." Layla's anxiety evaporated with her amusement.

"*Arrested Development*? I have never heard of this show." Allora smiled at the giggling pair. "I guess you had to see it."

"You really should watch an episode or two. I'll get you the DVD." Sebastian glanced at the actresses on stage. "Time to get to business. I don't think everyone is enjoying bonding time." He projected his voice to fill the theater. "All right, ladies. From this day forward, we work on motivation, blocking, and the actual scenes. Scripts out."

Layla and Allora followed him onto the stage.

"Rehearsals are going to be pretty casual. So, no need for those"—he pointed down to Mira's five-inch heels— "or fancy clothes. We're going to move around a lot and probably even get on the floor every now and then. You're welcome to wear a dress if you must. Otherwise, look to Layla's sweatsuit for inspiration. Since I forgot to mention this a few days ago, we'll skip the yoga portion of this rehearsal."

"Yoga?" Mira piped up.

"Yep," he replied. "My acting coach used to start every class with a three-minute session to release all the pressures of the day and get our minds into the task at hand. I still like that drill. Mostly because it works."

"Oh, I had a coach do that, too." Blythe's smile brightened her face. "It does work. Fun!"

"Today we'll try a different exercise to get into our blocking. As you know, 'blocking' is the positioning of your bodies on the stage, where and how you move around. We'll read through this scene together. This is a bit far into the play, but it's the only scene with all five of you in it. Okay, the Spaniards are about to invade and Ceiba gathers her daughters to provide emergency instructions. You all want to preserve your way of life and family—each other—at whatever cost. After every line, I want you to address each other as 'love.' As in, 'Please turn to page eighty-two and start us off, Layla, love.'"

"*Mother, you sent for me*—Wait, where do you want me to go? Where am I coming in?" Layla asked the director.

He snapped his head up as he made his way back into the audience section. "Um, let's assume the forest is stage-left and the city is stage-right. Huayra is returning from gathering herbs, so you'll enter stage-left."

Allora spoke up. "I understand stage-left is to the left of the actor when he is on stage looking out at the back of the theater. But—" She twirled around with her arms in the air. "This stage is surrounded by seats. Where is the 'back' of this theater?"

"Good question," Mira mumbled.

"The bleachers will be rearranged. The stage will only

have seating on three sides," he answered. "The back of the theater's behind me where the door is. That'll be clear once these guys are done with the set. For now, just remember to face me. I'm your audience."

"I can do that." Allora said as the other actresses nodded.

"Mother, you sent for me, love?" Layla wasted no time getting back to the script. She rushed across the stage, where Allora sat on a bench, and kneeled at her mother's feet.

"Yes, Huayra, love." Ceiba placed her hand on her daughter's cheek. "Come, sit with your sisters, love." The four young women moved together, sitting on the floor beneath Ceiba as she continued.

"Atahualpa has fallen. Many say the new king is nothing more than a puppet of the Spaniards. We know something much more sinister controls him. The evil within him will seek our knowledge. Our warriors are preparing for battle. We must prepare the rest of the city, loves."

"We have seen the Spaniards' weapons. They are too powerful, love—" Chasca interrupted.

"We have been over this already, love." Cocha turned to her sister. "Grandfather's charts foretold of this battle. We ignored the signs the Spaniards were not to be trusted, love."

"Cocha is right, love." Ceiba rose to pace in front of her daughters. "We've got to move quickly. Zara, take your daughter and the rest of the city's children to the caverns. Those mothers with babes still at the breast shall help and go with you, love."

"Yes, Mother, love." Zara rose, embraced Ceiba, and exited.

Sebastian scribbled on his script.

"Cocha, mobilize the young women into the second wave of defense. The men have taken all the proper weapons. Have the young

women search for anything else that can be used as such, love. Chasca, we need food in the caverns. Have the old women and old men help you gather it, love. Huayra, pack up your herbs. You will come with me. Machu Picchu must not fall into enemy hands, love."

Mira and Blythe embraced their mother, gathering purses and impromptu items before leaving the stage.

"Sebastian?" Jennifer, the stage manager, appeared in the aisle. The director waved her off as he wrote the actresses' movements on his script. This was the most fascinating part of the theater process. If left alone, a good actor set more than half her movements during the first few times on her feet. And adding the word "love" to each line was already making the actresses relate to one another on a more personal level.

"No, Sebastian, listen to me."

He looked up at Jennifer. Tears ran down her face. "What's wrong?" He'd known his stage manager for all of the six years he lived in D.C. She was a solid, no-nonsense kind of woman who rarely laughed, never cried.

"I don't know how to say this. Ariel's dead."

Chapter Seven

As she ran errands, Layla kept telling herself that Sebastian's ex-wife was a stranger. Therefore, her eyes should not have leaked tears. She didn't know if Ariel was short or tall. Was she a kind soul or a raving lunatic? Layla knew nothing of the woman. Perhaps that was why she couldn't stop thinking about her.

She wondered how long they were married. A Google search revealed Sebastian was thirty-two years old and graduated from New York University's graduate drama program seven years ago. Did he get hitched while in school? Divorced or not, Layla couldn't imagine losing someone she once pledged to love forever. Sebastian must be crushed. She still couldn't get Jennifer's tear-streaked face out of her mind.

Layla's science fiction brain had been convinced the stage manager was a secret, phase-one robot. Jennifer's face never moved from its deadpan stare throughout auditions or the first few rehearsals. But sobs shook her stocky frame as she interrupted the acting on stage. Ariel, her good friend, had been hit by a cab and died on a street downtown. Sebastian had already left; and the actors and crew were subsequently released. Jennifer didn't know when rehearsals or tech-time would recommence.

Layla spent the day picking up groceries and wandering. The city bloomed new life in every crevice, errant sprouts of grass peeking from cracks in the sidewalk. A quick ride on the Metro brought her to D.C.'s tidal basin and cherry blossoms. Pink and white flowers fell from trees, showering her with the fragrant smells of spring.

She wasn't overly religious. Her mother's Catholicism never quite caught on, and father insisted on sending her to Jewish camp every summer in her pre-teens. But that was as far as it went. Though organized religion did nothing for her, she had a strong belief that God was found in nature. Twenty minutes walking through the aromatic new blossoms and watching the geese were enough to restore her spirit. She hopped back on the Metro toward home.

As usual, Eastern Market tempted her when she emerged from the underground tunnels. Today, she gave in. She stopped at each outdoor kiosk, feeling soft alpaca sweaters, reading inspirational posters, sniffing heady incense and candles. The handmade jewelry cost more than a full night's waiting tables, and she reminded herself not to spend money that should be saved for the imaginary place of her own. Perhaps she should take her frozen dinners directly home.

Suddenly, the wind picked up, and the day got a little chillier. She increased her pace, almost pushed by the forceful breeze at her back. A woman wrapped in a bright yellow sari stepped into her path. Layla skidded to a halt and the wind ceased its force. Not a second later, the day was sunny and spring-like again.

"Need a pot?" The woman smiled as her face transformed from ominous to warm beauty. She was older, maybe sixty, dark-skinned, and spoke with a light Spanish accent. She held a silk-draped arm out. "Come look. You may find one of my pieces speaks to you."

Layla glanced around, wondering why the shopkeeper chose her. Though it was late on a Wednesday afternoon, the market was full. Tourists in shorts, stay-at-home moms with strollers, and Hill staffers on BlackBerries all appeared to have more cash in their wallets.

"Come in, child." The woman placed her arm around Layla's shoulders, coaxing her into the stall. After a second's hesitation, Layla ducked under the midnight blue awning and became immersed in a new world. Clay pots in rich earth tones sat on the canvas-covered ground. Muddy yellow urns matched squat, sage green bowls. A large, terra cotta container held ceramic spoons. Glass vials lined the shelves. Most were filled and labeled: "Black cohosh," "Echinacea,"and "White willow." Others had numbers and letters marked in what looked like charcoal.

A long, wooden table held baskets full of empty vials and smaller baskets. A small, mahogany display block featured a painted black, clay ball. Layla ran her fingers along its smooth surface. It felt warm.

"What's this?" she asked without taking her eyes from the object.

"It is a prayer sphere," the woman answered. "You like it?" Layla nodded as she lifted the baseball-sized orb, cupping it in the palm of her hands. Bringing it to her chest, she closed her eyes and exhaled. The earth beneath her feet breathed a sigh of peace.

Wind gusted, blowing up the awning fabric. Layla's loose hair lifted into a black halo around her head. The smell of the mountains filled her nose as she inhaled. Her eyes snapped open and betrayed her. No longer at Eastern Market, she was standing before an altar at the top of a mountain. Tornado-force gales whipped around her, and she knew if she dropped the prayer sphere, the storm would consume them all. She lifted up the sphere, observing that her brown arms were covered in fresh drawings and letters, as she began her chant.

"What did you say?" asked the shopkeeper.

Layla shook her head and the vision cleared. *What the hell was that?* She could have sworn she was sleeping again, or in one of the play's scenes. Method acting was useful—getting drawn into her characters always ensured a terrific performance—but she didn't want to become one of those crazy actors who couldn't tell real life from a role.

"How much for the prayer sphere?" Layla couldn't say what just happened. It was almost definitely nothing, and she refused to indulge her overactive imagination. In any case, she had to have that sphere.

"There is no charge." The woman steadied herself with a hand on the table, beaming. "It is yours."

"What do you mean?"

"I cannot exchange the prayer sphere for money. Take it. It is yours."

"No, I can't. This looks really expensive—" Layla stopped herself when an expression of displeasure flickered across the shopkeeper's features. "I mean, thank you. That's very kind. How much for four of the vials?" She didn't want to insult the nice lady, but she had to pay for something.

"They are not for sale."

Well, that made no sense. Why would the shopkeeper refuse to sell her the glass vials, yet give away a precious prayer sphere? Maybe the woman wasn't all there.

"Um," Layla began. "The prayer sphere is lovely. But, I don't think it's right for me to take it without paying."

"All right. If you must give me money, you can buy this." She rolled up her sleeves, bent over, and retrieved the biggest serving bowl Layla had ever seen from under the table. "It is a pot for stew."

"Oh! A stew pot. Okay, then. How much is it?"

"For you? Twenty-five dollars."

"That's it?"

"Yes, child." A light twinkled in the woman's golden eyes; she chuckled. "You keep the prayer sphere and buy the stew pot. It is pretty, yes?"

It was beautiful. A muted rainbow danced on the ivory-colored clay pot. Iridescent blues, purples, reds, and oranges swirled around. About two feet tall and two feet wide, the stew pot belonged in a museum. As she paid, she wondered where she would keep the thing. She shouldn't close it away in a cabinet, but there was no place to properly display it in Anne's small townhome.

No matter, she thought, as the woman wrapped the prayer sphere in brown paper. She would have bought a dozen regal stew pots for the chance to keep that sphere. Crazy method acting mishaps aside, Layla felt a little bit closer to God when she held it, which she didn't question too much, since it *was* a prayer sphere. She thanked the shopkeeper and carried her parcels away from the market before she could purchase anything else.

What the hell am I supposed to do with this thing? Walking home became a chore. The sphere fit into her messenger bag, but the stupid stew pot was cumbersome. Though relatively light for a giant clay bowl, its shape made it difficult to carry. She was swearing by the time she reached the doorway of O'Malley's, only a few blocks from her house.

Screw it! She had nowhere to be. Turning around to push with her butt, she backed through the pub's door with the rainbow stew pot in her arms.

"Layla." Tom greeted her as she waddled in. "'Tis a bit early for you, isn't it?" He glanced at the clock above the cash register. "Only four-thirty. Happy hour hasna even started yet."

"Yeah, I know. But it's five o'clock somewhere, right?" She set the pot on the bar top, careful not to let it bump into the row of beer taps.

"Hardy har. 'After five somewhere,' eh? Everyone 'as the same line. Usually the drunks, though." He peered at her over his wire-framed glasses. "You becomin' a drunk, Layla?"

"No, Tom. You're supposed to be friendly, y'know. You're a bartender. Gimme a Yuengling and shut up."

"Draught or bottle?"

"Do I need to answer that?"

He smiled and set a glass under the tap. "Good girl. I've taught ya well. You're not scheduled to work tonight, are ya?" He squinted at the spreadsheet tacked to the back wall and scratched the bald spot on his head.

"Nope."

"Ya gonna explain the artwork ya plunked on me bar?"

"Nope."

"Glad you're here." He placed the beer in front of her and turned back to the television. A night game of soccer was on, broadcast from the U.K. Layla knew enough not to bother the Irishman while soccer—ahem, football!—was on the telly. Assorted Europeans perched on bar stools several feet away. Regulars, their eyes remained focused on the screen.

She sat at one of the rickety bar stools, prepared to nurse her beer until her arms regained their strength.

"Hi, Layla. Mind if I sit?"

A tingle ran up Layla's spine. The deep voice reverberating in her bones could only come from one man, and it wasn't her overly-enthusiastic acting partner this time. What was Sebastian doing in her pub?

She swiveled around, and seeing his weary expression, felt compassion flooding through her. "Please sit." She pointed to the stool beside her. "Sebastian, I'm so sorry about your ex-wife."

"Thanks." He slumped onto the bar stool and put up his hand to hail the bartender. "I need a drink."

"Jennifer told us she was in an accident?"

"Yeah. She was crossing the street and got hit by a cab." He ran his fingers through the mop on his head, massaging his temples. The curly hair was a mess, obviously suffering from the repeated punishment all day. His whole body frowned, from the creases on his forehead to his sagging shoulders. "The driver swears his light was green, but witnesses say hers was too. How is that even possible?" He turned to her.

"I don't know." She reached out and lightly squeezed his forearm sympathetically. "Well, you know how lights in D.C. are. Sometimes the series of lights blur together. Maybe he thought the green light ahead was his own... That's all I can think of."

"That makes more sense than anything else I've heard today."

He seemed to take some comfort in solving that mystery. She could offer that much, though she had no idea what to say now.

"What'll ya have?" Tom narrowed his eyes at the intruder.

"Guinness, please."

"Bottle?"

"Tom," Layla interrupted. Sebastian didn't need to be put through the wringer tonight. "This is Sebastian, the director of my new play. Sebastian, this is Tom, my boss here. Tom, please give the man a draft."

The bar owner grumbled his greeting as he poured the drink and returned his attention to the game.

She watched Sebastian sip his beer. Simple conversation might relax his mind. "So, um, what brings you to O'Malley's?" she asked. "I don't think I've ever seen you in here."

"Hmm?" He was staring into the swirls of froth, lost in his thoughts.

"O'Malley's. Do you come here often?" Layla immediately regretted her words. *Do you come here often?* She was spouting pick-up lines worse than Alex's. A flush traveled from her neck up to her cheeks. Her face was probably as bright as her clothes.

Sebastian glanced up at her. He tried a smile, but it didn't reach his eyes. "O'Malley's? Is that the name of this place? I was walking around and saw you come in from a few blocks back. You're not hard to spot in your red sweatsuit."

Layla scrunched her nose and tried not to blush again. She knew he was teasing her. At least her embarrassment brought a semi-smile to his face.

"You work here?" he asked, his mood seeming to get a little lighter.

"Yeah." She shrugged. "I've got to pay the bills somehow."

He nodded. "I didn't picture you as a waitress."

"No?"

"I guess in my mind, you're 'Layla, the fabulous actress.' You don't need to pay bills." Looking down at his napkin, he curled the edge around a finger.

"You're serious, aren't you?" Layla laughed. She felt flattered for a moment, and then realized his comment probably meant he only viewed her as one of the actresses, not as a real person. She tried to suppress a sting of disappointment. A professional distance was safer for their working relationship, she reminded herself.

She watched him pull the napkin out from under his glass and fold it in half. "I didn't mean to make you feel uncomfortable," he said.

"No, I'm fine." Layla mentally frowned. He was perceptive; she was sure she hadn't let her discomfort show. "Anyway, you were a few blocks away when you saw me? What brings you to my neck of the woods?"

"I walked home from the hospital, but when I reached my house, I kept walking. Didn't stop until I reached the Capitol."

"G.W. Hospital, right? That's twenty blocks."

"I know." He took a swig from his beer. "I had to verify her identity there. She hasn't changed her name yet, so they called me. I'm one of the two other people in her cell phone with the same last name. Guess my mom didn't answer."

Layla kept her mouth shut. Sebastian had a lot more to say. And though she was too timid to support him with a hug, she intended to be the ear he needed right now.

"Call me morbid," he continued. "But when we were married, I used to imagine the horror of Ariel dying. How could I handle that pain? I never realized it would be this bad even though I'm not in love with her anymore... I've been walking around thinking she deserved to have someone cry out and scream over her death. Everyone does."

"What about her parents?"

"She wasn't close to her mom. And her dad passed away a few years ago. He was sick for a long time. I hate to say it, but he's part of the reason we split."

"How so?"

"Ariel wanted to leave New York and move back home - to Arlington - when her father was diagnosed with cancer, and I was all for it. We rented a townhouse in

D.C., fifteen minutes away from her dad. She traveled back to New York for her consulting job on weekdays, while I stayed in D.C. full-time. At first, it was practical. I could check in on her dad when she couldn't. She came home on weekends, and we were a nice, happy family."

"It sounds sweet."

"It was." Sebastian smiled, lost in memories of a good relationship. "Then, her father died and our marriage went with him. She skipped coming home a few times, and didn't call as much. She told me she needed some space to grieve. I should have gone up to New York anyway. I never should have left her alone."

"Why? What happened?" Layla turned closer to him, her leg brushing against his beneath the bar. His fingers bent the napkin in half once more as the corners of his mouth turned down.

"Nothing happened. That was the problem. We kept living our lives separately. I already had my theater company in D.C. by that point. Ariel leaned on her friends in New York for support, instead of me. We ignored the fact that we weren't truly living together for about six months before she came to visit Jennifer and didn't stop in to see me."

"Ouch."

He shook his head. "Yeah, it sounds bad. But that was Ariel. She didn't mean to upset me. She had plans with her friend and didn't want to 'bother' me. That was her story." He sighed. "Ariel lived in her own world. It's too bad we didn't try harder to make it work. She was a good person."

"I'm so sorry, Sebastian." Layla downed the last of her

third beer and Tom appeared with a fourth.

Sebastian's eyebrows rose as he watched her move. "So, what about you? Have you ever been married?" He looked into the bottom of his empty glass. "Hey, Tom, another Guinness, please?" Tom handed him a fresh one seconds later.

"Nope. I've had a few serious relationships, but nothing stuck."

"Let's hear it." He leaned forward. "Tell me your failures so I can forget about mine for a few minutes."

"Well, if you insist. Two years ago, I lived with my boyfriend in New York. Are you sure you want to know?"

"Absolutely." The Guinness must have finally caught up with Sebastian. The crease in his forehead was relaxing; and an air of peace settled into his features. Layla tensed over the prospect of rehashing old details. But she'd do just about anything to keep the frown off his face.

She took a deep breath and began. "Jonathan and I met in college—G.W. We were both theater majors. He was the big man in the program. Got every leading male role. Finally, he was Hamlet and I won the role of Ophelia. Cheesy, huh?"

Sebastian placed his glass on the bar and stilled her tapping fingers with his calm ones. She looked at the big hand, noting his bitten fingernails. The small contact between them generated so much heat, she wanted to fan herself. She didn't pull away this time.

"No," he said. "It's cute. Go on."

"Well." She concentrated on her story. "It was my first big part, even in a school production. I threw myself into getting it right. I knew that script inside and out. I can still recite most of the play now."

Sebastian smiled. "Yeah, I was the same way with my first role. I was Stanley in *A Streetcar Named Desire*. I tried to channel Marlon Brando."

Layla chuckled. "I can't picture you yelling 'Stella!' in a tight, white tank top…" Her voice trailed off as an image popped into her mind of his golden skin next to thin white fabric, the muscular chest from her dreams above her…

Sebastian was staring at her—that unnerving look again, as if he could read her thoughts. He squeezed her fingers and said lightly, "Don't change the subject. You instantly fell in love with your Romeo, right?"

"Hamlet. And, no." She cleared her throat, banishing Sebastian's half-naked body from her subconscious. "No, I hated him through rehearsals. I worked my butt off while he showed up late and was barely off-book by opening night. But in the end, I was a sucker for his raw talent. On stage and off, he looked at me like we really were star-crossed lovers. By closing night, I was a useless, girly sack of hormones, tripping over myself to say yes to a date. It's kind of embarrassing now, looking back on it."

"I'm sure it wasn't all one-sided." He peered at her from heavy eyelids. Layla wondered if he knew how sexy his bedroom eyes were.

"You're right." She urged herself to continue instead of being drawn into his gaze. She might do something stupid, like kiss her grieving boss. "It wasn't one-sided. On our first date, he admitted his feelings for me. We dated through the rest of senior year, and a few years after that. Things were going well, so we pooled our money and moved to New York together."

"Ah, the destination of all theater wannabes."

She lightly shoved his shoulder. "Shut up, you were there, too."

"I know. I know. Go on. You and Jonathan shacked up."

"Yeah, we lived in a posh apartment in Chelsea, paid for by Jonathan's dad. I wasn't thrilled at taking his money, but Jonathan talked me into it."

"Must have been rough," he teased.

"No, really. It was weird having someone else pay all the bills, especially someone else's parent. That's not how I was raised. And, my gosh, you don't truly know a person until you're stuck stumbling over his mountain of dirty clothes every day. It was annoying, at best.

"Then," she continued. "The banking industry collapsed and Jonathan's dad lost his job. Sucked for Mr. Rieger, but I was kinda glad Jonathan and I were forced to depend on each other and grow up. I started waiting tables. He started smoking weed between rehearsals. I worked early morning and late night shifts to cover the rent. Jonathan used grocery money to buy cocaine. We partied with Broadway stars, but couldn't afford dinner. I couldn't audition anymore because I was working all the time. I figured it was worth it; he had all the talent. I planned to get back into theater once he made it big enough to support us. I finally left when he got fired from a play for showing up stoned too many times."

"Layla, you're a brilliant actress. You could have made it on your own all along."

"Thanks." She noted his open, adoring face. Her

director had respect for her acting chops. It was a good ego boost. "Well, having no money, I came here. Anne, my best friend, took me in and I've been saving up ever since. The plan was to move back to New York as soon as I saved a couple grand. But after a few months, I missed theater and started performing again. Tom's great. He lets me schedule work around auditions and rehearsals. And now that I'm not supporting an addict, I don't have to wait tables as much. Saving is a little slower than I expected, since I don't work as much as I perform. I pay Anne when I can."

"You're happy with life as it is, though. That's good."

Surprised by his accurate assessment, Layla returned Sebastian's stare.

"Yes, I guess I am happy. I like D.C. I love seeing cherry blossoms down the road and being able to buy a giant stew pot on my way home." She pointed to the rainbow bowl on the bar.

"I saw you lugging that down the street. Good God, woman. What made you buy that thing? You make that much stew?"

"Ha! No, it's a long story. I kinda like it though."

He laughed. "It looks like something my mother would drag in. It's nice."

"Thank you. I have no idea how I'm going to get it home. I nearly had a heart attack carrying it this far."

He pursed his lips as he considered. "I'll carry it for you. How far do you live?"

"Oh!" How could Layla not see this coming? Of course he'd offer to carry the stupid stew pot. There was no way any nice guy would ignore her near plea for help.

She could only blame the alcohol for her myopia. "You don't have to do that. I wasn't trying to get you to carry it for me. I'll manage."

"I know you can do it." He calmed her panic with a hand on her upper arm. "Let me help. It's the least I can do. You let me smile a little tonight. If it weren't for you, I would have spent the evening wandering the streets aimlessly. You probably saved me from getting mugged or something."

He *was* headed into Southeast, the most dangerous quadrant of the city. Still, Layla couldn't imagine any thief who'd willingly attack the six-foot-three, muscled man.

"Okay, I guess I could use your help." She would walk home with Sebastian, have him set the pot on the kitchen counter, and bid him farewell. That would be the end of the evening.

"It's getting dark out anyway." He paid Tom and they gathered their bags to leave.

He was just her boss, doing her a simple favor. She wouldn't read anything into this; she could keep it professional. The plan was in place and she'd stick to it.

Then, Sebastian's hand fell to the small of her back as she hopped down from the stool. The heat sent tendrils of desire coursing through her.

Crap!

* * *

Layla never realized how small her home environment was. She and Anne were both under five-feet-four and their furniture was sized accordingly. Sebastian was a

Titan sitting at the delicate kitchenette set. A deliciously taut, sex-drenched Titan, watching her sip coffee. He attempted to cross his legs and nearly banged his knee on the glass tabletop.

"Thanks for carrying my stew pot."

"No problem," he said. "Nice place. Again, it's not quite what I expected, though." He stretched, one of his feet reaching to rest against hers under her side of the table.

"You've got a lot of preconceived notions about me." Her roommate favored contemporary styles and crisp colors. The kitchen was painted blue with white cabinets and stainless steel appliances. The rest of the apartment featured chrome, white couches, splotches of red accents, and Anne's Picasso prints.

"Maybe. As I said, it's a nice place. I just pictured something less stark. A little more emotion. More giant, rainbow stew pot, less untouchable museum."

She laughed. "Hey, Anne's got great taste!"

"Yes, but I was right. It's not you."

"Yeah, this is my best friend's stuff. My things are in storage, waiting for when I finally have a place of my own."

"I see you in a shabby-chic home. Off-beat paintings. Wild things to go with that hair of yours."

"'Shabby-chic?' You've been watching too much HGTV."

"It was the Do-It-Yourself network, and I had to get some pointers when Ariel moved out." His jovial mood faltered as he remembered his ex-wife. The smile turned down, and his eyes glassed over with unshed tears.

Rushing around the table, Layla embraced his large frame. "Sebastian, I'm so sorry." She cradled his head to her chest and held him.

Exhaling, he stood, crushing her in a hug. "I just saw her two days ago. She can't be gone."

The breath from her lungs was literally squeezed out, but she didn't complain. He needed this release. When he lightened his grip, she gasped for air, feeling her breasts swelling against his torso. He looked down, need darkening his green eyes. His tongue moistened his lips, and this time, she knew nothing would stop him.

Tilting her face up, she let her eyelids slip shut and felt the firmness of his lips meeting hers. Softly at first, he pulled her closer with one hand buried in her tresses. His tongue entered her mouth, gently exploring, asking for permission. Her body acquiesced, ignoring common sense and her perfect plan to remain professional. She deepened the kiss and caressed his sinewy back.

His hand dropped to cup her bottom and he pulled her up the length of his body so she was better positioned. His hardness pressed against her pelvis. Her knee lifted on its own, compressing her center to its match.

Sebastian moved his magical mouth to her neck, nibbling a path to her collarbone. The feathery sensation traveled to her core, fully awakening her passion. She opened her eyes, eager to see the beautiful man and gasped.

It couldn't be. Over his shoulder she watched her messenger bag—the one holding her new prayer sphere—hovering three feet above the floor in mid-air.

Layla disentangled herself and stepped toward the bag.

What the hell? It dropped back to the rug without a sound.

"You're right." Sebastian panted as he held up his hands. "We should stop."

"What? No, that's not—" Her head swiveled from the now-innocent bag to the man straightening his clothes.

"I'm sorry. I was sure you felt the same way. Damn, now you're scared. I'll go." He picked up his jacket and rushed out while she crept toward her bag.

"Wait, Sebastian!"

He was at the street already. And what could she say if she caught up with him? She was going bat-shit crazy. First, the weirdness at the market, and now she was seeing things. She had to figure it out before trying to explain anything to anyone else.

Chapter Eight

Sebastian jogged down Georgetown's streets. Seven o'clock on a Saturday morning always had a peaceful emptiness. Devoid of college students or partiers, the only pedestrians he passed were other residents, clad in workout gear, all single-mindedly pursuing thought-clearing endurance.

Feet hitting pavement, he thought of his whirlwind week. Ariel was laid to rest in her hometown of Arlington, Virginia, minutes away. As had been the case for the three years of his marriage, he still felt uneasy around her mother. He frequently insisted Mrs. Houst didn't like him. But at the wake, he finally got a whiff of her true feelings. The guilt seeping from her perfect, polished façade nearly made him stumble. She gave him her usual icy, half-smile and tried to dismiss him with a curt nod. This time, Sebastian knew her haughty attitude had nothing to do with him. The guilt over leaving her husband and daughter decades ago was destroying her ability to remain cordial.

He dared to approach her. "She knew you loved her," he offered.

"What's that, Sebastian?" Mrs. Houst narrowed her eyes.

"Ariel." Years ago, he might have fled seeing the look the ice queen threw at him. Instead, he now perceived her thawing. A flicker of hope blossoming in her heart. "Ariel said you were the right mom for her. She always admired your ability to follow your dreams and be true to yourself. You were a great role model for her. And she knew you loved her."

The ruby red lip quivered, taking the cool mask down. Relief and gratitude poured from her, filling Sebastian's senses like a powerful drug. She stepped forward, pulling him into a hug as she sobbed.

"Thank you for saying that," she whispered into his chest. "You were always such a dear."

Footsteps sounded in the hall of the funeral home. Mrs. Houst pulled away, wiping her eyes before retrieving a compact. She brushed a dab of creamy powder under each eye. In seconds, she looked ever the wicked stepmother she always had. But the calmness exuding from her was palpable.

Up Wisconsin Avenue, Sebastian turned right onto P Street. Providing closure with her mother might have been the greatest gift he could give his ex-wife. He was lucky he shared such a good relationship with his own mother. He saw her at the funeral, but still hadn't heard the rest of her revelations about his play and their Incan ancestors. He let several calls from her go to voicemail, not in the mood for her brand of theatrics.

He had his own drama with Layla. Going to Capitol Hill that night was a dumb move. There were dozens of other places he could have wandered. Hell, there were three bars on his block that kept tabs open for him. Would he let himself admit the truth? After hours of walking the streets, his soul needed solace from more than a bottle. And Layla drew him.

Maybe his new heightened emotional telepathy thing wasn't real. He might have gotten Layla's signals wrong. It turned out that all-consuming lust was only coming from him. If she felt what he thought she was—what *he* felt— she wouldn't have jerked away.

Even worse, since he was wrong about her carnal desire, he was also mistaken about the beginnings of something more. He wouldn't call it love. Not yet. But, the attraction wasn't all physical. She radiated an intense caring and passion. He kissed her thinking life was so much simpler now that he finally knew what women felt. She liked him. And he could tell because he was Super-Sebastian.

Oh how the hero had fallen! He needed no super-senses to decode the terror in her shocked brown eyes. And, she was right to pull away. He *was* her boss after all. What kind of scum puts the moves on his employee? He should never have taken advantage of the situation.

Sebastian bounded up the three front stairs to his townhome. Rehearsal started in ninety minutes. Just enough time to shower, shave, and forget he ever contemplated a relationship with an actress in his play.

* * *

Actors are cattle.

It was his internal mantra for the day. There was no reason to stare at the curly-haired woman any more than the other actors or crew. Ignore the heat coming off her. Even if he could trust his new power, he'd have to recognize Layla was feeling a sharp sense of confusion and fear, along with the familiar lust and infatuation. And Sebastian knew he was to blame for that. He had to keep it professional from here on out.

"Sebastian." The deep voice was right behind him. He didn't hear Alex approaching the table. His preoccupation with Layla had to stop. "We heard about your ex-wife. My condolences to you and your family."

"Thank you. I really appreciate that."

The young man gave Sebastian's shoulder a quick squeeze before dropping into the chair beside him. Both watched the curly-haired beauty chatting with a lighting technician. She flicked a strand away from her eyes and smiled, an outward picture of calm. She made her beige linen pants look comfortable, yet classy. The rainbow-striped shirt was just weird enough to say she was special. It also reminded him of her rainbow stew pot, and how he should have never let himself go to her house. Common sense and self-control flew out the window around that woman.

"My uncle was right, man. Layla is stacked," Alex whispered.

Sebastian readied a snide comment, then stopped himself before the words left his mouth. Who was he to judge? He may not have used the sophomoric word *stacked.* But he ogled her just as openly.

"Yes," he responded in a hushed tone. "Layla Cohen is beautiful... We might as well get started." He stood, script in hand, and walked to the center of the stage. "Layla, Alex, join me please."

After one week off, he started rehearsals again yesterday with the completion of the ladies' bonding period. Now it was time to have each couple from the play get to know each other in order to develop the necessary chemistry. Layla and Alex portrayed the oldest couple. Though her character was only twenty-five, she and Alex's character had three daughters, and had been mates for several years. They had to get friendly enough to give off the "old-married-couple" vibe. And Sebastian still needed to figure out how to tone down the importance of the mating, as he promised his mother.

"Stand facing each other and hold hands." Sebastian suppressed a wince as Alex entwined Layla's tiny fingers into his. "Alex, pull her toward you. Layla, follow him wherever he leads you. This is to build trust."

Layla's eyes locked onto Alex's as he tugged her hands. She seemed to be avoiding Sebastian. Probably a good thing. He had to concentrate on directing the couple.

"Lock your arms," the director interjected. "Let yourself be moved by Alex. By Kon, your mate."

Alex leaned back with his arms straight out, holding her. He slowly pulled her forward until she went onto her toes, then guided her back down. Taking a step to the side, he lifted her hand up and began a gliding dance across the floor. Faster, he swept them around while taking care to keep her from falling.

Sebastian felt Layla's apprehension ebbing away. Her smile became genuine as she enjoyed the impromptu jig. Alex pulled her hands up over her head and stepped in closer. Her breasts pressed against his chest and he started to bend down.

"That was great," Sebastian interrupted. "Just… great."

The actors looked to him for further instruction. He intended for the exercise to last ten minutes - not ninety seconds. But Layla's ever-present libido was only slightly dampened from its usual heightened state, and he didn't want Alex anywhere near her. Again, he couldn't pick up any emotion at all from the actor. Either way, the exercise was over because it was working too well for Sebastian's comfort.

The biggest play of his career, and he would rather ruin the chemistry than have someone else pawing over his favorite actress. Unacceptable.

"Cattle," he muttered.

"What?" Both actors stared at him.

"Nothing. Get your scripts out and turn to your first scene together. Page…"

"Seventy-two." Jennifer was a handy stage manager.

"So we're already done with this exercise?" Alex raised his eyebrows in question. "That was quick."

"Yep." He plastered the politician smile to his face and left the stage. After finding his usual perch in the audience, he called out to the actors. "I think we'll make more progress if we get right into the scenes."

"Sounds good." Layla retrieved her battered script from her messenger bag. The pages were dog-eared, and yellow highlighter marked all of her lines. Alex didn't move from his spot. "Forget your script?" she asked.

"No, it's all up here." He tapped the kinky, blond hair covering his head.

"You're off-book already?" Sebastian called out.

"I'm a professional." He beamed and Sebastian realized the kid was doing everything he could to please his director. Alex wasn't to blame for having an obnoxious uncle or being cast opposite the woman Sebastian couldn't stop thinking about. Even his dancing and flirting would have been appreciated if Sebastian hadn't gotten involved with the cattle.

He returned the smile. "Good job."

"Suck up," Layla teased.

"Don't be jealous." Sebastian laughed before looking up into the rafters. "David, Nikki, up there on lights, this is a morning scene. Near dawn." The lights dimmed and came back with the faint orange tinges of daybreak. "Anytime Layla—Huayra. You're entering stage-right. Remember, you just found out you and your family are destined to preserve the world's balance and deliver the Inca from doom. You have to convince your mate—Kon here—that he's magical. Kon, you want your wife and your lives to be normal." He would revise the script later.

"Right," Alex answered. Layla rushed off the stage, leaving her co-actor in a spotlight, framed in a soft halo.

"Excellent!" Sebastian called to the lighting technicians. Having expert crew was an unmatched gift.

Layla peeked around the corner. Then, with head held high, she glided into the light.

"Huayra, where have you been? Where are the children?" Kon

uncrossed his arms, turning to his mate.

"The girls are with my sister. I was in the temple."

"The temple again? I told you to stay away from there. It was fine before we married, but now we have responsibilities."

"Kon, with all you have seen, all we have been through, you cannot ignore the prophecies any longer." Layla stepped out of the spotlight, reached for one of the big black rehearsal blocks, and began to drag it back to the scene. Alex picked up the other end as he started his next line. Sebastian noted the placement on his script and nodded at Jennifer. The set-master would have to place a bench or something else there in the real set.

"What have I seen?" Kon straddled the block as he sat and pulled his wife to sit in front of him. "We have only followed your grandfather's teachings. Astrological charts are useful, but they are not magic. The correct mixtures of herbs can cure illness. This is not a miracle. We are smart, Huayra. Your mother, your sisters and their mates, you and I - together we are brilliant. But we are not gods." He stroked her temple as he pushed an errant lock of hair behind her ear. "You must see that."

Huayra stood, letting her hand linger in Kon's. Brows pinched together and chest thrust out, she searched his face for acceptance. "You don't understand. Cocha has found her mate. The prophecy has begun. Once they have bonded, we will be strong enough to defeat the intruders and heal the damage to our land."

"Your mother has brainwashed you. The answer to forcing these intruders to leave is more weapons. Better weapons. And our land will be cured when it rains again."

"But—"

"No matter what your mother says, you are better served helping the other women fashion more spears. If you must follow your

teachings, gather herbs for medicines. You will stop wasting your time in that temple, praying and writing spells."

"Kon—"

"Huayra!" He stood up so that he towered over her. The large man should have intimidated anyone, especially a woman half his size. But she tilted her head up to meet his glare and put her hands on her hips. Kon recaptured her hands in his own and pulled her close, his expression softening. He pressed their bodies together with only their clasped hands between them. "Huayra," he repeated, his tone a husky plea. "We must do everything we can to protect our daughters."

"Yes, Kon, this is what I am doing. Is it too much to believe that our love is capable of stirring the elements themselves?" Her smile quirking, she bit her lower lip.

Just as Sebastian found himself wishing he could taste those lips again, Alex lowered his head to Layla's. He claimed her mouth in an embrace worthy of applause. It was appropriate; hell, the script practically begged for the kiss. All work in the theater paused as the two actors mesmerized the crew. The director scratched out his notes, waiting for the kiss to end.

Alex moved his hands up into Layla's hair, plunging his tongue deep into her mouth. Was that a moan?

"That's enough," Sebastian called out. Layla pulled away and looked into the darkened audience toward his voice. Her lips were slightly swollen from the mauling, but she didn't appear nearly as shaken as she was when he kissed her.

Sebastian hated himself for interfering with a perfectly good scene. They both stared out, squinting, while they waited for direction. He said the first thing that came to mind. "Layla—Huayra, we can barely see your face. Kon, when you grab her, you need to turn her so she's not upstaged by you."

"Oh, okay." Alex shifted his body so Layla was half-facing the audience and he looked at the back of the stage. "But now no one can see me."

"Right. Now you turn so you're facing us too." Both actors were angled toward the audience. A gap separated them.

"This isn't very natural," Alex complained. "We can't get into the scene like this." He reached across the space and patted Layla's shoulder in illustration.

"It'll work. Try it out." Sebastian silently chastised himself for letting his emotions screw with his play. "Go on," he instructed the actors.

Alex delivered a half-hearted attempt at an awkward embrace. As he kissed her, Layla's eyes seemed to find Sebastian's in the dark.

"Don't you feel that?" Huayra asked.

"A warm breeze," Kon murmured, pulling her closer as he closed the gap.

"It's us. It's the prophecy." Still staring into the audience, Layla lifted her arms.

Script pages, scenery sawdust, and discarded sweaters took to the air. Everything not nailed down swooshed around the theater.

Sebastian leaned forward to watch the actress. The vibrant brown energy that normally radiated from her eyes was gone. Her gaze, which reflected heat only moments before, was now a vacant stare. She held her arms high to the side of her body, hair flowing into the air with everything else.

"Shut the door!" A crew member yelled.

"That was perfect timing," Alex said as laughter rang out. "Can we cue the wind like that every time?" Papers drifted down, and a hammer clattered to the floor.

"I wish," Nikki's voice rang out from the rafters.

Sebastian jumped from his seat and ran toward the stage. "Layla! What's wrong with her?" His heart pounded as he neared the statue-like woman.

Her skin a deadly white, Layla's eyes came back from whatever trance she was under. "I'm fine." Her voice sounded scratchy.

"What do you mean?" Still smiling, Alex looked down at his acting partner.

"She was…" Sebastian reached the stage, hurrying to the trembling actress. Her terror was cloying, clogging his brain with every step he took closer.

"I'm fine." She visibly pulled herself together, forcing a deep inhalation through her nostrils and hugging herself.

"You don't look fine." He stepped between the two actors and cupped her cheek in his hand.

She flinched at his attention. "I said I'm okay." Backing away, she rubbed her cheek where his hand just touched. "I need some air. I mean—" She glanced at the mess from the breeze. "I have to go. I'm sorry."

"He's right, y'know," Alex said. "You don't look right."

"I'll take you home." Sebastian moved to get his keys.

"No!" Layla nearly shouted her refusal.

He stopped, getting a whiff of the panic that crept into her emotions alongside the terror. She was scared shitless, and he was at least part of the reason. He wasn't such a monster as to jump a sick woman in the back of a cab, or hump her in the subway. She must really have a low opinion of him.

"I'll take her home." Alex offered his arm in a mock-gallant fashion. With a half-smile, she retrieved her messenger bag from the corner of the stage and allowed herself to be led away. Eyes wide, she glanced back at Sebastian one last time before exiting through the back door.

"Well, that was certainly dramatic." Allora stepped into the spotlight. "She looked like she saw a ghost. What was the matter with Layla?" Lights flickered as the technicians adjusted settings. The movie star's skin glowed in a golden hue, then red, and was finally bathed in a dazzling white that appeared to make her sparkle. She stepped closer to the director and rested her freshly-manicured fingers on his upper arm.

Marveling at his selective self-control, Sebastian barely glanced at the world's most attractive woman while staring at the empty doorframe through which Layla disappeared. He sank down onto a rehearsal block. "She looked right through me."

"When you were in the audience? Yes, I noticed that she appeared to be looking at you while kissing Alex. But, no one can see anything with these dreadful lights blinding them on stage."

"Hey!" David yelled out.

Allora blew a kiss up to the rafters in response.

Sebastian remembered he literally had an audience for his curious display. Partially collapsed on the rehearsal block, he was still reeling over the out-pouring of panic, fear, and confusion coming from Layla. No one ever had such an effect on him. But he couldn't very well explain that to the handful of technicians, or the actress next to him. They only saw an actress fall ill and leave. There was no logical reason for his behavior. Taking a cue from Layla, he inhaled a deep breath and composed himself.

Allora sat down next to him and stretched her legs in front of her. "You may have noticed I am quite early."

He hadn't. He never wore a watch. "Jennifer keeps me on schedule. How early are you?"

Her long hair was loose today. She swept the now wind-blown, tangled mess behind her back. "About an hour. I was hoping to ask about some of the spells my character says during the play."

"Mmm-hmm?" He wondered why Layla seemed so focused on him when there was no way she could have seen more than his body's silhouette.

"Did you know I am from Peru, too?"

"Yes." He felt a connection to Layla just before her eyes went blank, almost like he could sense her emotions from across the audience.

"There is one line that Ceiba says, a spell: 'Full of light, full of charm.' The funny thing is, my grandmother used to say that 'spell' before I went to sleep every night. It was a lullaby. Where did you find these words?"

Sebastian's attention snapped back to the woman standing next to him. "Your grandmother used to say that? So did my mother. And my mother's grandma said it to her."

"Interesting. Where is your mother from?"

"Cuzco, near Machu Picchu. There are about three hundred fifty thousand people living there now. You're from Lima, right?"

"Yes." She smiled. "You have done your homework. But, my parents were born in the Ollachea District, not too far from Cuzco. We used to pass through Cuzco on our way to my grandma's for the holidays."

"So we're neighbors. Maybe that spell was a community saying of sorts."

Allora's smile faltered as she raised an eyebrow. "A community saying? This would not have been spoken lightly." The older woman paused as she studied him, and pursed her lips before continuing. "You do not believe in the words of your play, do you?"

"Of course not. It's a fairy tale." He absorbed the look of disappointment on her face. "Should I? Do you?"

Though her anger sparked, a polite, blank look replaced her honesty. "No, I do not believe in fairy tales. I only believe in what I see and hear. I do respect the old ways. And one who exposes the ancient prophecy to the eyes of the public ought to know the danger he invites."

Chapter Nine

Layla was bat-shit crazy. It was official. Glowing eyes and spells and kisses. And, Holy Batman, the sex. Her episode on the stage was unexplainable. One second, she was kissing Alex and doing a fine job at channeling the energy from her encounter with Sebastian into a believably passionate performance. The next, she was staring across the darkened theater into glowing green eyes.

And screw her, it didn't stop at the freaky eye bit. As soon as she locked eyes with Day-Glo Sebastian, she was transported to another reality where she lay horizontal under the man who was kissing her lips, nibbling her neck, and compelling her to watch, to stare, to *mate* with him as he thrust himself into her.

Green eyes glowing and waking sex dreams. Rehearsal was a nightmare. Now, hours later, Layla stabbed at the lettuce on her miniature plate with a chopstick. "I need a therapist."

"No, sweetie, you need to get laid." Anne scooped up

the last of her miso soup. She had convinced Layla to dine at a Japanese steakhouse.

The popular chain restaurant was the perfect place to drown one's sorrows in huge servings and chef theatrics. Decorated in Americanized-Asian themes, black and white silk banners hung from the ceiling, scrawled with Japanese characters. Nearly every inch of the red walls was covered by tapestries and framed prints of serene landscapes. It would have been a relaxing atmosphere, but the tradition of hibachi chefs preparing the meals at a huge grill in front of the patrons attracted families. Each table sat up to twelve people, and grouped the diners together to save room.

The noisy den lent itself a feeling of anonymity for Layla. The place was crowded and chaotic. No one but Anne would hear her words, or care that she was the freak, carried out of a theater just a few hours ago.

She freely confided in her best friend. "The sex dreams were great when I was actually dreaming, y'know, dreaming in bed and not on stage with half a dozen people watching me."

"You're having sex dreams on stage?" The blond lawyer slurped at her soup. "As I said, you need to get laid."

Layla stuck out her tongue.

Anne laughed and wrinkled her nose as she put down the tiny porcelain bowl. "Seriously, though, when was the last time you saw a doctor? Maybe you need some blood work. Regardless of your dreams or whatever you thought you saw, Alex said you blacked out. That could be serious."

"Oh God! How embarrassing for my acting partner to have to bring me home like an invalid." She glanced at her friend's raised eyebrows. "No, I haven't seen a doctor. What would I say? 'Hey, I'm a sex-starved girl who can't stop fantasizing about mating with her boss?'"

"Who cares about the weirdness? You had what could be classified as an epileptic seizure. You're seeing things. I'm not the only one worried about you."

I also made the wind blow indoors. Layla didn't share that tidbit with anyone. While staring at his glowing eyes, she raised her arms, and felt Sebastian mating with her in another reality, so she pushed the resulting energy through her body and into the atmosphere. She called upon the wind. She knew it as surely as her diaphragm pulled oxygen into her lungs.

Anne sat munching on a sliced carrot. She tried again. "You mentioned 'mating' in your dreams. Assuming you're not a dog, that's something from your play, right?"

"I thought you didn't read the play."

"You got the part. I read the play. Isn't mating a huge part of it?"

"Yeah," she mumbled around a mouthful.

"Good evening." The chef wheeled his cart, piled high with rice, onions, eggs, raw meats, and a mountain of seasoned butter, into the hibachi area. He just saved Layla from a barrage of questions by counsel.

"My name is Kenny and I will be cooking for you tonight. You're having monkey's brains, right?" The tall, young Asian man teased as he verified the customers' orders.

Across from Layla and Anne sat a young family—

father, mother, a cute toddler boy in a wooden high chair, and a precocious five- or six-year-old girl. Precocious Daughter chattered non-stop into her father's ear while the mother concentrated on shoveling smashed carrots into Cute Toddler before he ungratefully threw them onto the floor.

Layla swallowed her food and chose a subject to tackle before her friend argued it all out of her. "Okay, so we haven't gotten a chance to talk much in the past week. Part of my obsession with Sebastian is that we almost 'mated' the other night."

"No!" Her jaw dropped. "How did that happen?"

"He was upset and I comforted him." Layla kept her gaze on her plate.

"'Comforted,' huh? Where did this happen, young lady?"

"The kitchen." She ducked her head as she covered her face with her fingers.

"*My* kitchen? What was your boss doing at our house?"

Kenny poured oil onto the steaming grill into the shape of a smiley face. He grabbed three eggs and juggled them before setting one to spin in the oil. "Egg roll!"

Precocious Daughter giggled while the adults smiled.

Layla turned to her friend. "It wasn't my fault. He carried my new stew pot home for me and things kinda got out of control."

"Yeah, I've been meaning ask about that giant, rainbow stew pot. What the hell, Layla?" Anne shook her head before pinning her with one of the assessing looks she always used when coming up with a grand solution.

"Anyway, it appears your crush isn't one-sided. He's your boss, but you may as well go for it. What stopped you from, y'know, *going* for it that night?"

Layla hated to keep secrets from her best friend, but didn't feel ready to explain floating objects any more than sharing her ability to influence the wind. "Oh, I knew he wasn't really into me. I told you his ex-wife just died. He needed a shoulder to cry on and I lent him mine." Once the lie left her mouth, it sounded plausible. She got so wrapped up in her own panic, she hadn't considered that Sebastian hadn't attempted to contact her since that night either.

Kenny chopped an onion and piled the circular pieces on top of each other. Dowsing it with oil, he used a long, electric match to set it ablaze, flames licking down the dome. "Volcano!"

Cute Toddler clapped his little hands, provoking everyone to join him.

"Are you sure?" Anne leaned in so her voice would be heard.

"Yeah, he never called. And rehearsal was all business this morning. He directed Alex in the best way to feel me up." She took a swig from her Sapporo, savoring the Japanese beer. Maybe she'd have a few more of these tonight.

"That doesn't mean that much. So he's professional. You're the one who turned him down that night?"

"Yes."

"Then I think it's up to you to reach out."

"No, I can't. It was a mistake. We got carried away. He was all messed up and emotional; and I took advantage of that. He hasn't called because he doesn't want to get involved. I need to stop my stupid little crush and get my head back into my role."

"If you say so. This *is* a huge career opportunity for you."

Kenny whipped out a second knife. Brandishing both, he slashed them across one another, making sharp metallic sounds as he juggled them from one hand to the next.

"You're right, it is. The only problem is the more I concentrate on the play, the more the play and my life get intertwined." Layla frowned as Kenny took a step closer with the knives. Everyone leaned back in anticipation as his theatrics spiked.

"You mean the mating?"

"Yeah. I told you I'm dreaming about him all the time. It started even before I met him."

"Wait. What?" Anne dropped the bean sprout she was toying with. "You dreamed about him before you met him? How is that possible? You must have seen pictures online."

"No." She knew she should have kept that to herself.

"You had to. It's not possible otherwise." Sometimes her friend's legal brain was infuriatingly logical. She wrinkled her brows as she pondered. "Nope. But maybe you *should* see a shrink."

Layla's chopstick slipped from her fingers. She made a face in response to her friend, then bent down to retrieve it.

Phwpt!

One of Kenny's knives stuck into the wall where her

head was only seconds ago.

"Holy fuck!" yelled the father across the table.

She kept her head down, but peered up at Anne's blanched face.

Her friend shrank back, holding her hand over her heart. "Oh my God," she choked out.

"I'm so sorry, ma'am!" Kenny rushed over and pried the knife from its spot. He had to brace his boot against the wall to extricate it.

Precocious Daughter looked up at her red-faced daddy and started to wail.

Cute Toddler raised his fists in the air, grinned, and shouted, "Hoe fuck! Hoe fuck!"

The mother patted her son on the head and reached for her little girl.

"Kenny!" A tiny, old Asian woman ran out of the kitchen. She yelled an admonishment in Japanese, grabbing the knives from Kenny's hands and pushing him away from the table. She hit him on the small of his back, and he stooped lower so she could deliver a motherly swat to his head.

"We're really sorry about this, ma'am." A younger version of the old Japanese woman appeared, and taking Layla's hand, guided her from the floor.

For one instant, she considered refusing the help. It was safer under the table. "It's okay," she mumbled as she stood.

"No, it's not okay," the father rumbled at the young hostess. "That idiot damn near decapitated that woman. And he ruined my little girl's birthday."

"Honey, stop shouting." The mother cradled her

daughter in her lap while still attempting to feed Cute Toddler.

"Hoe fuck!"

"We sincerely apologize." The hostess flushed as she picked up the beer glass that fell onto the carpet. "All of your dinners are on us. We'll have another chef out in just a moment." She left before the father could berate her further.

"Dinner's not enough for that kind of mishap. You could have been killed." The father waved his fork at Layla. "I know a good lawyer, if you're interested."

She glanced at Anne. "So do I. But I think we'll be okay."

* * *

"So explain this again," Anne demanded. "I get why you stopped your hot boss from going for it. But why are you pushing Alex away? He's the perfect fling and—" She thumped the steering wheel. "—You need to get laid!"

"Alex is a child." Layla watched cars weaving through the intersection. Saturday night D.C. traffic was as bad as regular rush hour, especially in Georgetown where a lot of nightclubs were situated. Traffic was getting worse as Anne's white Corolla inched its way toward the Key Bridge.

"He was man enough to get you home after you spazzed out this morning."

"He's twenty-four."

"And how old do you think you are? I know you read for the mother's role, but you're only twenty-eight, sweets.

Eek!" She lay on her car horn as a sleek, black BMW pushed its way in front of her.

"I know how old *we* are. Alex is a nice enough kid—"

"He's a grown man who couldn't take his eyes off you."

"—but he doesn't do it for me. He's too thin." She had to grasp for a reason not to find the handsome man attractive.

"He's fit. You want unhealthy?" Turning onto the Key Bridge, she zoomed past the BMW.

"No, I want…" Layla lifted her hands and felt the imaginary pecs of her dream man.

"You want Sebastian. NO!" Anne clutched the steering wheel as the BMW slammed into her side of the car.

Metal screeched and tires squealed as they moved sideways across pavement. The vehicle's speed increased with the assault of the black car, and they crashed into the guardrail.

Layla looked over. Her friend's head was slumped down, the airbag still pressed against her face. Pushing at the big, steel gray poof ball, she tried to force it away from Anne's nostrils, lest it suffocate her. The ball began to deflate, and Layla could place her hand on Anne's chest to feel for breathing. She was alive.

The metallic crinkling sound in the background grew louder. Layla's stomach dipped down into her pelvis as the realization hit her. That sound was the guardrail collapsing. And, they would soon plunge into the river.

She pushed forward, scrambling to get her own airbag out of the way. Closing her eyes, she felt her side of the car tipping over the edge. With a deep breath, she thought of glowing green eyes as she held her hands up and out toward the river, expelling her energy in an exhalation.

Glass shattered. The side mirror blasted away. The car scraped back up through the remnants of the guardrail and onto the street, landing with a thud.

Silence. But not really. As if she were underwater, Layla picked out the sounds of voices yelling, tires screeching, and the river rushing below. She shook her head, hoping to bring life back into focus.

"Child, are you okay?" To her left, peering into the open driver's window, was the dark brown face of an elderly man. His gray beard was twisted and unkempt. A raggedy hat was perched atop his head. Forehead creased and eyes wide, he reached a steady hand down to check Anne for a pulse.

The sight of her friend's blossoming deep purple bruises fully roused Layla. She tried to leap out of her seat to examine the blood-spattered nose tilted at an unnatural angle, but she was held back. Fumbling with her seatbelt, she released herself and scrambled over just as the homeless man pulled Anne out through the open window.

"Hurry up! Take my hand." Laying the small blond woman on the ground, he reached for Layla. Two weathered hands grasped under her arms and pulled her out before she could respond.

The white Corolla—now etched with deep black grooves in its side—tilted over the jersey wall and scraped the bridge as it plummeted down to the river.

"Child, you've got an angel with you." The old man rested his hand on Layla's head. "That car should have gone over a long time ago." He knelt beside Anne and placed two fingers on her jugular vein.

"Does she have a pulse? Is she okay?" She dropped to her knees, tears streaming down her face, and put her head on her friend's chest. Careful not to let her weight fall on the unconscious woman, she listened to the regular inhalations.

"She'll be fine. No lasting injuries."

"Are you sure?"

A stocky, balding businessman stepped in front of the old man. "Did anyone call the paramedics? This woman needs medical help."

The gathering crowd began speaking at once.

"I called as soon as I saw that Beemer pull away."

"Did you see how the car hovered in the air like that? It should have fallen!"

"How did they get out of the car?"

"Stupid Virginia drivers!"

"Hey, I'm from Virginia. It didn't even have a license plate, jerk!"

"—push a car into the river and just drive off?"

Fingers trembling, Layla swept blond wisps of hair from Anne's face. Her friend would be in pain when she awoke, but instinct told her to believe the old man, who quietly disappeared. There would be no lasting injuries.

Should she think about what else instinct had done for her today? She and Anne should be at the bottom of the Potomac River with the battered vehicle. But she used the air to push back against gravity. The wind was in her fingertips, at her control. She wasn't bat-shit crazy or delusional. Her new freaky power saved her best friend and her. Okay. Super-human was better than super-nuts.

What else could she do? Maybe she could heal Anne.

Willing her fingers to cease their quaking, she rubbed Anne's temples and concentrated. "Wake up. Get better. Wake up. Get better."

"I'm awake, for God's sake, Layla. Quit squeezing my head," the wounded woman mumbled.

"I did it! You're healed!"

"You did what, crazy-girl? I've been awake, piecing this together for a while now. My car is gone. There's a hole in the jersey wall. My nose is killing me. You look like hell. Car accident, right?"

"Yes, it was a very bad car accident." She laughed as she hugged her as much as she could without causing possible damage. At least her friend's personality was intact. "I'm so glad you're okay."

"Yeah, I'm good. Is anybody else hurt?" She tried to move her head to look, then groaned before laying it back down.

Layla placed a gentle restraining hand on her forehead. "Be still, Annie. No, just you."

"I'm not at fault, am I?"

"You don't remember?"

"The last thing I remember is ordering another natural ginger ale at the restaurant."

"Oh, well no, you're not at fault. Another car pushed us off the road." Layla explained the accident, and how the homeless man pulled them from the wreckage before it plummeted into the water. There was so much more, but she knew her logical friend would dismiss the unexplainable forces at work here.

"Give us room here." An official looking woman

wearing black Scooby-Doo scrubs with her purple hair cropped short shoved looky-loos aside. She bent down. Peering into Layla's gaze, she squinted her green eyes.

"At least your eyes aren't glowing," Layla mumbled.

"Two stretchers!" the EMT yelled over her patient's head as she snapped her fingers twice.

"No, I'm fine, doctor, ma'am." Layla put her arm out to stop the EMT.

"No, she's not." The blond traitor pushed herself into a sitting position. "She keeps staring off, looking at nothing. I think she bumped her head. And it's probably exacerbating what may have been a seizure earlier today."

"I did not have a seizure! Nor did I bump my head! You bumped your head, Anne!"

"Yes, I know I did. I'm going to the doctor. And so are you."

"I'm fine."

The EMT placed a hand on Layla's arm. The heat seeped into her limbs, making her realize how cold she was. It was a chilly evening and her jacket was in the backseat - the backseat now at the bottom of the river.

"I'm sure you're fine." The EMT's voice was a soothing balm. "But humor me, okay? What are your names?"

"Anne."

"Layla."

"Okay, Anne, please lie back down. We don't know how badly you're injured, so let's be as careful as possible. Layla, you're feeling fine, so lie down on this stretcher on your own while we lift Anne onto hers. We'll all head to the hospital and get checked out."

They would take her straight to the mental ward if she told them she wasn't injured since her windy summons kept her from feeling the impact of anything. Best to take the ride to the hospital.

She closed her eyes as the EMT wheeled her to the ambulance. Glowing green eyes appeared in her darkness. "Sebastian." Her whisper flew into the wind. Glass skittered across the street in a sudden, brisk breeze. A breeze *she* called forth.

Chapter Ten

"Guinness, please."

"Make that two!"

Glancing in the mirror above the bar, Sebastian watched his brother claim the seat next to him. The petite bartender did a double take. He almost laughed at the sexual heat she threw off when she caught sight of the pair. Kinky girl. She was turned on by the twins. His brother winked.

The bartender smiled. "Coming right up."

"Did you have to cut your hair like mine?" Sebastian asked his twin without turning. "We look ridiculous."

"Who told you to wear all black? You know this is my clubbing gear. Besides, I make this style look good." He rubbed a hand through his curls.

"This looks planned, Trystan. *I* can barely tell us apart." Sebastian stared at their reflections. "You're getting a little tubby though." He tapped at the imaginary extra flesh under his brother's chin.

Trystan slapped away the hand and flipped his middle

finger at the mirror. "Be nice. I'm leaving tomorrow."

"Yeah, I know. How's Mom handling that?" He took a swig of his recently served beer and tried not to make eye contact.

"Better than you. At least she can admit she'll miss me."

"I won't miss you, asshole." He shoved his brother.

"Yeah, you will. I'll miss you, too." Trystan righted himself on the stool. "Mom is pissed at you. Why haven't you finished talking to her about your damn play?"

"I tried." Sebastian did call his mother a time or two those first few days. Then Ariel passed away and he forgot about his mother's disapproval.

"Well, try harder. She says you're exposing things that are meant to stay private. You're making life dangerous or something." He turned in his seat to scan the crowd.

Sebastian followed suit. "You believe in the old stories?"

"No, but my mother is upset and it's your fault." He poked his brother's chest as his tone grew serious. "So, you better fix it."

He held his hands up in surrender. "Point taken." Swiping away his brother's finger, he continued. "Now lay off."

Both men leaned against the bar, sipping their dark beers.

"Nice place. Great name," Trystan offered.

"Great place. Awful name." Sebastian delivered his joking jab with a straight face. He'd never admit to first being drawn to the hang-out *because* of its moniker. Now Tryst was one of his favorite spots. Not only was the popular coffeehouse/bar within walking distance of his house, it was one of the best places to people-watch in his Adams Morgan neighborhood.

At nine o'clock on Saturday night, the establishment was making room for the upcoming live musicians. Waiters shoved tables and chairs away from the little stage. Lights were dimmed to a sepia-toned ambiance. Patrons lounged on the over-stuffed lime green and rust orange couches and loveseats. And the average female garb went from sundress and sandals to skin-tight pants and strappy heels.

Sebastian's brother nudged him as three college-aged women in halter tops and black pants walked by. The women openly stared at the pair, eyes wide. One let her jaw drop open.

"Too young." The director was feeling drunk with the raw desire emanating from every woman who spotted the twins.

"Still nice to watch. You seem off. Are you nervous?" Trystan teased as his eyebrows shot up.

"Why would I be nervous?" He downed his beer before signaling the waitress for a refill. "I work with Allora. She invited me to dinner because she doesn't know anyone else in town."

"Allora Delaney is ridiculously beautiful. Any man with half a brain and half a package would be nervous if she asked him out. Straight or gay." He raised his glass at a man in a tight pink t-shirt who stopped to look.

"She's just a woman, Tryst. I have no interest in dating my actresses." He smiled at a gawking couple passing by. He and his brother were a carnival act together. It had been this way since they were tiny boys dressed in matching Osh Kosh B'Gosh overalls. People couldn't help staring at twins. Sebastian was used to that. But now, all the lust waves coming his way nearly floored him.

"Yeah, yeah, actors are cattle. I know. What good is being a famous director if you're not going to enjoy it?"

"Shut up. She's coming." Sebastian stood to greet the cow in question. Looking every inch the movie star she was, Allora glided into the room wearing a gauzy white pantsuit. It was so sheer that if he looked hard enough, he could probably see through the material. He noticed his brother trying and stifled his laugh with a cough.

"Allora, you look wonderful." Trystan stood up and hugged her. "Have you met my brother Trystan?" He swung her around to face his mirror image.

"You are a twin?!" Allora gasped. Sputtering, she looked from one brother to the other, her huge, dark sunglasses doing little to hide her confusion. She held onto Trystan and stared at her director. "Why, he looks just like you. It is uncanny."

Sebastian couldn't believe his brother was pulling this old stunt when his career was involved. He inhaled, counting to ten before he spoke. "That's because I *am* Sebastian." He held up his script as proof. "My brother lives in London and only came here for Ariel's funeral. I hope you don't mind him crashing our evening."

"Not at all." Letting her hands fall away, she stepped back, switching her scrutiny to the man who was holding her. "Yes, this makes more sense. I can see the difference now. You, Trystan, you have more laughter in your eyes. I like you."

Join the club, thought Sebastian. His brother had always drawn more women. That used to bother him before an ocean separated them. These days, he liked to sit back and observe his extroverted doppelganger. Luckily, Allora was amused by his antics.

"I like you, too. Let's get you a drink, Ms. Delaney." Trystan offered his arm to the beaming woman and pulled her to the bar. Holding up his hand, he signaled for the waitress to come over. "The lady will have a…"

"Mojito." Smiling, she kept her eyes glued to her companion.

Sebastian had seen Allora's public persona before. She usually kept her head ducked down, as if trying to avoid being identified. Two minutes with his brother, and her head was held high, already forgetting the plagues of fame. Glancing around, he realized most eyes still landed on his brother and him. Unwittingly, he provided the perfect diversion for his star actress.

Drinks in hand, the trio headed for one of the unoccupied couches. Allora in all white, her black hair cascading down her back in a river of silk, and he and his brother clad in black with golden curls topping their heads, created an artistic image when they assembled on the rust-colored couch. The director made a mental note to include these colors in his set and wardrobe. Perhaps he could have the four daughters in flimsy white dresses and their mates in all black. Did they have black fabric in the 1500s? Pure white?

"…no?" Allora was asking a question.

Next to her, Trystan shook his head as a small smile tugged at his mouth. "Where'd you go this time?"

"I was thinking about the set."

"You have the world's most beautiful woman sitting across from you—literally, the most beautiful, there was an article—and all you can think about is work? Shame on you, little brother."

"Little brother?" The beautiful woman twirled a mint leaf in her drink. "I thought you were twins."

"Yes, we are. Trystan likes to think his seven-minute head start gave him an advantage."

"And vast knowledge. Don't forget 'vast knowledge.'" Trystan stretched his legs across the floor and draped his arms over the sofa. Step one of the three-part series for getting a woman into his arms was complete. Sebastian hadn't seen his brother in action like this since college.

"Oh, so you are the smart one." Allora leaned toward Trystan. "Your brother knows nothing about the play he has written. Are you aware that he reveals secrets with this show?"

"Really?" He raised an eyebrow. "Have you been talking to our mother?"

"Your mother? No, but perhaps I should. Does she know what he is doing?"

Sebastian sighed. "She knows what I'm doing and she's angry. But I still don't fully understand why." He refused to believe his mother's ludicrous explanation. There had to be something more. "Well, Allora, we're away from the theater as you wished. Tell me, what's wrong with my play?"

His brother reinforced his inquisitiveness. "Yeah, someone needs to spill and it may as well be you, gorgeous."

"Such a nice invitation." Allora's sarcasm was doused in her flirtatious charm. "This may all be folklore to you, or bedtime stories your mother told before she tucked you in at night. But for some, this is history."

Sebastian rubbed his temple. "You said you don't believe in all the spells and magic." He didn't miss the irony of trying to convince a woman that magic didn't exist while supernaturally feeling her frustration.

"My beliefs are not the point. There are people in this world who *do* believe in the spells and the magic. And they are dangerous people."

"It's just a play." He almost gasped at the spark of anger that instantly lashed from her.

"Dammit, Sebastian! You wrote your play based on real events. Whether you believe in magic or not, there was once a woman named Ceiba who had four daughters. They were high priestesses. The Spanish destroyed their home."

"My mother already told me that."

"Of course. That much is fact. I've seen the records—"

"You've seen records?" He interrupted. "Why are you researching this?"

She ignored him. "And just as you were told in your 'fairy tales,' many others believe Ceiba and her descendants have special powers."

"What are you saying? There are some wackos searching for superheroes?"

This time Allora glared at her director. "It is not only their abilities, it is what they represent. These descendants and their mates are the only things that prevent the collapse of the corporeal world."

Both men stared at the actress.

"You know this isn't some ridiculous Mayan catastrophe story, right?" Sebastian asked. "The world isn't going to end at a predestined date."

"We are not Mayan. We are Incan, or Tawantinsuyu as the old customs said. You must know that. Your last name, Tawanti, retains some of the old moniker. Our old religion tells of the world being split into three realms: Uku Pacha is the realm of the dead and of new life, the spiritual realm. Hanan Pacha is the realm of the sky, where the sun and moon reside. And Kay Pacha is the corporeal realm, where humans and nature live. Some believe that Ceiba was Pachamama, the goddess of the corporeal realm. And her descendants are responsible for maintaining balance here. Wind, fire, earth, water."

"The building blocks of the physical world. I see the tie-in to the play. But if you can find that much from your research, why does it matter that I've written about elementals in my play?"

Allora swiped back the hair that had fallen into her face. With a little hop, she folded her legs under her bottom. Incan lore was more than research to her. Excitement leapt from her limbs. "Do you not see? You are publicly revealing what Ceiba's descendants can do and exactly how they do it. Nobody was certain before now. You have helped those that would destroy the earth by sharing secrets that should remain with the priestesses and their mates."

"My play is about one Incan family and their belief system. It has nothing to do with the destruction of the world."

Allora's mouth dropped open. "Yes, it does!"

"Okay." Sebastian held up his hands before she could further object. "I added conflict between the evil ones and the main characters, but I made up that part. None of it is true."

"Well, your words—your little fibs—are attracting the wrong kinds of attention. You should not toy with that which you do not understand."

Trystan had been silently watching the conversation. "I have a question. How do you know all this? Why have you researched Ceiba's story? And what exactly is the wrong kind of attention?" He rubbed the stubble on his chin as his eyes slightly narrowed.

She smiled and the apprehension melted away when Sebastian would have expected it to grow. "That is three questions, dear. I am playing the role of Ceiba. Of course, I researched her. Google is useful." She tapped Trystan's knee. "And as I told your brother, my grandmother relayed the play's spells to me when I was a child."

She gave a mirthless laugh as she continued her story. "You call the ones against Ceiba 'evil.' I call them family. My grandmother lived in a village that worshipped the god, Supay, the ruler of the realm of Uku Pacha. Perhaps you have seen the parades for the Day of the Dead even today. My family, members of the Supay followers, honors the spiritual realm."

Sebastian recoiled. "Your family is the evil that wants to destroy the world?"

"Of course not! That is why the other day I asked if you had any idea who these 'evil ones' are in your play.

They do not want to destroy the world. They are a peaceful culture, same as yours... minus a few human sacrifices."

"Sounds great." Trystan rolled his eyes.

"Just as in Christianity, a few zealots go too far. Some of the Supay followers believed that human beings are spirits trapped in the corporeal form. They strove to free us from the disgusting human body so we could all be closer to Supay, to God."

Sebastian understood where she was headed. "So, Pachamama—Ceiba—would represent evil to them because she fights to maintain the physical world."

"Right." Allora nodded. "Her elementals are the embodiment of all that is wrong. Fire, earth, air, water. For the Supay zealots the elementals exist to keep the spiritual realm encased in a physical prison. And now, you have told these people how to weaken the elementals."

Trystan exhaled loudly. "Well, that explains why Mom's so pissed."

Sebastian sat back in his seat, letting the full weight of the revelations settle on his shoulders.

"And the attention…" Allora continued, reaching into the big, camel-colored bag beside her and retrieving an envelope. "I received this at the theater yesterday." She handed it to her director.

"There's no stamp on it." Sebastian turned it over, lifted the flap, and pulled out the half-sheet of notebook paper.

"Right," she said. "Someone must have walked it in."

He read the block letters out loud. "'We know the real you. Deliver the sphere and no one else will be hurt.'"

"What the hell does that mean?" Trystan clenched his fists.

"I am not positive." The actress sat back on her feet. "I called my cousin. She remembers a prayer sphere that was crucial in the old stories. There were four. But the important part is someone is connecting these old stories to your theater."

"I don't have any prayer spheres in my play... It's addressed to 'Ceiba.' Where did you find this?"

"In the audience area where I usually sit to watch rehearsals. Now you see that someone out there still believes in these old stories though you do not. There may be truth to them." Her eyes twinkled.

"Who cares if they're true? Someone is threatening you." Trystan caressed Allora's hand on his knee as his voice tightened. "Did you take this to the police? It's not likely that the Supay followers have traveled here to harass actors in a small D.C. theater. This may be a stalker."

"No!" The actress snatched the letter out of Sebastian's hand. "The police are never any help in stalker situations. I have been 'threatened' before. Such men only worsen when the police get involved. Then they know you are scared. If it *is* a stalker, I have my weapons."

The twins' eyebrows rose to the same level.

"Weapons?" the director asked.

"With an 's.'" Despite his concern, the corners of Trystan's mouth quirked up. His attraction was growing; Sebastian could feel the admiration pouring from him.

"Yes, I protect myself," the waif-like woman continued. "I am more concerned that an organized unit—the Supay cult—is responsible. Whether or not there is any truth behind your story, there is someone who thinks there is. And he or they are willing to hurt people to get what they want."

"So call the police if you don't think it's a stalker." Trystan pulled his cell phone from his front pocket.

"No! Honestly, I cannot have my name linked to this mess. I did not get any good roles for five years after it came out I am pagan. Your country mistakenly thinks anything besides Christianity is devil worship."

"Allora, someone threatened your life."

She cut off Trystan's pleas. "No, they did not threaten my life, just 'someone else's.' I will be fine. I brought it up because I wanted to see if your brother meant to reveal so much. Now I see you both are less informed than I." She gave a little wave of her hand, putting an end to further argument.

She was right about that part. Sebastian sank into his overstuffed armchair. He wrote the play to educate the public about Incan people. He wanted to honor his mother and her heritage. Instead, he somehow managed to anger his mom, expose ancient secrets, and set a psychotic cult on an innocent woman. Bang up job.

The music swelled in the establishment, making it impossible for him to hear the conversation between Allora and Trystan, which continued. They forgot him as they spoke, holding hands while fingers grazed each other's arms and legs. Luckily, he liked to people-watch. And since the arrival of his sixth sense, his favorite pastime had become especially interesting. The average person wore an expressionless mask while concealing a tumult of emotion within.

Allora's earlier apprehension gave way to excitement. The director knew she loved the thrill of having a stalker or "cult" after her. There was caution and a bit of fear mixed into her emotional bag, but the actress was a gunslinger at heart, anticipating her match. He made a mental note to get some scary-looking security guys for the theater and Allora's hotel. Philip would gladly pay for it.

Sebastian chuckled as he watched his brother resume his goal of draping an arm around Allora. Whatever they were discussing, he could feel Trystan's admiration wrestling with physical desire as the dominant sentiment. The actress flipped her hair again and flapped her hands to describe something. Then she gave that radiant, scene-stealing smile and Sebastian knew his brother was lost. Trystan's eyes went out of focus as he tilted his head and stared. Lovesick puppy. It didn't seem like Allora noticed; she kept gabbing.

He wondered if he looked the same way when Layla was around. She was addictive. The more he saw her, the more he wanted to see her. He'd held her twice, kissed her once, and had a need for more contact that could put all the love songs ever written to shame.

He'd watched Layla get ill in the morning and knew he was in trouble. She was a little woozy and he nearly jumped on stage to carry her to safety. Before he walked into Tryst, he left a voicemail for her. And he used the business-like words, "inquiring after your health." When she pushed him away during their kiss, she made it clear her focus was professional. He wouldn't make a fool of himself again.

Would he let himself consider the possibility that every word in his play was fact? A whiff of every patron's inner feelings assaulted him if they passed within ten feet. He was getting used to the foreign emotions, almost as if they belonged. Maybe magic and spells weren't mumbo-jumbo. But where did that leave him with the crazy cult and super-human destiny? That still didn't make much sense.

"Another round?" A waitress in an impossibly short, black mini-dress stooped down to his eye level.

"Yes, please. Two Guinnesses and a Mojito."

She followed his gaze to the couple. "Is that Allora Delaney?!"

"Yes, but—"

"OMG! It's Allora Delaney!" Her screech might have broken glass if the music hadn't been so loud.

Sebastian jumped up and put his hands on her shoulders. "Shh! They're having fun. We don't want to ruin it for them." He walked the waitress—still slack-jawed and pointing—back to the bar. "If you promise to keep it quiet, I'll get you her autograph."

Disappointment mixed with defiance clawed at him from the woman. She snapped her mouth shut, then looked at Sebastian. "You're that theater guy, right?"

He narrowed his eyes. "Yes…"

"You work with her then. I want to meet her. I think we could be friends. Ooh, I'll get a picture with her!" She jumped up and down, body parts close to falling out of the little dress.

Allora and Trystan could both take care of themselves. Trystan would probably enjoy the woman's antics, and Allora was well-practiced in putting off overly exuberant fans. They didn't need him to babysit.

"You can try," he told the waitress. "I've got to go." Turning, he pushed his way through the crowded club. The rust-colored couches were now occupied by squealing college girls. With the not-so-supernatural sense he always had that allowed him to locate his twin anywhere, he zeroed in on Trystan and Allora dancing to the music.

Bodies heaved and swayed to the techno / hip-hop pulse. Trystan held his partner close as they gyrated with the beat. She laughed openly without the reserve Sebastian had come to associate with her. He caught his brother's eye and gave a nod. Time for him to go.

He pushed his way through the crowd and out the door, giving a half smile of acknowledgement to the bouncer now carding patrons as they entered. Party-goers spilled from every establishment on the block. Normally, he would wander into another bar. Tonight, he made his way back to his house in solitude as he fingered the cell phone in his pocket.

It was too late to seek more answers from his mother. And he shouldn't call Layla again. She was probably out having a great time with friends. She wouldn't want her boss calling.

He reached his front door and paused to retrieve his key.

"Sebastian," Layla whispered his name.

He spun around, looking for her though he knew she wasn't there.

Again, he ran to the G.W. Hospital.

Chapter Eleven

Key lime pie Jell-O. Where could the fancy Jell-O be hiding? Layla walked up and down the supermarket's aisles. She passed boxed gelatin and frozen Jell-O pops, but still couldn't find the deluxe, gourmet key lime pie-flavored Jell-O Anne requested.

They escaped their date with the Potomac River approximately thirty-six hours ago. Anne's car was still underwater; Anne, however, was doing well. Suffering only a broken nose and a concussion, she was in super shape. But the painkillers made her a cranky, woozy mess and Layla was trying everything to keep her friend happy and away from the law firm.

That meant running her roommate's errands on a Monday morning. She picked up the dry cleaning (including her own green blouse), dropped off a deposition to the firm's paralegal's apartment (anything to keep Anne from stepping foot in the office and getting sucked into work), was completing the grocery store run (stupid Jell-O), and still needed to stop at Starbucks.

She looked at her cell phone again. The text from Sebastian came in shortly after she arrived at Georgetown University Hospital on Saturday night. *Are you OK? Inquiring after your health again…*

That was a nice, professional text from her boss. He must have been referring to her spastic episode during rehearsal, so she responded with: *Better now. Alex got me home. Thx for checking!* Sebastian had interesting timing. Just as she needed him, he was thinking about her as well. Maybe Anne was right. She shouldn't throw away a chance at love because she was going nuts.

And now that she was alive, thanks to "going nuts," she was rethinking her precarious mental status. The wind was definitely under her command. And it started the day she was in Eastern Market with the shopkeeper. That was the night her messenger bag floated. Or was the bag floating because it contained a magical prayer sphere?

The sphere bumped against her leg in her bag as she pushed her cart. There was the key lime pie Jell-O. She tossed two cartons on top of the ice cream and headed to the checkout. The day's agenda formulated in her mind: Get Anne's shopping done and go to Eastern Market to question the woman in the yellow sari.

"Do you have a shopper's card?" the cashier asked as she dragged the snacks across the conveyer belt.

As Layla reached into her bag, a tabloid magazine caught her eye. "Allora's New Beau!" read the headline. The cover image showed her co-star in a lip-lock with a golden-haired, tanned man. Layla didn't need to flip the pages to find the name of the lucky guy. Sebastian.

"Do you have a shopper's card?" The groceries bagged, the cashier drummed her nails on the register as she repeated her question.

"What? Um, yeah." She snatched the tabloid and handed it to the woman. "This too."

The cashier smiled. "She's fabulous, isn't she? I've always loved her. Looks like she found someone as hot as she is this time."

"Yeah." The contents of Layla's stomach boiled to liquid. The need to vomit almost overwhelmed her as she grabbed her bags to rush outside. Gulping in the fresh air of the spring day, she placed the groceries on the pavement and leaned back against the building.

He wasn't her boyfriend. She rejected him. Of course he made out with Allora as soon as he got the chance. Sebastian didn't owe her anything. And she shouldn't feel like she just lost her dream man.

But that's what he was. He was her dream, her fantasy, her imagination's Adonis come to life. He was her inspiration for love scenes. She was connected to Sebastian. She dreamt about him before they met and saw his glowing green eyes whenever her magic kicked in. They were meant for each other. How could he be sleeping with Allora?

Maybe he wasn't. She fished the magazine, *Page Seven*, out of the plastic bag and flipped to its table of contents. "Allora's New Beau!" on page thirty boasted more pictures to tell the tale. Allora and Sebastian dancing. Allora and Sebastian giggling on a couch. Allora and Sebastian making out on a couch. And Allora and

Sebastian getting into a cab together, his hand on her bottom as he helped her get in.

The accompanying article spelled it out in case she didn't see the obvious: "Our sources tell us Allora Delaney's new beau is Sebastian Tawanti, owner and artistic director of Sylph Theater in D.C. Delaney is in our nation's capital rehearsing for Tawanti's new play. Love is in the air. The hot new couple pawed each other all night before leaving hand in hand. The sheets will sizzle!"

It made sense. Layla picked up Anne's groceries and started home. No use brooding over a man that was never hers anyway. Yes, he was gorgeous. And sweet. And funny. And the star of her fantasies and magical flair. But she had her shot and blew it. Now he was with über-hot Allora Delaney.

She walked three steps past Starbucks before remembering her roommate's caffeine addiction. Of all the items on the list, Anne's morning coffee would be the worst to forget. Backtracking, she pushed through the door and made her way to the end of the long line.

"Back from the temple already?" The deep voice startled her.

She turned and looked into the handsome, unassuming face of her acting partner. "Alex!"

"Sorry! I didn't mean to scare you." His nose wrinkled, making him look younger.

"No, I'm in my own little world. What are you doing here?"

He glanced around. "Getting coffee." The white sweater he wore complimented his dark skin, as he raised one eyebrow over a sparkling brown eye.

Now it was her turn to be embarrassed. "Yeah, that makes sense. You live around here?"

"No, I live in New York. I figured I'd see some sights on my day off. The Capitol is around here, right?"

"Yep." Layla reached the counter. "Two cappuccinos, please. A venti with skim milk and two extra shots of espresso, and a plain tall one."

Alex raised his eyebrows.

"It's for my roommate. She needs her dosage."

Laughing, Alex nodded. "I understand." He ordered his own heavily caffeinated beverage and stood aside to wait with her.

"So," he started. "I really have no idea where I'm going."

"It's easy. The Capitol is the center of D.C. All roads lead away from it. We're at 8th and D Streets, so go toward 1st and A. Keep walking. The Capitol would be at Zero if there were such a street." She twiddled the thumbs clutching her shopping bags. She was a twerp for not volunteering to walk him there, but she knew he was really asking her on a date. And she was determined not to start a relationship—or a fling as her sex-obsessed friend suggested—with her acting partner. She already had a bad case of unrequited love for Sebastian. There didn't need to be another awkward situation at work. She reminded herself that visiting the Capitol on a workday during rush hour was about as much fun as getting her armpits waxed.

"I guess that's easy enough," he mumbled.

"Venti skinny cappuccino, two shots! Tall cap!" the barista yelled out.

"That's me." Layla smiled as she maneuvered her way back to the front, Alex right behind her. She stopped at the counter with groceries gathered in her left hand and dry cleaning slung over her right arm. Her heart sank as she stared at the two drinks. She wanted to kick her own butt for not realizing she wouldn't be able to carry everything on her own.

Alex grabbed a cardboard drink holder and put the three drinks inside. "Come on. I'll help you. Again." He tossed a smile back at her as he held the door open.

He was such a nice guy. She briefly considered running in the opposite direction, screaming. Instead, she used her acting skills and put on a happy face.

"So, why isn't Anne helping you with these errands?" He pulled three of the four grocery bags from her hand as they walked toward her house. "You're supposed to be resting."

"Oh, we've gotten into way more trouble since we last saw you." She remembered that the last time she saw Alex he was bringing her home from the theater two days ago. It seemed like a lifetime.

"What happened?"

She sighed. How much should she share? "Well, we went out that night since I was feeling better. First, a chef nearly killed me with his flying knife."

"Huh?"

"It was a Japanese steakhouse where they cook at your table?"

He nodded, hanging onto her words as they walked down the cherry blossom tree-lined street.

"Kenny-the-chef was dicing veggies and showing off when one of his knives slipped and almost impaled me. I bent down to pick up my chopstick a fraction of a second before I would have gotten hit."

"Amazing you were so lucky." He shook his head.

"I know, right? But that wasn't the end. We were driving across the Key Bridge after dinner and almost got sideswiped into the river!"

His mouth gaped open. "How?"

"A BMW slammed into the side of Anne's car and pushed us through the guardrail. We got out of the car just before it went off the bridge."

He stopped and stared at her. "Jesus, Layla, you were in a car accident? Why didn't you tell me?" Lowering her bags to the sidewalk, he pulled her closer into a hug. "Were you hurt?"

Um, she didn't tell him because she didn't realize she was supposed to. He never entered her mind. That wasn't a nice thing to say, though. She stepped out of his embrace and decided to focus on Anne. It was better to transfer his concern than to address his questions. "I'm fine. Not even a scratch. But Anne got a pretty bad concussion and a broken nose."

"Oh, no wonder you're running her errands." He picked up the groceries and looked down at her, a bit closer than purely platonically. "You two are a danger to yourselves. You should stay in bed."

Layla could feel the heat coming off the close young man. Did he mean the double entendre? Putting distance between them, she took a step back again. "Anne's in bed. No worries." She started to walk again.

"All the same, I think I'll look after you today."

"No, there's no need to do that!"

"You were already sick, and now you're trying to take care of your injured friend. Out running errands when you should be at home resting. Somebody needs to step in and it's going to be me." He walked ahead of her without waiting for her answer, a grin on his face.

"I don't want to be a burden. I mean, don't you have somewhere you'd rather be instead of taking care of injured, afflicted women?" She stopped herself before she reached out to touch him. *No flirting.* But, having a guy openly pursue her was a nice change. Sebastian was no longer an option now that he chose to shack up with Allora. Maybe her roommate was right: There was no good reason to keep pushing away her good-looking, nice, available co-star.

He gave a pout as she caught up. "No, I'm pathetic. I have no friends here and nothing to do unless I want to hang out with my uncle's friends all day. And I'm tired of getting hit on by women who used to babysit me."

"Ew!"

"Exactly. Save me, Layla!" He leapt in front of her and dropped to his knees, balancing drinks and groceries at his sides. "Please let me spend the day fetching you bonbons and refereeing pillow fights. I'm begging!"

"Get up! Pillow fights?" She laughed out loud for the first time in days.

"Yes, pillow fights. I know you female roommates strip down and pillow fight every night. I won't accept any denial from you. Don't try." He hopped up in a fluid display of masculine grace without touching the ground.

"Let me watch and I'll be your servant. In every way." This time he wiggled his eyebrows, making his meaning clear.

Laughter bubbled out of her. "I hate to disappoint you, but Anne and I do not have nightly pillow fights."

"Weekly, then? Promise me you'll call the next time she gets frisky."

"Whatever, weirdo." She stopped at the old Victorian townhouse she called home. "This is me."

"Yeah, I know, invalid." He unlatched the little, black gate in front of her walkway and held it open. "I brought you home two days ago, remember?"

"I know that." Holding her nose in the air, she wished she could put her hands on her hips as she jostled bags and dry cleaning up the walkway. The scary truth was she barely remembered coming home with Alex. She recalled the theater and causing wind to blow. That would forever be etched in her mind. And she remembered lying in her bed later with Anne bringing water. But she didn't fully understand how she got from the theater to her bed. Alex was involved. She had fuzzy memories of his face looming in front of hers. Did they take the Metro? A cab? Did he hitch her to the back of a unicycle and tow her in a rickshaw? She had no idea. Maybe she *should* go to the doctor. She wrinkled her forehead with a frown.

"Hey, everything was innocent when I brought you home. I promise I didn't even feel you up." He gave a sly smile.

"No, I'm sure." She returned his smile to hide how creepy his accurate reading of her concern was. "I'm thinking you may be right, anyway. I need to see a doctor." Using her key, she opened the front door and pushed her way in.

"Now? Should we go?" He stepped back out of the house.

"Not right this minute. Come on in." And just like that, Layla asked him to stay.

Sitting on the couch covered in ugly, plaid blankets and gossip magazines, Anne raised her eyebrows. "And here I thought I'd have to console you over Sebastian. You move quick, girl." She smiled at the visitor. "Good to see you again, Alex. What brings you here?"

"Nice to see you again, too." He closed the door behind him. "I'm the knight in shining armor here to rescue the damsels in distress."

"Oh? And Layla is letting you rescue her?"

"She has no choice. There's no resisting my charm. But what's this about Sebastian?" He returned his attention to Layla. "Why do you need consolation?"

She lay the dry cleaning over a white armchair, the plastic instantly clinging to its metal back. Taking the grocery bags from Alex, she avoided eye contact. "Oh, Anne's just being funny. She thinks Sebastian is cute. And it appears she read about his dalliance with Allora in today's *Page Seven*." She grabbed the open magazine from her roommate's lap, rolled it up and thumped her on the head with it. "She just loves—" *thump* "—this kind of gossip."

"So much it hurts." Anne covered her head. "Concussion here!"

"Sebastian's with Allora? Really?" He reached for the tabloid.

"Pictures don't lie." Layla kept her face emotionless as she handed over the magazine. The last thing she needed was for a rumor to get started that she had a thing for the director. The prospect of having to watch Sebastian cuddle up with Allora for the rest of rehearsals was bad enough. She certainly didn't want everyone thinking she was the jilted ex-lover.

Her co-worker thumbed through the pages, a smirk on his face. "That dog. He is my new hero." He shook his head, lost in admiration. "He did it."

"You think this is nothing more than a fling, then?" Anne piped up from the couch. "See, nothing to worry about, sweetie." The drugs loosened her tongue.

Layla rested her hands on her friend's shoulder. "Why don't you get some rest in your room?"

Finally getting the message, the lawyer gathered her magazines and stood. "Yeah, that's probably a good idea. My brain isn't working right. No filter on my mouth today."

Unhearing, Alex looked up from the magazine. "You're leaving?" He gave back the tabloid and walked the few steps to the adjacent kitchen. "Don't forget your coffee. Let me put it in a mug for you. It'll taste better."

Layla watched him open cabinet doors until he found the right one. He selected three oversized mugs and went to the refrigerator. "What do you need now?" she asked as he rifled through organic eggs and condiments.

"Whipped cream. Everything is better with whipped cream." His bottom was in the air as he bent over.

"Sure is." Anne paused to stare as she made her way to the stairs. "Bottom shelf on the door." She winked at her roommate and mouthed the words, "You need to get laid."

Shameless hussy. Layla couldn't hold back her giggles.

"Such dirty minds! I like the way you two think." He straightened, putting the whipped cream on the counter with the mugs. The high, breakfast bar ledge obstructed the view as he prepared the drinks. "Here you go, Anne. Do you need help getting into bed? Please say yes."

She swatted him on the shoulder. "No, I'm fine. But, I think Layla could use your... assistance."

"Anne!" The blush crept into her cheeks as giggles turned into laughter. "Go to bed, you loopy lunatic. And don't come out until you have some sense!"

"I'm going." She pouted. "But you know I'm right. About everything." Her drugged friend held the magazines in one hand, her coffee in the other, and dragged her hideous blanket under her arm as she made her way up the stairs.

"She's nice." Alex came around the counter and handed Layla a pink mug with frothy cream peeking over its edges.

"She's a crackpot."

"Is she right?" He stepped into her space, looking down with big, brown eyes as their bodies met. "Is there something I can help you with?"

Young or not, Alex was all male and seemed to know how to get her heart pumping. Fingers lightly brushing her arm, he used his free hand to palm the small of her back and pull her closer.

She blinked and broke the spell. This wasn't what she wanted. Chocolate skin, solid body, and a taut bottom -

yes, he was attractive. But he was her acting partner and she did not want tension between *two* men on the set. Stepping back, she put up her hand. "No, my roommate is over-zealous at the moment. I'm fine. No help needed here."

He tilted his head and studied her. "That's probably a good choice. I don't think you could handle me, little miss."

What a cocky bastard! Layla almost wanted to kiss the grin off his face. "Is that so?"

"That's so. It's okay. We can start our relationship by feeling each other up at rehearsals. You'll change your mind." He stuck his finger in the whipped cream of his cappuccino and smudged her bottom lip with it. "Drink your coffee."

Well, damn. She watched him raise his mug to his mouth. Licking the froth from her own lip, she couldn't help imagining him kissing her again, this time without a spotlight. Sebastian *was* with Allora. What would be the harm in having a little fun with Alex?

She raised the pink mug to take a sip. It halted in mid-air, sloshing hot liquid onto her hand as she tried to lift it higher. *Oh no! Not again!* Crazy things happened every time she decided to ignore propriety and get intimate. She placed the cup on the counter. Maybe she could start over. Switching hands, she slowly lifted the mug to her mouth. It stopped three inches away. She could not bring the stupid cup any closer to her face. She tried lowering herself to the mug, aware that Alex was watching.

This time, a wind blew through the room. *Stop!* She tried commanding the element. It grew stronger, pushing her hand and the mug away until she dropped it onto the floor, coffee soaking into the cream-colored plush rug.

"Holy crap!" She rushed to the sink to retrieve cleaning supplies.

"You didn't have to drink it if you didn't want any whipped cream. No need to throw it on the floor." His voice held an odd edge to it.

"Oh, I didn't mean to." She bent to get cleanser and paper towels under the sink and found him picking up pieces of the mug.

"Just kidding. Is there a window open? There was a breeze in here." He flashed a mega-watt smile.

"There must be one open somewhere." She lied.

"Let me help with that." He soaked up the coffee with the paper towels.

"No, that's okay." Layla looked at the handsome young man. Perhaps this was for the best. She didn't want to have a fling or a relationship with her co-worker. "Alex, maybe you should go. I'm going to take a nap."

"Oh." His shoulders drooped a bit before he caught himself. "Well, don't forget, we have rehearsal soon. You'll change your mind." He leaned forward and planted a quick kiss on her lips. "Sweet dreams."

Leaving his drink on the table, Alex made a hasty exit.

Alone, Layla thought about that promise. Everyone was right. She did need to get laid. And if she had to handle countless rehearsals of Alex kissing and pressing himself against her, she'd probably let that someone be him. Why resist?

Chapter Twelve

"But I did not know there were photographers present! This Tryst place is *your* neighborhood pub. You said it would be safe!" Flushed, the actress jabbed a finger at Sebastian's chest.

Few people got to see the cool, mysterious, unflappable star irate. This fact did not lessen his annoyance.

"You're Allora Delaney. Someone will always snap a picture of you."

"'Someone?' Not just 'someone!' It was a photographer for *Page Seven*! How could you take me to a club frequented by the paparazzi?"

"I didn't!" Throwing up his hands, he walked across his office. In the tiny, converted dressing room, the trip took six steps. "Paparazzi were probably following you as usual. Why did you have to kiss my twin brother?"

"He kissed me! And it is none of your business whom I kiss! How dare you!" Her hands flew up as her face turned an alarming shade of red.

"Normally, I wouldn't care whom you choose to kiss, or if you kiss him on the White House lawn. But in case you didn't notice, this article assumes it was me!" He held up the tabloid and pointed to *Sebastian Tawanti* written in big, bold letters.

"Yes, well…" Allora wrapped her arms around herself and looked to the side. "That is not my fault."

"Not your fault?"

"No, it is not my fault. Who told you to bring him anyway? It was supposed to be a private conversation between the two of us."

"Trystan wanted to meet you."

"Well, he met me." She plopped onto the guest chair in front of the small mahogany desk.

"Yes, everyone can see that. Only, they think it's me. Allora, you have to clear this up." He cringed as he tried again to figure out how to explain the mix-up to Layla. Every time he dialed her number, he reminded himself that he didn't owe her an explanation. She rejected him, and he'd probably make a fool of himself concocting excuses where none were warranted.

"Oh no! I cannot do that!" She jumped to her feet. "I cannot clear this up and neither will you."

"Why the hell not?"

"Because right now, it is a cute little story of an actress falling in love with her director. We are so in love, we do not care who is watching. And so on. If you tell them the truth, the headlines become, 'Allora Shags a Stranger!'" Her hardened eyes flashed. "I will be lucky if they do not call me a whore. You cannot tell anyone!"

The waves of panic from the actress began to chip away his resolve. "Allora, I understand the situation you're in. It's a double standard for women. I get it. But I have a life here. I don't want people thinking I'm involved with you when I'm not."

She crossed her arms. "It is Layla, yes? You are in love with her."

"No. It has nothing to do with Layla." He wondered if his nose was growing. "I don't get involved with actresses. Everyone who knows me knows that."

"Oh good." She clapped her hands. "Then it is settled. The elusive Sebastian Tawanti has fallen for me. We are perfect together. A pretty picture, no? Then it can quietly end after the show. Those kinds of relationships happen all the time."

"No."

"Yes, Sebastian. This will be good for the play. People will come because of the back story."

"The back story is that these are stories passed from generation to Incan generation. It's culture!" He wanted to scream.

"That is not a very interesting back story to me, and I am Incan. Besides, you must change the more private parts of the play as we discussed."

"I still don't—" Sebastian took a deep breath. "That's not the point. What about my brother?"

"What about him?"

"Don't you care how he feels about this? Aren't you planning on seeing him again?"

"Well…" She shrugged one shoulder.

"What the hell? He likes you!" Sebastian recalled the fuzzy stirrings of real feeling wafting from his brother that night.

"Oh he did not! He wanted to sleep with Allora Delaney." She hugged herself, eyes blazing and mouth set.

He wondered if she remained single by choice or tossed away all men like Trystan. There was a hurt, little girl quality about her. He stopped focusing on his own anger and felt the fear and insecurity oozing from her.

"That may be true. You're beautiful," he started. "But I know my brother, and it was more than that for him. He was laughing with you when I left. He was captivated by your childhood stories, hanging onto every word from your mouth. There were no scripts involved and he wasn't preoccupied by stardom. He liked you."

She looked up. "You think so?"

"Yes."

She sighed. "Well, that is nice. But it does not change the fact that I cannot be seen as a whore."

"Okay…"

"You have to do this for me. For your theater. Play along." Allora stepped closer, her hands together in a plea. "Or simply say nothing. Do not confirm or deny anything. That is what my publicist always does. Can you do that?"

He crossed his arms. She shouldn't be called a whore; that was unfair. But he still didn't like the idea of taking the blame for actions he never committed.

"Please, Sebastian. I will beg if I must." Now standing inches from him, she looked up and batted her eyelashes. "Please, please help me."

"Fine."

She hugged him, and her relief flooded the room.

"Two conditions." He gently pushed away.

"Anything!"

"Neither of us ever confirms this lie. I won't deny it if you don't confirm it."

"Done."

"And you have to call my brother."

She smiled. "Done."

"Okay, it's time for rehearsal." He opened his office door. The one-on-one scheduled for the star of the play should have been on stage. Regrettably, their private time only strengthened the illusion that the pair had a relationship. Nothing could be done now. He walked ahead into the theater.

"There's the celebrity couple!" Alex stood and applauded as they entered. "Philip says this stunt has generated more press than anything he could have paid his PR team to do. Well done."

An open copy of *Page Seven* lay on the table, Trystan's and Allora's lips locked in a passionate embrace for all the world to see. Layla sat with her back ramrod straight, a plastic smile stuck on her face. Chatting quietly with Blythe, she made a point to ignore the display. As he got closer to the actors, he felt the sharp pang from her. It was a sense of betrayal.

That brought two facts to Sebastian's mind in an instant. First, Layla wanted him. She could pretend to be professional and hold him at arm's length, but the idea of him shacking up with someone else devastated her. He almost grabbed the woman out of her seat to kiss her.

Second, he was able to control whose feelings invaded his psyche. There were five actors plus crew in the room at the moment, and Sebastian was zeroed in on the small, curly-haired woman in the ivory sweatsuit. Nice! No more teenage angst from the neighbor boy, or lusty vibes from the checkout lady. He could turn his sixth sense on and off at will now.

He tested it on the table's occupants. Focusing on Blythe, he felt boredom and repressed fury. Weird, but moving on. Antonio, her partner, was over-the-top excited. The young man stared at Allora. Oh right, it was his first time working with her. Allora remained relieved. Alex was… still nothing from Alex. But, otherwise he controlled his sixth sense. He smiled.

"Look at the proud grin!" Alex slapped the director on the back. "Well done, sir. It's good to see you two so happy."

"No, that's not why I'm smiling." He frowned at the misunderstanding.

"You're not together?" Alex raised his eyebrows.

Layla stopped feigning interest in Blythe's chatter and looked up at him with a glint of hope. He wanted to bend down and kiss away her pain. Behind him, Allora kicked his Achilles heel with her pointed shoe.

"Ow! I can neither confirm nor deny that." He gritted his teeth. "Please get rid of the tabloid trash, Alex." He winced as Layla's eyes returned to their dull, downcast state. *Get through rehearsal. Then screw the agreement and tell Layla the truth,* he thought. "Moving on, today is special effects day. Layla, you control fire, so there's obviously some danger in the execution of that. Blythe, your water works aren't necessarily dangerous, but it's going to be tricky."

"I thought Layla was the wind," Alex interrupted.

"No, I'm not wind. Why would you say that?" There was a hitch in Layla's voice. "Didn't you already memorize the play?" Her slightly widening eyes hinted at the alarm Sebastian perceived from her.

Whatever the problem could be, he started to come to her aid, but her acting partner beat him to it.

"My bad. Sorry, babe." Alex draped an arm around her shoulders and squeezed.

Sebastian waited for her to throw off the arm, yell at the kid, or at least raise an eyebrow. She did nothing, but stared at her script while Alex hugged her to his side.

"Right." He felt Allora snake an arm around his own shoulders. "So, Layla is fire and Blythe is water. Glad we cleared that up. Smitty here is my special effects lead." A well-built black guy in a gray jumpsuit sat in the audience with his feet on the chair in front of him. "Listen to Smitty and he'll make sure we live and don't burn or flood the house."

Smitty made his way to the stage, pointing out various nozzles from which water would spurt or fire would leap. He kept the actors' attention, showing them how they should handle canisters of lighter fluid and water jets. This presentation was mainly for the women. Their mates would be responsible for ending the special effects should anything ever go wrong.

Allora was special because her character could control everything. At least, that's how it was in Sebastian's version. He invented her powers since none of the stories he'd heard ever mentioned them. As the actress sat back watching Smitty, he wondered if Allora wasn't more like his version of Ceiba than he originally thought. She controlled too much in real life as well. Layla was cozy with Alex and Sebastian wasn't supposed to say anything.

The special effects technician fit the actresses with fire-shooting and water-squirting belts. They practiced their crafts, Layla releasing flames on cue while Blythe doused them with her fancy water gun. Jennifer held her stopwatch, barking out orders until the timing worked with the script.

An hour passed with the director taking notes, absorbed in his creation. He tried not to think about his personal qualms, but just as he couldn't get a sense of Alex's feelings at all, he couldn't turn off Layla's. Every time she approached him, he got walloped with a dose of misery.

Jennifer finally called the end of rehearsal. Blythe, Antonio, and half the crew filed out. Allora gave him a wistful smile as she flicked her fingers in a little wave and left. Alex tried to hold Layla's hand, but she dodged him as she reached for her messenger bag.

Sebastian seized the opportunity. "Layla, can I see you in my office for a minute?"

Alex glared at the director.

"Bye, Alex," he called. "See you tomorrow or whenever you're here next." He dismissed the actor, not bothering to hide his smile.

"What do you want, Sebastian?" Layla looked at him with cold eyes.

"Let's chat in my office."

"You just had Allora in there. You need me, too?" Her meaning was not lost on him.

"I did *not* have Allora in there. I have never *had* Allora," he whispered. "Can we talk in private for a moment?" He steered her out of the theater and down the hall to his little office.

"You didn't sleep with Allora?"

"Nope. I'm only interested in you." He closed the door as she paced the room. It was time to make his heart as plain to her as hers was to him.

"This isn't you?" She pulled her own copy of the tabloid from her bag, already folded to the picture of his brother.

"No."

"What? You have an evil twin?" She stopped and shook her head at him.

"Yes."

"What?" She stared at him, a mixture of disbelief and confusion. These feelings were better than the misery.

"Trystan's not evil, but he *is* my twin, and that's him."

"How stupid do you think I am?" She yanked the magazine back, stuffing it into her bag.

"I don't think you're stupid. I think you're a beautiful, intelligent, talented woman. That's why I want you."

She shook her head again, leaning on his desk for support. "You want me to believe you have a long, lost twin?"

"He's not lost. He lives in London."

A mirthless laugh escaped her. "You're not making any sense."

"Yes, I am..." He moved so he was right in front of her. He had to make her believe him. "Listen to me, Layla. My ex-wife died. My brother—my twin—was in town for the funeral. He met Allora and kissed her. Pictures were taken and the reporters assumed it was me. I don't want her. I want you."

She threw up her hands. "Then why don't you tell them it's not you?"

"Because Allora is afraid of people calling her a whore for sleeping with a guy she just met."

She frowned. "Hmm, I understand that." Pushing him away, she placed her hands on his chest. "But I still don't think I can believe a twin showed up and bonked Allora so you'd get blamed for it."

Why was it so hard for people to accept twins? He pulled his iPhone from his pocket and scrolled through the photo gallery. "Look, here's me and Trystan. His hair was long until three days ago. Now the asshole is my mirror image."

"Holy Batman! You have a twin!" Joy blossomed, erasing the misery within her. "That wasn't you..."

"No. I only want you." He stepped closer again, although something still bothered him. "What's going on with Alex?"

"Nothing. You know he took me home the other day."

"And nothing happened?" He gave in to the urge to touch her. Running his thumb along her upper lip, he felt the familiar desire coursing through her.

"Not then."

"When?"

"Yesterday, we ran into each other at Starbucks. He helped me get my groceries home."

"Preying on the kindness of your co-workers again, are you? So what happened?" He let his other hand reach into her hair.

"He poured me a cappuccino and kissed me." She licked his thumb. "It didn't go far."

"That's all?" He freed her hair from its clasp, letting the unbound mane tumble past her shoulders.

She nodded. "Why? Do I owe you anything? Should I save myself for you?"

He bent down and captured her lips with his, intent on erasing the other man. Probing her mouth with his tongue, he reveled in their passion. "Are you listening, woman? I want you. Save it all for me. You're mine." He lifted her onto his desk and moved between her thighs.

She gasped. "Yours, huh? Well, that would make you all mine."

"Yours." He pressed himself against her, hoping she could feel a fraction of their joint arousal. Melding her body to his own, he pulled her closer until there was no space left between them. Her breasts flattened against his chest and he reached down to cup her buttocks in his hands. Her moans filled the room.

The door flung open, Jennifer already in mid-sentence. "…to sign these purchase—" She took one look at the couple and tossed the papers onto the chair closest to the door. "Geez, Sebastian! Can't you keep it in your pants for one day? Mira and Marcos are here for the next rehearsal." Turning on her boot heel, she fled the office.

With a smile, he took a deep breath, inhaling the heady scent of Layla's patchouli shampoo. Placing her delectable bottom back on the desk, he pulled away from her. "I should go." Or, maybe he would cancel rehearsals for the rest of the day and stay in his office with his new girlfriend.

"Go." She bit her now-puffy bottom lip, her face tilted up, bedroom brown eyes peering into his own. "We have time."

* * *

"Sebastian, we are running out of time!" His mother's voice trilled into the earpiece as he walked home from the theater. Nighttime in the city was calm. Just after rush hour, drivers were less frantic and the car horns had ceased their medley. The air was uncharacteristically warm, still above eighty degrees, and the sun set hours ago. He would have enjoyed this stroll if his mother weren't being her usual dramatic self.

"Mom, I already know about the Supay cult. I'll get rid of the references to the elementals' mates… But you don't believe any of this, do you?"

"I know what is true, child, and so should you." His mother's crisp words were clear through the earpiece. "It is not superstition. Not only have you exposed family secrets, you have exposed me. I wanted to have this conversation in person…"

"Well, that hasn't happened so please get on with it."

"*Ch'inyay!* I have known for some time I am the vessel of Pachamama. Some call her the tree of life, some Mother Nature. Whatever the name, I am Ceiba."

"Mom…" He didn't know what to say. His mother had finally gone too far. Was it early onset dementia? She was only sixty-four.

"Do not 'Mom' me! I know what I am saying. I am Ceiba. I am the vessel of the goddess Pachamama. That has been true for many lifetimes. More importantly, from what I can tell, you and your brothers are the elementals' mates, the cardinals."

"I'm a little red bird?" He wondered how much the mental institution would cost.

"No! Shut up and listen! You are a cardinal, one of the sun's compasses of the earth. Part of the sun god's spirit has chosen to course through you. You borrow upon his power."

"Right." Perhaps he could hire an in-home nurse and have her therapy sessions done on an out-patient basis.

"And I am guessing you have developed your empathic abilities by now, yes?"

Sebastian stopped calculating expenses. The businesswoman behind him bumped into him and he realized he had actually stopped walking as well.

"My dear," she continued. "Did you not question this gift? Where did it come from? Why now? Or are you so wrapped up in your play and your comic book fantasies, you imagined yourself Superman? He was your favorite, no?" Her amusement carried through the phone.

"No, I didn't think I was Superman." He wouldn't give her the satisfaction.

"Nevertheless, you are a cardinal - an empath - and it appears you have found your mate. Her proximity awakens your powers."

"My mate?" He thought of his increasing ability to zone in on Layla's emotions above all others.

"Which do you find harder to believe? That you have a mate? Or that you have empathic powers?"

"I've had the empathic powers for a while now, though I didn't know what to call them."

"Yes, so having a mate is more incredulous for you?"

"No," he hedged. "Yes, actually it is, Mom. This isn't a story. This is life. That stuff isn't real."

"Yes, Sebastian Tawanti, it is! I've been trying to tell you that your little play is real. You have taken family secrets, family tools, and exposed them not only to the public, but to the evil ones. Now they know who you are. And they will try to kill you."

"Okay, Mom, I get it."

"You are not the only one in danger. Your mate is as well. In fact, she is in more danger than you. I have protected you and your brothers with spells and potions since you were born. There is not much to be done to you, unless they harm your mates. And, oh yes, they can harm your mates. They have proven that."

"Ariel." The name dropped from his mouth on a whisper. She was the "else" reference in Allora's note.

"I believe her death was the first blow. The poor dear. I tried to protect her, taught her as much as I could. But it wasn't enough." Her voice caught.

Head reeling, he leaned against the nearest building and let the truth sink in. This wasn't a joke or superstition.

His mother wasn't crazy. He had all the proof he needed in his Super-sense and his ex-wife's untimely death.

"How can I fight what I can't see? How could they kill a woman who has nothing to do with any of this at all?" He slid to the ground, partially blocking the sidewalk. Passers-by shifted their courses, walking around him without pause. The city kept moving as his reality morphed into science fiction.

"I'll change the play." He remembered that was what Ariel had urged him to do.

"The damage has been done. Now we must train your true mate to protect herself."

"I can't see Layla with a gun."

"She doesn't need one. Her power is protection enough."

"Power? She can read emotions, too?"

"No, dear. Think of your play. She is an elemental."

Chapter Thirteen

The front door was ajar. Layla tried to remember safety tips from her self-defense class. Never enter the house if you suspect intruders may be present. She walked back down the path and out the gate.

Grabbing her cell phone from the front compartment of her messenger bag, she hit the button to speed dial her roommate. Two rings… four rings… voicemail answered. She hung up and dialed again. No answer.

Maybe Anne went back to work. She was on medical leave with strict instructions to rest, but the office may have proven too much of a draw. Layla called and was put through to the workaholic's assistant.

"No, we haven't seen her." Anne's assistant hadn't received an email response from her boss in more than four hours either.

That BlackBerry was practically attached to her roommate's hand. Layla called the police.

They gave her a five-minute estimated time of arrival and told her to wait outside. So she stood on the curb, staring at the house. A man passed by walking his dog. The shih-tzu sniffed her leg; and the man looked her up and down. Who stands around watching a house in the middle of the evening? She managed a nod and a weak smile.

Screw it! Stupid or not, she wasn't leaving her best friend in a possibly dangerous situation. Arming herself with the biggest stick she could find, she charged to the front door and peeked inside, still hoping there was a benign explanation. Ideally, she'd find her friend zonked out with the television blaring.

No such luck. The living room had been tossed. The pristine white couches were overturned, their stuffing freely flowing from deep gashes in the cushions. Drawers from the coffee table were spilled onto the floor. Bookshelves were emptied, while pages and papers rose into the air.

Wind. Layla's powers stirred as she ran. Her heart thumping in her chest, she barely felt her feet racing across the hardwood. Spinning in the new breeze, couch stuffing and knick-knacks flew after her. She was vaguely aware she was calling a gale into the house. Neither the errant wind nor the fact that her feet no longer hit the floor mattered as she made her way up the stairs. Flying now, she pushed open Anne's bedroom door and encountered a tousled scene.

The intruders ravaged this room as well: dresser toppled, mattress flipped, clothes strewn. But Anne's shiny new laptop sat on her desk. Why would thieves leave behind a two-thousand dollar computer? More disturbing was the BlackBerry next to it. Her friend would never voluntarily leave that.

Still hovering, she moved to the desk. There was a note on plain, white paper in block letters: "Deliver the prayer sphere to the SW corner of the Washington Monument by midnight. No police or the lawyer dies."

The prayer sphere? Layla patted the round bulge in the messenger bag strapped to her chest. Her friend was kidnapped because of a clay ball. She looked at the clock radio. Thirteen minutes after seven.

"Police! Your door is open. We are coming in!"

The wind evaporated under Layla's feet and she fell to the floor, the big stick clattering on hardwood.

"Identify yourself!" The police officer's voice was menacing, his steps rapidly approaching.

"It's Layla Cohen. I'm upstairs!" She shouted her response, hoping to avoid being accidentally shot. She looked at the note in her hands. If she didn't hide it right now, the meeting spot would be crawling with cops and Anne could be killed. But should she trust these kidnappers not to harm her friend if she complied?

"Are you alone, ma'am?" The police officer was already upstairs.

She shoved the note in her bag with the prayer sphere and stood. "Yes."

The officer walked in, glaring at her from icy, blue eyes. "You called this in?" Average height and build, the cop had his pistol drawn.

She was glad she identified herself. "Yes, I got home about five minutes ago and found the door open." She wondered how much she should say. If she planned to rescue Anne herself, did the police need to be involved at all? Making the right choice here was critical. Some book or television show said missing people have only about twenty-four hours from the time of their abduction before they were usually murdered.

"Weren't you told to stay outside and wait?" His eyes twitched. He holstered his weapon and looked down at her. "A stick? Did you bring a stick in here to protect yourself? Didn't even grab a knife from the kitchen?" He exhaled loudly. Taking the wide-brimmed hat off his head, he ran his fingers through graying hair. "You could have been killed, little girl. What the hell was so important you couldn't wait outside the damned house?"

Layla wanted to yell back, to demand she be treated like the woman—the adult—she was, instead of a wayward teenager. But after seeing the way his hands trembled, she could tell he had seen more than she wanted to know. And he was right; she should have stayed outside. She would have if she'd been able to reach Anne.

"My roommate," she started to explain. "My best friend was home sick. She didn't answer her phone. And now she's gone." That was all she would say about the disappearance.

"Does she have a boyfriend? Anyone who would know where she is?"

"No boyfriend. I called her office."

"Any answer?"

"No." She looked at the floor.

"Layla!" The voice sent a warm ripple through her system. "Where is she? Is Layla all right?" Shouting, Sebastian questioned someone downstairs. "Layla!" He was running now, footsteps squeaking on the hardwood floor as he searched her house.

"I'm upstairs!" she called, making her way around the officer and out the bedroom.

"Sir!" A woman yelled after him. "Do you live here? This is a crime scene and we can't have you—"

"Layla!" He reached the top of the stairs. Rushing toward his outstretched arms, she fell into his embrace.

"I thought they got you." He murmured into her hair. Kissing the top of her head, he crushed her face into his chest. The smell of cedar and fear assaulted her senses. All she could do—all she wanted to do—was be held by this man who had miraculously appeared when she needed him.

"Excuse me," the officer interrupted. "Who are you? And who did you think 'got' Ms. Cohen?"

The warm embrace stiffened. Sebastian relaxed his hold and looked over her shoulder. He held out his hand. "Sebastian Tawanti. I'm Layla's boyfriend."

She wished circumstances were different so she could properly rejoice in hearing him say "boyfriend" for the first time. As it was, she turned and looked into the cop's narrowed eyes.

"Uh huh. I'm Officer Brull. Who did you think 'got' Ms. Cohen? Do you know who has taken her roommate?"

Sebastian squeezed her arms as he looked down at her. "Someone took your roommate?" He noticed the officer staring expectantly at him. "I don't know who did it. I meant whoever broke in."

Officer Brull narrowed his eyes as he watched the couple. "Something's not right."

The female cop yelled from the bottom of the stairs. "They need to get out of my crime scene. It's like a tornado went off in here. We've got a lot of work."

"Come on, follow me to the station, please. We need to get the facts so we can find your friend."

* * *

Two hours later, Layla and Sebastian exited the doors of the Capitol Hill precinct. Officer Brull was sure they were hiding something, but Layla had no desire to share her supernatural windy abilities or anything else that could get her locked in an asylum; and her boyfriend couldn't tell them anything he didn't know. So they were free to go.

They trotted down the steps in silence. She had to tell him something. Less than a day together and she'd already gotten him dragged down to a police station. And she was about to involve him in a ransom exchange. He may not want to be with her after tonight.

"You're afraid. And it's not entirely about Anne." Sebastian stopped and pulled her to face him.

"Again, you know exactly what I'm feeling." She fidgeted with the little, pink puppy charm on her jacket's zipper. "I need to tell you something. I wasn't completely honest with the police. Or with you."

He didn't look surprised. Face impassive, he waited for her to continue.

"The kidnappers left a note. I'm going to get her back by trading a clay ball I have. They demanded the prayer sphere—"

"*You* have the prayer sphere?!" The transformation was almost humorous. Green eyes going round, his mouth dropped open. "No wonder they trashed your place!"

"What do you know about the prayer sphere? Who are 'they?' Do you know who did this?" She pushed him away so she could get to a proper yelling distance. "And I was just about to apologize for getting you mixed up in my drama."

"Wait!" He held up his hands. "I have an idea who's behind this." With an apologetic shrug, he explained about the three realms in Incan religion and the Supay cult. Layla's head swam as she tried to figure out where to start her questions.

"Allora got a note, too," he continued. "Her note said to deliver the prayer sphere and no one else would be hurt, but we didn't know what that meant... So you have the prayer sphere?"

"I still don't understand. Are you saying your play is real?" None of this made any sense.

He rubbed his brow. "Maybe. I think I can perceive when you're in danger. I was on my way to your house when I was hit by a blast of terror so thick... all wrapped up in your essence. It was just like the other night when I thought I heard you whisper my name."

"Saturday night?" Layla gasped, recalling her urgent need for Sebastian to be by her side as she was lifted into the ambulance.

"Yeah, you sounded so lost and scared." He bit his lip. "I ran to the G.W. Hospital looking for you. Nobody heard of you. You texted back that you were fine, so I thought I was crazy and just hearing things. Was that you?"

"Yes, it was me." She tilted her head as she stared at her new boyfriend. He came for her. That knowledge settled into her heart, easing some of her lingering doubts about his affection and his sanity. "I was at Georgetown Hospital. Someone ran us off the road."

He swore. "They're already after you... Can I try something?" He closed the distance between them, planting a kiss on her lips.

All at once, nothing mattered but having him hold her. His tongue entered her mouth, and began dueling with hers. One of his hands cupped her bottom and pulled her up, pressing her core against his. She moaned as his other hand went to the back of her head and squeezed her closer still, deepening the kiss.

Sebastian lowered her to the ground. "This isn't normal, Layla," he panted. "This pull we have ... You must be my ... mate."

She looked up to see his glowing, green eyes peering into hers. As ridiculous as it sounded, the facts finally clicked into place. "You're my mate and I can blow things around with my mind. The play is real." She dug her nails into the palms of her hands, more pain to convince her this was reality. "So that means there *are* evil forces after us." And that also meant she was in *way* over her head.

He frowned, nodding his head. "And I'm guessing they have your roommate."

"We have to get this prayer sphere to them before they hurt her." She looked at her watch. "Five minutes 'til ten. We still have a little over two hours."

He grabbed her hand as she started toward the Metro station. "Layla, we can't walk into this without knowing what we're getting into."

"We're giving them this ball of clay so Anne can come home."

"No, we don't know what will happen if we hand over something like that. What does the prayer sphere do?"

"I don't know." And she didn't care. She didn't ask for this elemental destiny crap. Getting Anne back was most important.

"Right. But I'm sure my mother knows. She can probably help with your new wind powers, too."

"Why? Is she the tutor to troubled superheroes?"

Smiling, he said, "Better. She's Ceiba, Pachamama or the vessel of the tree of life or something."

"Holy Batman!" Mind reeling, she leaned against the building. "This is too much. Your mother is Ceiba?"

Layla stared at her reflection in the glass wall of the building. This morning, her biggest problem was whether or not the guy she liked would like her back. Now she was supposed to accept she was a part of a big Incan destiny. What did that make her? Was she just a vessel for some ancient Incan being? Her heart started to hammer as she thought of the wind that blew whenever it chose. How was she supposed to handle this? She covered the rising panic with a smile, happy she was an actress and able to hide her true emotions. If Sebastian could remain sane in the face of this lunacy, she would try as well.

"I know it's a lot to take." He reached over, hugging her to his chest. "Just breathe. The anxiety will pass."

She froze at his words. "How do you know about my

'anxiety'? I know I'm not that obvious." She looked up at the guilty look on his face. "You keep doing that. Can you read my mind?"

He winced. "Not exactly. I can feel your emotions."

"That's not in your play," she sputtered. Vulnerable, Layla tried to remember all the embarrassing moments she'd had since meeting him. It had mostly been one sex-filled thought after another. She couldn't recall a time when she hadn't wanted to screw him on the spot. "You must think I am the horniest woman in the world!"

"The feeling is mutual when I'm around you." As his eyes took on an iridescent tinge, she figured out what made him glow.

Forcing herself to step away from her mate and his rising libido, she concentrated on the most pressing issue. "Let's focus, Sebastian. The prayer sphere. Whatever it is, we've got to get Anne away from the Supay followers."

He pulled his iPhone from his pocket to check its clock display. "We have exactly two hours. Whether or not we give away this ball, we need to arm ourselves. We're not walking into an obvious trap with nothing but fistfuls of wind and feelings to save us. First, we're going to Smitty's to get a gun or two."

"Smitty? He's got guns? I thought he was your special effects guy."

"The guy blows things up for a living." Sebastian gave his radiant smile. "He's got guns."

* * *

A thirty-minute cab ride later, they pulled in front of a sprawling rambler in Temple Hills, Maryland. The homes were set back far from the winding street. Two forgotten bicycles lay in the driveway, and a basketball hoop hung near the side garage. A minivan was parked at the curb.

"Are we at the right house?" Layla couldn't believe an arms dealer lived in such a suburban setting. Taking Sebastian's helping hand, she climbed from the backseat of the taxi.

"Yep. Perfect cover. Smitty's a great technician. Theater combat is his hobby. I ask no questions and get a free resource."

And she was worried about dragging him into trouble. She looked at her new "mate." He was a magical Incan descendant, capable of sharing her emotions, and friendly with an arms dealer who liked to make things go boom. The fact that he was her boss seemed so trivial now.

He laughed. "Smitty is ex-CIA. He's a *legal* contractor for the Pentagon now—legit. But that's all I'm allowed to know." He poked her in the ribs. "Try not to be so worried."

This empathic boyfriend thing was pretty handy. Layla hadn't figured out how to articulate her concerns, before Sebastian had already defused them. She watched the sexy man walk up to the front door, his muscles outlined by the thin black material of his shirt. Again, his curly hair was unkempt from his fingers running through it so often.

She reached up and twisted one of the locks. *Boy, the curls on our kids will be out of control,* she thought.

His eyes widened as he looked down at her. Then he cupped her face in one big hand, planting a chaste kiss on her nose.

"Wait!" She felt the blush take over her face. "You heard that, didn't you? You *can* hear thoughts!"

He flashed one of those heart-stopping, world-ending, make-love-to-me-now smiles, and kissed her lips. "Only *your* thoughts and only for the last hour. Shh."

The door opened. A ten-year-old girl with two afro puffs sticking from her head peered out. "Dad!" She walked back to a blaring, flat-screen television, leaving the door wide open. A ballet tutorial was playing, and the child pirouetted with the video instructor, her bright orange tutu spinning.

"Christy, don't open the door for strangers." Smitty came down the massive staircase.

"But, don't you know them, Dad?" She continued twirling without pause.

"Yes, but you don't."

"You do. So, they're not strangers."

"Christy…" He shook his head and muttered. "Thousands of dollars on a security system, but it's still not Christy-proof." Turning to the pair, he stepped aside. "Come on in. What brings you here, Sebastian? Layla?"

He led them into a room with the biggest dining table she'd ever seen. It had to seat sixteen people, with the china arranged in ready settings. The place was pristine except for a hot pink backpack on the floor close to the kitchen.

"Did we forget to go over something in rehearsal today? Catch yourself on fire?" Smitty still wore his gray jumpsuit.

Layla looked closely at her special effects coach. At the theater, she was so preoccupied with simultaneously trying to ignore her disappointment over the *Page Seven* article while paying attention to the proper handling of flames that she barely took in the man himself. He was older, maybe forty-five or fifty, with a few gray hairs sprinkled into his short black hair. Ex-CIA made sense; he was still in shape, his broad chest boasting defined pecs. She suspected she'd feel nothing but steel if she hugged him.

Sebastian coughed and narrowed his eyes at her.

That wasn't fair. She couldn't be blamed for noticing that a guy was fit. *No fair!* She shot that thought at her mate. He caressed her hand in recognition.

Then he smiled at Smitty. "No, this isn't theater-related. Can we talk about your other business?"

The intelligence agent missed none of this. "My other business, huh? Okay, Mr. Tawanti, walk this way." He shouted to his daughter before they left the room. "Christy… Christy! I'll be working in the basement. Call my cell if you need me."

"Okay, Daddy!" The little girl leapt across the room, mirroring the on-screen video.

They walked in silence down the hall, Layla dwarfed by men at least a foot taller than she. Head held high, she guesstimated they each weighed about seventy-five pounds more than she as well. Sebastian rubbed her bottom.

The arms dealer stopped in front of an iron door featuring a lock that belonged in a spy movie. Placing his palm on the scanner, he spoke into a little box. "Three one nine eight two Matthew Elijah." He hopped twice on his left foot and the door opened.

She looked around for the camera and couldn't resist asking. "What was the hop for? Is there a sensory plate in the floor?"

"No. Just keeping you on your toes." He let out a deep belly laugh. "Don't be so serious, girl. Come on in. Now, what do you kids need from Uncle Smitty? Sebastian, what good reason do you have for bringing this nice young lady into my shop?"

He flicked a light switch, illuminating walls covered in firearms and ammunition. Little guns, big guns, machine guns. Was that a cannon? If it used gunpowder, it was in this room.

"It's true." Her mate shook his head. "You've got a freaking arsenal down here."

"Who told you that?" Smitty frowned.

"Nikki, the lighting tech."

"She talks too much."

"Maybe," Layla interrupted, looking at her watch. Ten forty-five. Time was running out. "Smitty, we've got a situation and would feel much better if we had a gun or two. Can you please help us?"

The special effects technician shrugged. "You're down here already. I'll help. What kind of gun do you need?"

"One that won't knock me on my butt when I shoot it."

"Have you ever fired a gun?" He tapped the stubble on his chin.

"Once." She frowned. "I shot a baby deer when I was fifteen."

Sebastian piped up. "*You* shot a fawn?"

"I didn't think I'd hit it. My cousin gave me his rifle and let me try. I shocked us both. He said I had natural aim. I was so upset I killed Bambi, I haven't touched a gun since."

"Well, if you have a 'situation,' it's time to try again." Smitty selected two automatic loading Glocks from the wall, one slightly larger than the other. "Follow me."

"Um, Smitty," she called after his retreating back. "We're in a bit of a rush. Can we just take the guns?"

"No. Would you let a baby play with a grenade? You're not taking my guns until I'm positive you can handle them."

* * *

Nine holes between the eyes of the paper dummy. The tenth went wide when Sebastian squeezed her rear. She would have been proud of herself, but she knew the wind aided her accuracy. Bullets changed their trajectory as the air buffeted them to her goal. It turned out "natural aim" was synonymous with "weird wind power." Nice development.

Her mate wasn't bad either. He hit the target seven out of ten times; four of those shots in the heart area.

Smitty gave them the two guns, refusing the director's money. "Find a play that lets me blow up a miniature town or something. You buy the explosives."

He called his car service to retrieve the couple. Layla was relieved when it arrived in five minutes. That left forty-five to get to the Washington Monument.

In the backseat of the car, Sebastian pulled out his phone. "Now, let's find out what a prayer sphere is." He dialed his mother and spoke into the receiver. "Yes, she's here."

The screeching could be heard from her seat next to him. He held the phone away from his ear. "She's fine. … I'm fine … Wait… Mom … Mom … Mom! We're on our way to the Washington Monument. They took Layla's friend and we're getting her back… The prayer sphere. That's why I'm calling. What exactly *is* it? …" He pressed the Speaker button. "Okay, we can both hear you now."

"Hello, child." The voice sounded familiar.

"Hello, Mrs. Tawanti."

"So you are carrying the prayer sphere with you. Good. The sphere is safest and can help most when it is with you. It is your soul's creation."

Layla didn't know what to say to that.

"You cannot trade such an object. Not even for your friend." The voice was soft, but firm, meant to serve as the last word.

"Mrs. Tawanti, I will not abandon my friend for a ball of clay."

"Ah, it is more than clay. I know you have felt its power, its promise. That prayer sphere holds the gift of wind. With it, you cannot be stopped."

Sebastian placed a calming hand on her knee before she could respond. "And what happens if we hand it over to the Supay followers?"

"That is not an option. You must not let that prayer sphere fall into the wrong hands!"

"Okay, Mom." He rubbed his temples.

"Sebastian! I am serious!"

"And so am I! A woman's life is at stake. I won't place a trinket—regardless of the superstitions wrapped around it—above her very real danger. We have weapons. We'll make the trade and regroup after Anne is safe."

"That is a mistake—"

The glass partition slid down and he disconnected the call. The driver announced their arrival, then got out.

They climbed from the car, looking at the Monument illuminated in white lights. Eleven forty-five.

Boom!

The car exploded.

Chapter Fourteen

Sebastian lay on his back in a ditch with Layla sprawled on top of him, facing the carnage. Debris was suspended mid-air, inches away from her nose. The car engine halted above his head. The carburetor still hummed, he almost reached out to touch it.

Instead, he shimmied out from under the woman who saved them, gently pulling her from danger. Slowly. He wasn't sure how she held the car parts in the air, and he made sure not to jostle her from her trance, lest the car and its parts come crashing down on her.

Once they were a good distance away, he shook her, cradling her in his arms. "Layla, baby, wake up." He kissed her mouth, cheeks and forehead, finally rousing her.

She blinked and stared at him. The debris hit the pavement with a racket to rival the initial explosion. Screaming, she turned in his arms and stared at the wreckage. "Is the driver okay?"

"He got out of the car well before it blew up. He had to be in on it." The director tried not to let his mind lead him to an unhappy conclusion about his colleague.

"We need to find Anne." *Please, God, let her be alive.* Her thoughts were as loud as her words.

Sebastian wasn't shocked when he first heard her inner monologue. True to the old stories, his mate made him stronger. She just stopped a car from landing on them. The tiny woman in his arms was becoming a powerhouse.

He hugged and released her. "Let's go." The idea of Layla being in the middle of such danger ate away at him. His plan was to leave her at Smitty's, but his old friend didn't quite smell right. There was an air of duplicity clinging to him that couldn't be trusted. Now that the car belonging to the former explosives expert had detonated, he was glad he didn't leave his mate there. But how, and more importantly, why was Smitty involved?

Pondering that question would take his head out of his present bucket of problems, so he dismissed it for later. He grasped Layla's hand as they started across the grass. Car alarms blared behind them, set off by the explosion. People began to gather at the wreckage and sirens wailed in the distance. That car would soon be a crime scene, full of detectives and possibly Homeland Security. You can't blow up a car in downtown D.C. without repercussions. He walked faster.

The last thing we need is to be detained and questioned for another two hours. Layla picked up her pace as well.

"Exactly. We'll be lucky if we don't wind up in jail cells. The southwest corner is this way." He pointed toward the giant obelisk.

"Okay, I know you can hear my thoughts, but responding to them is throwing me off."

"Do you want me to stop?" The connection with Layla made the whole save-the-world thing more bearable. He wasn't ready to shut her out.

She frowned into the night ahead of her. "No," she said. "Don't stop. I like having you with me…" Her voice trailed off as she looked at her watch. "Eleven fifty-two. Do you think Anne's still there?"

"If she ever was, she still is." He regretted his phrasing as soon as he felt her pang of panic. "She's there. They can't get the prayer sphere without her. So we need to be prepared. Can you secure this in your waistband?" Handing her the smaller gun, he noticed how inappropriate her white sweatsuit without pockets was.

She frowned again as she held the gun with her delicate hands. "I dressed for combat today, but it was supposed to be pretend. If I put this thing into my sweats, it'll probably fall to the ground." She wiggled her hips, illustrating the spare room in the soft fabric.

He tried not to focus on her curves. Putting a hand out, he stilled her movement. "I see your point."

"Your eyes are glowing again." She smiled and patted his hand. "I'm flattered. Now let's get Anne." She held the gun close to her body and sprinted ahead, surprisingly fast.

A breeze picked up, pushing their backs and aiding their journey. Sebastian had to run at full steam to keep up with her gait. They crossed the grassy field of the Washington Mall in silence, running into a perfect trap.

There was no way to approach the building without being noticed, but plenty of spots to conceal the kidnappers.

In her light sweatsuit, his mate was a beacon, visible for at least a mile. And his eyes glowed. He wished he could do something to even their chances of survival.

Grabbing Layla's hand to stop her, he whispered in her ear. "This is suicide. I want to get Anne back as much as you do. No one else can be hurt because of my play, but we have to be smart about this."

She hesitated, eyes darting to her watch. The backlit display read 11:58. "So what do you want to do?" Eyebrows raised, she tapped her foot, waiting for an answer.

"Let's go." They had to get out of the wide-open space. He shifted course and ran to the southeastern corner.

His mate followed. Crouching beside the building, she put the gun in one white-knuckled hand and fingered her bag with the other. "What's the plan?"

"The plan is now that they're sure to know where we are, at least they can't see us anymore." He watched her fiddling with the bag again. "Offer them the ball."

"You agree with me?" She nearly the dropped the bag as her head jerked up.

"No, we can't give it to them, but we can use it as leverage to see if Anne's here." He grasped her arm to steady her and felt a rush of warmth as she leaned in. "We'll get close enough to talk to them, so I can tell whether or not they're being truthful. When we see Anne, you blow away the bad guys and we'll run."

"Blow them away, shoot them, whichever works. Let's go. It's midnight." She held the sphere to her chest and turned toward their rendezvous point.

"Wind's cardinal," an other-worldly voice oozed against his eardrum.

Sebastian's skin broke out in a rash of hives, pins sticking into every pore. His sixth sense was assaulted by rage, misery, loathing, and fear. Nostrils flaring, he raised the gun and pulled Layla to his side.

She screamed as a black mist descended upon them, pervading the air. The breath left her lungs, swirling into a wind, and enclosing the couple inside a cocoon of purity while holding the cloying mist at arm's length.

The torture ended, leaving Sebastian wrapped in Layla's essence. The fragrance of her patchouli shampoo mixed with her natural scent filled his nostrils, and he would have closed his eyes to enjoy the sensation of being surrounded by the woman. But the mist was moving, coalescing into a shape in front of them.

"Wind's cardinal."

The sound reverberated in his head, and Layla dropped the prayer sphere into her bag so she could clutch his fingers. Her grip would have crushed the hand of a smaller man, and he had to rein in the terror threatening to cripple his own limbs.

"What do we do now?" She stood on tiptoe and whispered into his ear.

That was a good question. He instinctively knew the gun in his hand would be useless against the creature forming in the grass. Still mostly transparent, the eight-foot tall mist apparition now had six goat-like legs and was developing two heads. Those heads destroyed every rational thought left in his mind. One was shaped like a bulldog's, complete with slobber running down its snapping jowls. The other was Ariel's.

Her angelic, blue eyes peered at him from the massive monstrosity. As the creature solidified, her strawberry-blond hair framed sun-kissed cheeks. He wanted to close his eyes, praying for her image to disappear. Layla squeezed tighter as the thing opened his ex-wife's mouth.

"Sebastian, you failed me." Ariel's voice clawed into him. *"You didn't trust me enough. Wouldn't listen to my warnings. How long did you wait after getting me killed before you found someone else?"*

"Ariel." The thing was right. He didn't deserve—

"You don't deserve to be happy," his ex-wife's head continued.

He dropped Layla's hand, and immediately, his head began to pulse with a sick, rhythmic beat.

"You can fix it, Sebastian. Give me the prayer sphere. I can move on in peace." The thing took a step closer. Two of the goat legs turned into arms with monkey's paws at the ends. It reached for Layla.

"No," he mumbled, clutching his battered head. He looked over to find his mate's mouth open in a scream he couldn't hear. Tears streamed down her face and she beat at an invisible wall around him. He was encased in the black mist.

"No!" This time he yelled as guilt sank deeper into his soul. The thing continued its manipulation, Ariel's face transforming with a sneer unlike anything she was capable of in life. Shaking, Sebastian tried to throw off the intruder. It latched on even tighter and he fell to his knees.

His mate dropped with him, her shouts still failing to reach his ears.

"Elemental!" the thing shouted at her. *"Give me the sphere or this man will die, joining the woman he truly loves."*

Layla stood up as she retrieved the ball from her bag. She held it up, wind whipping her hair into a huge, black crown. She spoke, her brow furrowed as the tears continued to flow.

Sebastian still heard nothing but the creature's now-scratchy version of his ex-wife's voice. As his mate's lips moved in response, the thing reached into its folds of cloying mist and pulled out the limp form of a woman, dropping her onto the ground. Layla frowned, then pointed to Sebastian and mouthed more words.

Instantly, the mist evaporated around him, and his lungs inhaled the first pure breath he'd had in a dozen minutes. Scrambling from his hands and knees, he gulped in the night air as he rushed to join his mate.

"Take it!" Layla threw the prayer sphere at the creature and dropped onto her knees to grasp the female figure lying on the grass. "Anne! Annie, wake up." She brushed wisps of blond hair away from the woman's bruised face, lightly slapping her cheeks.

An ugly barking sound erupted from the creature. It tucked Layla's prayer sphere into its nothingness and smiled. This time, the canine head spoke. *"Stupid girl!"* The barking grew louder and Sebastian realized it was laughing. *"Stupid, stupid girl!"* It lifted a monkey's paw, shooting an inky mist toward the three people.

This time, a black veil fell over Sebastian's vision and he tasted and smelled raw power, malevolence, as the mist surrounded and entered his body. Beside him, Layla twitched with the same invasion. Her wind abandoned her.

"You gave away the only thing that could have saved you." The laughter intensified, blocking out all emotions except fear.

Sebastian pulled his mate and her friend closer to him, attempting to shield them from the creature. Layla clutched her head and he knew she was being attacked with the same mind-shattering, throbbing pain he felt. They could not withstand the assault much longer. Their brains would implode.

The canine smiled, and Sebastian remembered he was a cardinal. If his mother were right, he was born to fight this thing, born to *defeat* this thing. He looked up into the canine's glowing, red eyes and focused his energy on deflecting the destructive pain back into the creature.

The creature's laugh died as the mist wavered.

His defense worked!

"Cardinal! You dare to reflect my power back at me!?" The thing grew taller, now resembling a baby elephant from hell. It shook its canine jowls. *"Your mate is useless without her sphere. And you are weak without her. You will die."* It stretched out its monkey's paws, assaulting them anew. Layla screamed and he felt both their minds splintering.

Lightning flashed from behind them, striking the creature in the center of its chest. The mist creature scattered, only to begin taking shape again a few feet away.

"Sebastian. Layla. Come quickly!" Thunder rumbled

with a crystal clear voice.

The darkness seeped from Sebastian's vision and his temples ceased their pounding. With a moan, Layla moved to touch her roommate's forehead.

"Quickly!"

Shielding his wounded mate and her friend in his arms, Sebastian turned in the direction of their savior. "Mom?"

"The shopkeeper?" His mate stared, jaw hanging open as she held onto him.

The vessel of the tree of life whirled her crimson sari and the world disappeared.

* * *

Seconds later, Sebastian and Layla found themselves reclining on paisley couches, sipping tea. The sitting room featured three large couches, two armchairs, and Incan pottery in muddy yellows, oranges, and blues. He and his mate each had a private sofa; Anne slept on the other. A portrait of Sebastian and his three brothers hung above the fireplace. They were in his childhood home.

Though he grew up in the hundred-year-old Colonial, his heart raced, and he was positive the expression on his face matched Layla's.

Eyes wide, brows raised almost to her hairline, her hands shook as she lifted the heirloom cup to her lips. "Well, at least I can get the cup to my mouth this time," she muttered.

"What?"

"Where the hell are we?" She thumped the china to the thick carpet. "How did we get here? Why didn't you tell me the shopkeeper was your mother? And where the hell did this tea come from?" She tried to get to her feet and fell back onto the couch.

He reached out a hand from the couch next to hers. Unable to move much more, he stroked her arm and laughed. She had precisely summed up the gist of his feelings.

"Why are you laughing? What's going on?"

"I don't know." His head still hurt. "This is my house, though. Or, rather, it's my mom's house. I grew up here. I don't know how the hell we got here. My mom wasn't a shopkeeper last time I checked. And I don't know where the hell this tea came from. I'm guessing she wants us to drink it." He sipped from his grandmother's china, noting it was the set he was forbidden to touch as a child. "Chamomile."

Eyeing him, she picked up her cup. "Why are you so calm?"

Sebastian wondered the same thing. Perhaps her outburst defused his own internal bomb. Now he flexed his legs on the couch he spilled grape juice on twenty years previously, and closed his eyes. "We're safe. Whatever else is going on, we're all safe." He pointed to Anne on the third couch and heard Layla sigh.

"I'm glad we're safe. I really am, but I need some kind of explanation. That ... thing... was not a guy from a crazy Incan cult. That was an evil cloud. A cloud!" Her discombobulation filled the room.

He understood. Though he was glad to be home, fear still permeated his bones as well. Abandoning the tea, he hefted himself off the couch and crawled to his mate.

Scooting her over, he pulled her into his lap and held her until she stopped shaking. "It's over. We're okay." He rocked her back and forth, kissing her forehead and cheeks.

His mate, the woman who stood up to a giant monster, was in tears. He loved that about her. She was unapologetically tough and fragile at the same time, an emotional badass. Since he now accepted his ancestors' folk tales as truth—and how could he not after what they endured in the last few hours—he had to learn to support a mate far more powerful than he wrote into his play. Layla was the wind guardian, the living vessel of the elemental wind deity. She sniffled into his t-shirt.

He hugged the sobbing woman tighter. She sacrificed herself for him tonight. When she could have—*should* have—run, she stayed and fought for him. "It's over," he murmured.

"I am afraid it is far from over." His mother stepped into the room, her red sari flowing behind her.

Layla pushed herself up. "You're the shopkeeper. Can you please tell me what's going on here?" Her voice cracked.

"Yes, I was a shopkeeper for one day. I had one customer. You." She strolled into the sitting room and sat down on the couch with Anne. Putting the unconscious woman's head in her lap, she brushed the blond hair out of her face.

"Why the charade? If you wanted me to have the prayer sphere, why not ask Sebastian to give it to me?"

"You two take too long. My goodness, I have never seen two people meant for each other find more reasons to stay apart. You needed the sphere and it needed you. I did what I had to do. Where is it?"

Sebastian hugged his mate. "We gave it to the thing trying to kill us."

"No! I told you not to give away that sphere!" Brows furrowed, she wore the same look as when he totaled her car at the age of fifteen.

He was no longer a child. "A clay ball is not more important than our lives, Mother. It would have taken the prayer sphere anyway."

"No, it could not." She shook her head. "The prayer sphere cannot be stolen or taken. As a manifestation of the soul, it will not function properly if such a transgression occurs. It must be given of free will, which you did. And that thing, the Filth, could have been defeated if you were properly trained. You must learn to close off your gift to protect yourself." Lips pursed, she looked at the couple.

"Mrs. Tawanti?" Layla cradled her head in her hands, shifting in her mate's lap. "Forgive me, but shouldn't Sebastian already know all of this? Shouldn't you have been preparing him for the Supay followers and filthy mist and whatever else is going to attack us? It's not fair to scold when we had no idea what we were up against."

His mother gave a wistful smile as she shook her head. "Yes, you are right. He should have been prepared. And you should have known enough to never give away your prayer sphere. But my son wrote a little play..."

"Mom." He heard enough about the damn play. "There is nothing I can do about that now."

"Yes, well," she continued. "I was waiting patiently for

my boys to find their mates. It is best to train a pair together. He is your source for strength and focus. You protect and guide him. His empathic powers create a connection that makes the two of you unstoppable. But you must be proper mates. It is best not to force this process."

"Oh. We have to mate…" Layla trailed off.

"Yes. You will figure that part out for yourselves." His mother stood.

"One more question."

"Anything, wind guardian."

"How did we get here so quickly?"

His mother's smile lit up the room. "Oh, you have your powers. I have mine." Stooping down, she laid the palms of her hands on Anne's cheeks. Her hands glowed an iridescent white where they touched the unconscious woman, and the room filled with the smell of lilacs and cinnamon.

Anne opened her eyes. "Ceiba."

His mother took her hand. "Come, child." She looked back at Layla. "As I told you on the bridge, your friend will have no lasting injuries." Raising an eyebrow, she left the room.

Layla's mouth hung open. "I think your mother was the old, homeless man."

His mate was drained more than he thought. He massaged her temples. "Shh, you'll feel better soon."

He always knew there was something other-worldly about his mother. Later, he would wonder if he'd ever learn all of her secrets. For now, he concentrated on his part of this mess.

Mating. Sebastian didn't put that ritual in his play because he hated wedding scenes. "Well, maybe we can get a quick wedding at the courthouse."

"You want to get married?" She turned so she could face him.

"We have to protect ourselves. It's not romantic, but I know I care for you a lot." He winced at his words. It wasn't the best proposal, but two weeks was too soon to fall in love with a woman. He shouldn't be in love with her yet. That would be ridiculous. Worse, it would be a betrayal of what he shared with poor Ariel.

She scrunched her nose. "Oh. I um, like you, too, Sebastian … Wait! What do you think mating is?"

He jumped at the opportunity to change the subject. "My mom said marriage mated the elementals and cardinals."

Layla laughed, holding her sides as she cracked up. Tears sprang to her eyes. "Oh my gosh!" She let one hand rest on his upper thigh as she steadied her teacup. "Of all the things for your mom to leave out. Mating isn't marriage."

His mother left out a lifetime (or ten) of things.

He tickled Layla's side. She was even cuter when she lost control like this. "What's so funny? This is *my* family's story. How do you know mating isn't marriage?"

She gasped as her giggles increased. "Because I've been dreaming about mating with you for a month." She twisted, straddling his waist as she leaned to put her cup on the floor. "And it's never in a church."

Mating was sex. That made sense. His mom had been telling them these stories since he and his brothers were still in bunk beds. There was no way she'd tell them about their ancestors getting busy.

He ground up into her heat. "We only met two weeks ago. How have you been dreaming about me for a month?"

"I have no idea." She ground her pelvis into his.

"You were dreaming of me… That *was* you in that field, wasn't it?" One more second of her movements and he would rip her clothes off in his mother's sitting room.

She bit her lip as she nodded. "This is so awesome. You *are* my mate. And your eyes are glowing again."

Enough of this. Sebastian picked up his woman and carried her down the hall to the room he once shared with Trystan. The space wasn't exactly where he planned to consummate their new relationship, but he wasn't waiting any longer.

Her legs wrapped around his waist, and he sat on the bed, gazing at the beautiful woman in his arms. Cheeks flushed and hair wild, she bit her bottom lip and stared back at him with wanton eyes. He needed no Super-sense to understand her primary desire.

"Kiss me." She didn't wait for an answer, tilting her head up and pressing her mouth to his.

His restraint ended. Flooded by pent-up craving and need, Sebastian gave into the carnal emotions driving them both. As his erection throbbed against his jeans, he felt her excitement grow and she ground her core onto his bulge.

He deepened the kiss, pushing his tongue into her mouth and taking as much as she was willing to give. His hands roved over her back, and he decided she was wearing far too many clothes. Still claiming her pouty lips, he leaned back and unzipped her jacket. She scrambled out of it, and broke their kiss to yank her t-shirt over her head, leaving only a lacy crimson bra.

She tugged at his shirt. He got the idea and pulled it off, tossing it onto the floor with her clothes. Reaching out, he cupped her breasts, reveling in finally being able to touch the full orbs. His cock pulsed again and Layla gasped.

She was a breathtaking sight; dark curls tumbling over her shoulders in contrast to fair skin. Her reddened lips opened, and she demanded, "Off."

He followed his lady's command with a smile, pushing her onto the pillows and stripping off his jeans. By the time he was nude, she lay in the buff as well.

Chapter Fifteen

Layla willed her mate to touch her. His glowing, green eyes covered every inch of her as she took in his sculpted golden body. The reality was better than her dreams. Soft, sandy brown hair curled atop a well-defined chest.

Rock hard abs led down to the V of his pelvis. And there, jutting from a nest of curls stood the most perfect penis she'd ever seen. As her hand reached up to stroke his erection, he closed his eyes and exhaled. She rubbed the smooth skin, wrapping her fingers around its mushroom head, and cupped his testicles. He shuddered as he lowered himself onto her.

Kneeling between her legs, he bent down and took one of her nipples into his mouth. The wet warmth sent waves of pleasure washing over her. Just as she was about to touch him, he captured her hand in his and pressed it to the bed. He pulled her other hand from his rod and held it down as well, raising his eyebrows in question until she nodded her consent.

She lay on the bed with Sebastian moving over her, no

way to stir, a slave to his ministrations. Tongue traveling from her left nipple to her right, he swirled each one before gently nipping with his teeth. The pleasure-pain had her arching her back in frenzied response. She longed to touch him, but he smiled and trailed his kisses lower, keeping a firm hold on her hands. His tongue flickered over her stomach, and a moan escaped as she bit her lip.

Now caressing the palms of her hands with his thumbs, he moved still lower, nuzzling his head between her legs. His tongue delved into her folds, tasting and probing until he found the spot to make her cry out in ecstasy. Over and over, he licked and lapped at her, caressing her hands as she thrashed about. When she could barely take anymore, he moved a hand down to insert one digit inside. And she came with gasps and moans, biting her lip to keep from screaming.

Shaking, Sebastian kissed her again before moving up to position his thick shaft against her opening. He claimed her mouth again, releasing her hands to brace himself on either side of her head.

With the newfound freedom, she took the opportunity to do some exploring of her own. Grasping his back, her hands traveled down to his solid butt. She pulled him closer with one hand, the other running through the curls on his head.

He stopped his kiss and she felt his stare. The glow of his eyes now seemed so normal, a part of this magnificent man, her mate.

"We don't have to do this, Layla." Sebastian's voice was husky, and his forehead creased as he poised himself above her entrance.

She lifted her hips and took the first inch of his manhood inside her. "Yes, we do. I want this."

At that, he dropped his lips to hers again, forcing his tongue deep inside her mouth as he pushed into her wet center. In an instant, she was so full, she would have woken the neighborhood with her scream if he hadn't muffled her cries. She adjusted to his ample girth and lifted up again, signaling for him to proceed.

He pulled out and thrust his way in again, over and over. Layla nibbled along his neckline, enjoying his shivering reaction. He built up a rhythm driving in and out, and it didn't take long for her to re-ascend the orgasmic mountain.

She clutched his back as she went over again. This time, her mate moaned with her, shuddering with the exact timing as her own release. He kept thrusting and she realized his empathic powers were allowing him to experience her orgasms. He smiled down at her and brushed his lips against hers with just the right amount of pressure to coax her center into fresh convulsions.

Her lover thrust inside her a final time and stayed there, both of them gasping. He rested his weight on top of her, skin to skin, while her legs remained wrapped around his waist, her heels digging into his bottom.

"I love being an empath." He planted his knees on either side of her and scooped her up in his arms.

"I'm sure you do." She laughed. "It doesn't seem fair that you can feel my orgasms and I can't feel yours, though." Come to think of it, it wasn't simply unfair, it wasn't right. If they were properly mated, they should share a connection that went both ways. Her dreams were so amazing because she experienced simultaneous orgasms in every sense.

He frowned. "Yeah, I think you're right. It was amazing, but we aren't bonded." He kissed her deeply.

She was so convinced the mating ritual was about sex.

"Don't worry," her mate said as his eyes began to glow again. "We can keep trying." Still inside her, his member throbbed and lengthened again. He rocked forward, rubbing against her special button while impaling her with his hardening manhood.

This would be a fun challenge.

* * *

Layla shuffled into a bright yellow kitchen. Gleaming granite countertops were stacked high with apples and bananas. A baking sheet of steaming cinnamon rolls sat cooling on the stove. The open window overlooked fields of grass and hay, and a horse trotted by.

Anne was sitting at a built-in kitchen nook, spooning Cheerios into her mouth as she watched CNN on a thirteen-inch television mounted on the wall. "Morning, sleepyhead." She wore the same pink flannel pajamas she donned the day before. "Get laid yet?"

Layla held her head as the million questions she neglected to ask last night crashed in.

"Whoa, slow down with the confusion. You're making me nauseous." Sebastian walked in behind her and patted her bottom. "What's wrong?"

"Yep." Answering her own question, Anne returned to the news.

"I remembered I still don't know where we are, what we're doing, or what's after us." She paced the room and pointed out the window. "There's a horse out there! We're not in D.C. anymore. Where are we? And don't say Oz!"

"Sorry, I guess I should have explained. We're not that far. I grew up in Leesburg, Virginia, about forty-five miles west of D.C. This is a horse farm." He kissed her cheek before going to retrieve the whistling kettle. "Tea?"

"No, thank you. Do you have any coffee?" Layla hated tea. Shouldn't her "mate" know that about her? She thought he grew up in D.C.; this place felt like another country. No wonder they hadn't bonded, they barely knew each other.

And he still wasn't answering her questions. Worse, Anne wasn't asking the right ones. Her friend would normally be the one badgering everyone until she figured things out. Layla was in the Twilight Zone.

"Layla." Sebastian moved behind her, enveloping her in a hug. "May I remind you that I can hear your thoughts?"

Dammit!

"Don't be embarrassed. You're right. We don't know each other well yet. I like what I see so far, and we'll learn more as time goes on." He kneaded the tension from her shoulders, turning her around to face him. "As far as everything else, I'm with you, remember? I don't know what's going on. There's that filthy creature out there, but I don't know if it's still after us, or if it'll leave us alone now that it has your prayer sphere."

"You've got to get that back, y'know." Anne sipped a glass of orange juice and pointed at the television screen.

"All hell's breaking loose."

"What do you mean?" Layla stepped over to her friend, stopping to look closely at her. "Are you okay? You seem to have no trouble accepting all of this."

Anne placed the glass onto the table and smiled. "When Ceiba healed me, she left a little piece of herself. I got a glimpse of what she knows. However illogical, however rooted in the supernatural and unproven theories, you two are at the center of this world's most transitional moment. What you do now affects us all. You can't force the mating process—though I'm glad you got laid, Layla—but you *can* get that prayer sphere back from the Supay followers. You've got to start taking this seriously." She ate another spoonful of cereal.

Sebastian huffed as he grabbed packets of instant coffee from the cupboard. "We almost got killed by a deranged cloud last night. We *are* taking it seriously."

Anne turned up the sound on the TV. "—death toll is now estimated to be approximately forty-two hundred people. Scientists are preparing an answer to explain why tornadoes are cropping up without storms. So far, three major cities have been hit. The wind has decimated Barcelona, Spain; Shanghai, China; and Portland, Oregon here in the States."

Layla sank into the seat closest to her. This was no coincidence.

Her friend turned to the couple. "They're trying to figure out if terrorism is involved in some way. Tornadoes are supposed to follow certain patterns: thunder, lightning, storms—and they tend to hit flat areas, like the Midwest. It's also odd only big cities seem targeted. There are undiverted wind tunnels spinning throughout major metropolitans. Everyone senses this isn't right. You two can do something about it."

Sebastian grabbed his mate's hand. "Let's go. We have to stop this."

Shaking her head, she slumped into her chair. "You did that reflecting thing and hurt the Filth once. But I have no idea what I'm doing. And the Filth was right, Sebastian." She swallowed as she admitted her real reason for all of her anger. "Giving away the prayer sphere *was* stupid. I have no powers now. Guns are useless against a morphing, diaphanous, misty, cloudy thing. I hate to say it, but I don't think I can do this." She hid her face in her hands, waiting for the backlash.

"No, you can't." Mrs. Tawanti walked into the kitchen. Leaning against the counter, she frowned as she shook her head. "Not as you are now. I must teach you to move in your new world. Without the prayer sphere. Learn to walk before you try to run."

"But more people will die! We don't have time for this." Sebastian clutched the back of the chair on which Layla sat.

"Yes, but if you die with them, we are all lost." The older woman retrieved a porcelain cup from the cupboard.

"Mom, screw the tea! Why aren't *you* doing something? You can stop this, can't you? You're Mother Earth for God's sake!" He slammed his hand on the table.

"No, child. I've only her vessel. And, if you noticed, I merely distracted the beast long enough to get away. And even that took its toll." Eyeing the tea kettle, his mother started to cross the room to the stove. Her gait was slow and halting, and she nearly fell.

Brows creased, Sebastian rushed to her aid, giving his arm for support as he half-carried her to a chair. "Mom, are you okay?"

Layla went to get the woman's tea. She had already caused the death of thousands of people, soon to be more. And the only thing she could think to do was fetch tea.

"I have used too much of my power. Sifting space, healing others takes a toll on me, uses my resources. And with the wind's prayer sphere gone, I am not at my best. Do not fret, child. Time will replenish me." She offered a weak smile as she took the tea from Layla. "Thank you."

"She gets stronger when her kids are bonded." Anne glared at the pair. "So you two need to figure your stuff out quickly."

"*Ch'inyay!* You talk too much." The older woman slapped the lawyer's arm next to her. "They cannot be rushed. Leave them alone."

"We tried to bond last night!" Layla felt her face grow hot as she realized she just told her boyfriend's mother she had sex with him down the hall.

"It didn't work." Sebastian continued without missing a beat. "I mean, it worked, but we're not joined."

She would have laughed at the man's need to make it clear their sex was good, but he was right. They both managed to achieve amazing, multiple orgasms. If the sex had to be better in order for them to mate, she wasn't sure that was possible.

Ceiba smiled. "You will figure it out. For now, we

must eat. You cannot train on an empty stomach."

* * *

"Focus. The wind is within. You need only tap into what already exists." Mrs. Tawanti sat on a bale of hay in her backyard, her teal sari tucked beneath her.

The view from the kitchen window left out the sweeping hills, expansive fields, and blooming vegetation covering the land. Tiny, green leaves spouted from rich brown tree branches. Yellow buds emerged from flowerbeds by the house. Two horses roamed the grounds, nibbling grass and loose bits of hay. Their black coats shone with obvious care. A calm lay over the farm like a soothing fog. Ceiba's home was nature in its most relaxed state.

Layla watched a family of blue jays perched in a magnolia tree. Chirping and flapping their wings, they challenged her to join them in flight. The amazing twist of life was that she could. She flew up the stairs in her house, so she could do it again if her mind would stop racing long enough to focus on Mother Earth's instructions.

Focus. The wind guardian took a deep breath and exhaled slowly. *One, two, three, four.* Again, she lifted her arms and pushed. And again, nothing happened. This was nothing like when she blew papers around or kept the car from falling into the river. At those times, she felt energy pulsing through her. Though she didn't know the prayer sphere was aiding her, it was always strapped to her body in her messenger bag every time she used her powers.

Now she was on her own. Another deep breath. *Up!* She willed the wind to flow through her arms. *Up! Focus!* And, again, nothing happened.

How could she do this without the prayer sphere? She took another deep breath. In and out. Closing her eyes, she imagined herself back in Anne's car when she commanded it to stay on the bridge. Glowing green eyes appeared in the darkness of her subconscious. That was it! She was focused on her mate. And she could do it again now.

"Sebastian?" She called him, interrupting the brush-down he was giving a magnificent brown horse fifty feet away. "Will you help me?" Maybe she needed to see his eyes for this to work.

He walked over. Clad in a faded black t-shirt, jeans, and a leather work-belt slung around his waist, he resembled a stable hand—a romance novel cover-worthy, yummy male specimen of a stable hand. Layla wanted to run her hands over the sculpted chest outlined under the shirt. Maybe she could convince him to throw her in the hay later and take her from behind.

His nostrils flared just before those green eyes began to glow. "Good God, woman, I heard that." He glanced at his mother, and the light weakened.

"That's what I was counting on. Eyes on me!" She pulled him close and gave him a squeeze, deliberately pressing her breasts against him. Pulling away, she ensured his eyes glowed again.

Watching her mate, staring into his eyes, she took a deep breath and exhaled the energy through her outstretched arms. Stray bits of hay scattered to either side. She summoned the wind!

"Bravo!" Mrs. Tawanti clapped her hands.

Layla bent in a mock curtsy. Great. Now she just had to keep Sebastian in a constant state of arousal and they'd be fine.

"That's going to be painful if you don't help out at some point." he whispered in her ear, lingering to nibble her lobe.

Ceiba cleared her throat and Sebastian straightened. "Are you two already communicating telepathically?"

"I can hear her thoughts. That's part of the empathy, right?"

"Yes, but usually a pair is mated before that happens. You two are very close." She stood. "I'm happy you found a way to access your power again, Layla. I did fear you would need your prayer sphere to accomplish it. Well done. Now we can get to the real training. Sebastian, whatever you did to help, keep it up. Layla, it is time to fly."

Keep it up, love, Layla thought to her mate.

He groaned, cupping her bottom behind them. "I'll get you for this," he whispered.

"You have to catch me first." Layla started to run. This was the aspect of her new gift she longed to explore. Last night at home, she was so set on getting to Anne's bedroom, she barely acknowledged that she literally flew up the stairs. At the mall, the wind was with her as she ran, and she outpaced her athletic boyfriend.

She pumped her legs, running as fast as her feet could carry her. Past the three-horse stable, past a small garden, down a path. As she entered an open field, she closed her eyes and pictured her randy mate's eyes. Then she exhaled and lifted off the ground.

Blinking, she saw the ground three feet below. Awesome! She kept running, this time stretching her arms in front of her. Calling forth the wind, she pushed up, and away she flew. Up, past the magnolia tree she sailed. The birds chirped their applause.

But what if she went too high? Turning around, she flew past the path, then past the small garden. She briefly considered taking a break on top of the horse stable until she realized she didn't know how to land.

Hovering above Sebastian and his mother, she yelled down. "How do I get down from here?"

Ceiba laughed. "Child, if you had stayed long enough for me to complete a sentence, I would have told you before you flew away. Never start if you do not know how to end."

A little late for that now. Flapping her arms only drove her higher. She was afraid to put down her arms lest she plummet to the ground. "Sorry, Mrs. Tawanti! What do I do?"

"You must control your power. Tell the wind to lighten, but not to cease. Yogic breathing helps." She tapped her son's back. "Help her, Sebastian."

"I can't with you touching me."

"Oh, for heaven's sake!" She returned to her perch on the bale of hay.

Layla hovered about thirty feet above ground, watching her mate for signs of arousal. *Come on. Fellatio. Cunnilingus. Help me!*

"Sorry. You're scaring me up there," he yelled. "Move. Fly over some hay or something so you don't hurt yourself if you do fall."

Obliging his request, she sailed to the mound of loose hay. Then she closed her eyes to block everyone out. If she couldn't command her element without Sebastian, she was a danger to herself and anyone near her. Her prayer sphere could create tornadoes. Could she do that without meaning to? Now that it had returned, she had to learn how to control her power.

Imagining his glowing, green eyes, she inhaled and pulled a bit of the wind back into herself. The buffer of air separating her from the ground lessened and she sank down a bit.

It was working! She did it again, this time using a yoga technique to slowly pull the air into her lungs while stretching her hands above her head. Her toes touched the hay first. Then, she got so excited to be on the ground, she forgot her concentration and would have collapsed in a heap if her mate hadn't caught her.

"I've got you." He held her close enough for her to feel his pounding heart.

Their instructor walked over. "Well done. That's it for the day. Sebastian, dear, run to the vet and get some horse feed for me, please."

He stared over his mate's head at his mother, jaw dropping open. "If we're not going after those evil spirits, we have to train, Mom. We don't have time to waste buying pet food."

"*Ch'inyay!* Go get the food. I know what I am doing!" The crazy old woman picked up her teacup and walked back to the house.

"Well, at least she's got her strength back." Layla wondered if they should leave and fight those creatures on their own.

"No, we can't leave," answered her annoyingly telepathic boyfriend. "The last time we ignored my mother, we lost the prayer sphere." He took her hand. "I guess we're going to the vet."

* * *

"We don't stock horse feed here. Mrs. Tawanti knows that." The veterinarian cocked her head as she spoke. "You could try Birds 'N' Things. You know where that is? Two blocks south?"

"Yes, I remember. Thank you, Dr. Corey."

Sebastian held her hand as they strolled down the cobblestone sidewalk of downtown Leesburg's Main Street. The historic district was full of little stores, most of the buildings two hundred years old. Fancy stationery boutiques nestled next to antique shops, and old-time diners competed with organic cafes. Near the courthouse, a few men and women wore business suits. The rest of the residents donned jeans and sweaters.

"I wonder what your mom is up to now. Will we be washing old cars next?"

"Wax on. Wax off." He completed her nod to the '80s movie, *Karate Kid*, in which the enigmatic teacher forces the student to complete seemingly unrelated tasks in preparation for martial arts training.

She raised her eyebrows, laughing. He was one of few people who understood all of her obscure movie and TV references. "No, I think I know."

Most couples passing by pushed strollers. The restaurants advertised "Kids Eat FREE!" And there were more children's clothing and toy stores than she'd seen in a one-block radius in years. "She's sending us into kid-central. It's a hint." Layla's last boyfriend's mom was grandchild-happy, too.

"Hmm, I don't think that's it. This is Leesburg. If we leave the house at all, it's here or other kid-friendly places."

"I never would have thought you grew up in such suburbia."

"Why? Where are you from?"

"Outside of Philly in a suburb. I'm not saying there's anything wrong with the 'burbs. I guess I pictured you as a city boy."

"Huh. I thought you were a city girl." He laughed.

"We don't know much about each other, do we?" She frowned.

"I know your eyes roll into the back of your head when I—"

"Sebastian!" She slapped his chest. "I'm serious."

"So am I. I may not know where you're from or your favorite color or your middle name, but I know who you *are*, Layla Cohen. You're the kind of woman who leaps headfirst into danger to save her friends. Your talent surpasses nearly every actress I've watched on any stage.

You have the hottest ass on the planet. And there is no one I'd rather have at my back when we fight an evil cloud than you."

Layla stopped walking, surprised she didn't melt into a puddle of girly goop. No man ever made her feel so accepted on so many levels. He really was her dream come true. She couldn't find the words to express herself.

"You just did." He bent down and planted a kiss on her lips, pulling her out of foot traffic so the strollers could get by.

"Ambler. Rainbow. And Marie," she answered when they stopped for air.

"Hmm?"

"I'm from Ambler. My favorite color is actually a rainbow. And my middle name is Marie."

"Oh." He smiled. "I'm from Leesburg. My favorite color is black. And my middle name is Charles."

Chapter Sixteen

"Hold your mate's hand and try again." Sebastian's mother had been coaching him in empathy for more than an hour.

The training session began as soon as Layla and he returned from their wild goose chase. No one sold the brand of horse feed his mother requested. After the third store, they found out she special-ordered the food online. He couldn't be mad at her though. By the time he drove his mother's old pick-up truck back to the farm, Layla was resting her head on his shoulder and he felt closer to her than he had to any woman in his life.

Wax off.

Most of the hang-ups Layla had were gone, her mind finally at ease where he was concerned. He still sensed a tumult of insecurity and unresolved guilt surrounding the prayer sphere. They had to stop the destruction for many reasons. With every life lost, his mate's soul grew a shade darker.

Now sitting in the kitchen, she held his hand and peered into his eyes. Her smile urged him to drag her into a private room. Maybe that feeling was useful. She used his libido to tap into her element. He pictured her naked, writhing beneath him, her wetness enveloping him as he pushed inside.

She opened that perfect mouth. "Your eyes are glowing." *Later.*

Ah, to be young and in love again. His mother's thoughts rang into his mind.

Sebastian clutched his head as his brain struggled to accommodate three sets of emotions and thought patterns. Layla's was a caress, a welcome companionship. His mother was an intrusion. He yelled as the pounding started in his skull.

Dammit, it's too soon. Please do not let this kill my baby. His mother's smile was tight. "You are fine. You can do this," she said out loud. "Focus."

Layla squeezed his hand as she moved to crouch between his knees, holding his cheek with her other hand. *What the hell am I supposed to do? How do I help him?* "What happened? Talk to me."

Head splitting, he looked from his mate between his legs to his mother across the table and almost laughed. Everyone was insecure. He shook his head. "I'm fine. Mom, is the aspirin still in your bedroom?"

"Yes, but try to rid yourself of the pain. Block me out." She folded her hands on the table. *I should get him the pills. There is no reason for him to be in pain.* She stared unblinking at him, and the only emotions emanating from her were love and determination. Such a paradox.

"Sebastian, you have already discovered outward appearance rarely matches emotion." His mother smiled. "Now you will learn that emotion is not ruled by thought. Feelings and thoughts are two different processes. Now concentrate. Block my thoughts from your psyche." *Because you don't need to know why I am so frightened for you.*

He gritted his teeth. Again, he took his mate's hand. Sex turned on the empathy; maybe sex could turn it off. He imagined Layla in her lacy black bra and a thong.

I wish I could be there when he fights that thing Malc has become, the Filth.

"Mom, please." He tried to shake his mother's words from his mind as he focused on his mate's body. Curly, dark hair cascading down her bare back.

The other boys' mates will be in danger by now. I wonder if they know each other yet. Should I give them their spheres? That didn't work out so well here.

"Mom! How am I supposed to concentrate with my mother's voice invading every two seconds?"

"You can't," she snapped. "When your full power is bestowed, you will have the thoughts of every person within fifty feet crashing relentlessly into your mind. If whatever you are trying now is insufficient to block out my words—and I *want* you to succeed—maybe you should try something else."

Layla leaned in and hugged him, blocking the view of his mother with her unruly hair. "Build a wall," she whispered. "Close everyone out. And then, when you're ready, give me the key." *I know you can—*

She vanished. He was alone in his brain for the first time in twenty-four hours. Peace. And loneliness. He took his hands from his temples and raised his head.

Layla leaned in, pecking a kiss on his cheek. "Whenever you're ready. Hey, I could use the privacy. I don't need you poking around my brain." She smiled. *But I like it. I miss you already.*

"I like it, too." He successfully brought only his mate back into his psyche.

She wrapped her arms around him.

"Congratulations, Sebastian." His mother stood. "I am proud of you. That was a feat not easily accomplished, especially when a couple has not mated." She raised her eyebrows. "Now, as you know, I must get to your brothers and help protect their partners before it is too late."

"Are we ready to fight?" He stood, still holding his mate in his arms.

"When you are ready, you will not need to ask. Remember all you have learned today. Your powers will grow exponentially once you are fully joined. And you will already have the proper tools to control and use them."

"Mrs. Tawanti." Layla stepped out of his embrace to face the vessel of the tree of life. "Thank you for giving me the prayer sphere. I would have died several times without it. I hope I can get it back and stop this."

"I know you will, child. Have confidence. Your soul has done this before. Now I think I will give a few more girls their 'clay balls.'" His mother lifted the bottom of her sari and began to twirl.

"Wait!" Layla yelled. "Why do you wear saris? You're Peruvian."

"Yes, now I am. But I have had many lives and belonged to many cultures. Now I wear what is comfortable." And she disappeared in a poof of teal silk.

* * *

Sebastian drove his mother's beat up pick-up truck down Route 66 toward the District of Columbia. A Top Twenty song scratched out of the ancient radio. Snoring, his mate rested her head in his lap. He played with loose tangles of her hair as he wove through traffic.

Layla was his true mate. He knew that as surely as he knew he recognized her in his dreams. Her soul belonged with him in this life, the ones before it, and any future ones. They would spend eternity together. That joyful thought brought a fresh surge of guilt.

Ariel was dead solely because she was unfortunate enough to fall in love with him in college. They both realized the mistake, but his negligence cost her life. The only thing he could do now was vow not to let anyone else lose their lives because of him.

He drummed his fingers on the dashboard as he drove. Missing a day of rehearsals was necessary for their developing personas, but he still had a theater to run. Jennifer oversaw today's technical rehearsal with Smitty and the remaining couples. They probably didn't miss him. He wondered if Smitty showed up. Did his old friend really try to kill him?

He pulled his cell phone from his pocket and plugged it into the spare car charger, careful not to wake the sleeping woman.

Jennifer left the first message: "Allora didn't show up for her wardrobe measuring. She's not with you, is she?"

He almost pounded his fist on the steering wheel as he remembered the charade he promised to live out with his star actress. There was no way he could pretend to be her lover now that he was with Layla.

"*Message Two!*" Jennifer again. "Allora skipped her voice coaching session this afternoon. It's great if you found the one, but you both have responsibilities."

"*Message Three!* Seriously, Sebastian." Jennifer's voice went one note higher. She must have been pissed. "Do you know where Allora is or not? She needs to check in with her assistant. People are starting to worry about her."

"*Message Four!* My friend, we have a situation." Philip's message was a jumble of words, ending with, "Allora's missing. There was a note in her hotel room. Something about the second prayer sphere, whatever that means. You've got to get here so we can spin this right."

This time, Sebastian's hand did slam the wheel.

"*Message Five!* Where are you? Shit, man, do I not pay you enough money to answer my calls?" Philip was screaming. "Meet me at your theater for tomorrow's rehearsal. We have to get the story—"

Sebastian hung up before the message ended.

Rubbing her eyes, Layla sat up in her seat. "What was that about? What's biting Philip's butt?"

"Allora's missing and there was another note. We've got to find her before something happens to her." He didn't waste words.

"But the Supay followers, the Filth, whoever already knows I'm your mate. And they have the prayer sphere. Why would they take Allora?"

"Because she might be my brother's mate. He really liked her and if they did enough digging, they'd discover that I have a twin. The note mentioned a second sphere." Head swimming, he swerved around a car moseying along, his foot on the accelerator. This mad rush was going to get tricky as they neared D.C. and its ever-present traffic.

Layla bit her lip. "Allora will be okay. If she's Trystan's mate, she's got an elemental power, too. And maybe your mom already gave her a prayer sphere so she can protect herself." *God, I hope that's true.* Her after-thought rang out as loud in his head as if she'd spoken.

Sebastian reached over to hold his mate's hand. "We'll get there."

The forgotten radio emitted a high-pitched wail as the emergency broadcast system took over the station. "This is a report from the National Weather Service. Tornadoes have been spotted in Asheville, North Carolina and Richmond, Virginia. Because of the unpredictable pattern of recent storms, authorities are urging everyone in the southeastern states to be alert for spinning funnel clouds, with or without rain. Get off the roads and into safe quarters. This warning is in effect until further notice." The report repeated itself.

Horns began blaring all over the highway as drivers who'd just heard the alert changed their destinations. A minivan cut them off, darting across three lanes of traffic to take the next exit.

"That report was a bad idea. They just panicked millions of people." Sebastian gripped the steering wheel.

"It's not their fault. They don't know what to do." She looked out the window. "We have to find my prayer sphere."

He hit the brakes as traffic slowed ten miles outside the city. Wednesday night was no exception to the phenomena that caused a constant backup on I-66 without accidents or any logical reason. "What good is being a super-hero if you still have to sit in traffic?"

"I could fly over it."

"And you'd be dissected by morning."

"Then what do you suggest?" She drummed her fingernails on the dashboard, just as he had while she slept.

"First we have to get Allora back—"

"I can't allow thousands of people to die just to save one woman! Not again," she interrupted.

"And I can't let someone else who trusted me die because of my actions!"

The truck at a standstill, they glared at each other. Sebastian tried to hear his mate's thoughts, but only found silence. Then he realized he couldn't feel anything from her either. She was a blank slate. No matter, he didn't need his empathic power to know they wouldn't agree.

Her face softened. "Look, I understand you lost Ariel. But—"

"No, you don't understand. I was married to her. And now she's dead because of me. If I can prevent that from happening to someone else—someone I promised to help just three days ago—I will do whatever I can."

"Even if it means screwing over thousands of other people?"

He rubbed his temple. "No... Are you saying you would have let Anne die if you'd known what would happen?"

She exhaled and her frustration, anger, confusion, helplessness, worry, and terror came tumbling out.

Sebastian gasped as he was hit with the force of her despair.

His mate grabbed his hand again. "Sorry. I couldn't hold it in any longer. Are you okay?"

He nodded, struggling to get his breath. "You can hide yourself from me?"

"I guess so. It's the first time I tried."

Something about this was important. But as he recovered, he couldn't figure out what that crucial thing was. Besides, he was not happy that she shut him out. "Answer the question," he demanded.

Traffic started moving again.

"Would I have let Anne die?"

"Yes."

"I..." She trailed off. *No. I couldn't let Anne die. No, there's no way I could choose a million strangers over my best friend. But I want to be a better person than that.* "I don't want to be selfish. Of course, we have to save Allora, but not at the expense of so many other people. I'm praying she has her own powers and the sense not to give away her own prayer sphere. She's okay, if that's the case."

He squeezed her hand. "We'll do the right thing. I have the feeling we'll get the prayer sphere back once we find Allora."

As usual for D.C. traffic, the congestion cleared enigmatically, and the truck sailed into the city.

* * *

"I'm telling you, I don't know if this is a nightmare or a gift from the PR gods." Philip leaned back in the guest chair of Sebastian's office, his legs crossed while his left hand incessantly clicked the top of a ballpoint pen.

"What did the police say?" The director sat behind his desk, hoping he wouldn't choke on the barely contained excitement oozing from the man in front of him.

"Nobody called them. Her assistant said not to. Apparently, Allora hates the police. She'd rather handle stalkers and other crazies on her own." He pulled a cell phone from his suit jacket and began a text message. "Just in case this gets out, you need to make an appointment with Lynn from the publicity team. She'll give—"

"Do you have the note, Philip?" He interrupted the producer's instructions. His hands were clenched and he needed to get rid of the scum before he did something he'd enjoy.

"The note? It's nonsense." He leaned in. "I'm wondering if Allora wrote it herself to get some attention. I heard she paid those *Page Seven* guys to snap those pictures of you two. How was she, by the way? Good in bed?"

Sebastian gritted his teeth and clutched the armrests of his chair. Going to jail for assault would cause a delay they could not afford. "Where is the damn note, Philip?"

"Calm down. I get it. You don't kiss and tell." He shook his head as he retrieved a crumpled piece of paper from his back pocket. "I could have sworn you were in on this little disappearing act. Don't get me wrong, I was livid yesterday. Livid. But Lynn can fix it. You'll talk to her?" He held the note away from the director as he waited for an answer.

"Yeah, just give me the note." He snatched and opened it, turning in his chair so he no longer faced the jerk.

More block letters: "Deliver the second prayer sphere or the actress dies." He flipped it over. Blank. It had no meeting spot or time. He crumpled the note. All of their plans depended on it telling them where to find Allora. If they had Allora, he figured they had a chance of getting Layla's prayer sphere back. Now, he had nothing but more riddles.

"You look devastated, man. You don't believe in your own fairy tales, do you?" Philip laughed.

"It's not a—" He smelled the joy coming off the producer. "Why are you so damned happy? Your star actress—a woman you claim is a friend—was kidnapped by someone who thinks my play is real. She's in danger." Maybe the producer was too dense to understand the gravity of Allora's situation.

Philip rested his elbow on the desk as he scrolled through messages on his smartphone. "Allora can be replaced. Publicity this good can't be bought, young friend."

"Get out." He stood, arms folded to keep from hitting the bastard.

"It's okay. You're upset because your little girlfriend took off without telling you. So you get this one time to disrespect me. Don't let it happen again. I own you and this matchbox theater." He left the office, slamming the door on his way out.

Sebastian sank back into his chair. A hundred Philips could take over his theater if he could have one clue how to rescue Allora, get Layla's ball back, and stop the tornadoes before the world was blown away.

Chapter Seventeen

They arrived at Sylph Theater together. But now Layla was on her own, trying to squelch the panic attack that started as soon as she watched her mate head into his meeting with the producer. Without Sebastian or the prayer sphere to ground her powers, she half-expected to accidentally blow away the building, or perhaps, be killed by an ancient assassin.

She peeked into the auditorium. Alex was already there, pacing the length of the stage, a purposeful step in his gait. Back straight and mouth set, he looked much older than the college kid she remembered.

"Hey Layla!" Mira walked in behind her. "Did you hear Allora went 'missing?'" The young hospital drama star held up her fingers in air quotes. "I heard she forged a hocus-pocus ransom note to plug the play, too. This is going to be off the hook." Her voice filled the theater.

Layla followed her in, careful to keep her arms at her sides and her breathing even. "Aren't you worried? She was kidnapped."

"Oh, please." Mira flipped her hair and walked to Marcos, her co-star.

"Layla!" Alex leapt off the stage and bounded into the audience toward her. "I tried to call, but your phone went straight to voicemail. Everything okay?" His shoulders slumped a bit, taking on the careless frat boy look he normally wore.

"I'm fine."

"How's Anne?" He reached her side and held his arms open for a hug.

She patted him on the arm closest to her and passed him. "She's fine, too. Back at work already." After Ceiba's healing, cured of her concussion, broken nose, and chipped nail, her best friend had taken a cab back to D.C. following breakfast yesterday and had since been working non-stop.

"Is she?" He followed her to the stage. "When did you get so fast? I can barely keep up, girl."

Oops. She stomped with her next step to make sure her feet were still on the floor. "Oh, um, I guess I'm just ready to get started."

He caught up with her and flashed a big smile. "Me too. I knew you'd change your mind."

"Okay, everyone on stage." Jennifer walked into the auditorium. "Sebastian is meeting with Philip, but we're going to get some blocking done while we wait." She waved at Mira and Marcos, trying to capture their attention as they cuddled.

Alex nudged Layla. "Love is in the air. Looks like everyone is pairing off." He tried to drape his arm around her shoulders.

She ducked. "Not everyone." Hopefully, he'd get the hint that they could not have a relationship. "We're not pairing off, okay? But I do value your friendship." She cringed at the overused line.

He smiled, lips pressed in a tight line. "Friends, huh? You'll change your mind. I'm not giving up on you."

Jennifer appeared on stage, breaking into their private conversation. "Alex, give up. Not gonna happen." She winked and Layla remembered the stage manager saw her making out with the director.

She felt the old blush creeping into her skin, but decided the outing was for the best. The theater troupe *should* know they were together.

"Scripts out. We're walking through Act Two, Scene Three. Give me full movements so I can track where the set and special effects need to change." Jennifer climbed down from the stage, heading for the audience.

"What about the parts where Allora's supposed to speak? Should we, like, skip over that?" Mira called after her.

"Yeah," Marcos added. "Will she be back by the first run?"

Jennifer blinked. "If this is a stunt, I assume she will return for rehearsals soon. If not…"

"OMG, are we in danger?" The young actress clasped her hands over her chest.

"You're fine. Nobody wants you." Alex's deep voice carried.

Layla shook her head at the mood in the theater. Self-absorbed and self-serving, not one of them showed concern for their missing co-worker. She wasn't sure which was worse—their apathy over Allora's disappearance, or their cavalier acceptance of faking a kidnapping to generate press.

Jennifer clapped her hands twice. "Let's go. Huayra, enter stage-right. You're fresh from the market."

Layla picked up a basket from the props table, left, and reentered.

Huayra pulled her sister aside. "I thought you'd be at the temple."

"You don't have to whisper. Paryaq and I have been showing Kon what our bonding can do." Cocha snuggled next to her mate, stroking his chest.

"Your sister started a wind tunnel. She has a gift." Kon stood up to approach Huayra.

"She is the wind. And she has a mate to help her though the process. Just think what we can accomplish if we embrace our destinies. Together, we are one." She turned to him, taking one of his hands and holding it to her heart.

Alex bent down, putting his free hand around Layla's waist, and, completing the swift movement, smashed his lips against hers.

She dropped the basket and shoved the actor. Her power kicked in, sending a gale with the shove, and he would have tumbled across the stage if she weren't holding his other hand.

"Whoa! What was that? Have you been lifting weights?" Alex felt her upper arm, his fingers brushing against the side of her breast.

"Alex! I told you there is nothing between us!"

"Calm down, Huayra. I'm Kon, we're acting. Remember?" He smirked.

What kind of damage would she do if she hit the twerp?

"No." Jennifer flipped through her script, head down as she read her notes. "There is no kiss in this scene. Huayra holds Kon's hand, Paryaq rubs Cocha's shoulders. Cue the wind effect. …What happened with the wind effect?" She turned in her seat and called to the technicians in the rafters.

Alex leaned down and whispered in Layla's ear. "C'mon, are you still hung up on the director? He's with Allora, was probably doing her all week. We belong together. You can call it rehearsal if you need an excuse." He reached for her again.

And the breeze began. Dammit, her arms were lifting! First, the basket at Alex's feet skittered away. Then his tracksuit pants began to ripple. *Stop! Bad wind!* She begged her powers to comply before she blew the idiot through the plywood set.

"My rehearsals are no excuse for you to molest my girlfriend." Sebastian stalked to the stage. "Look at me, Layla. Calm down."

His words were a soothing caress in her psyche. She focused on his face, an impossible mixture of fury and compassion. Thank God he could hear her thoughts, feel her emotions. She balled her fingers into fists and felt the breeze evaporating.

"I thought he was, like, with Allora."

"What's he talking about, anyway?" The other two actors, oblivious to Layla and Alex's private conversation, spoke at once.

"Sebastian and Layla are together. That was his twin, Trystan, in the tabloids." Jennifer delivered her deadpan revelation. "Yes, he has a twin. Shocker. Can we get back to rehearsal now?"

Alex stood tall. Pursing his lips, he turned to his acting partner again. "Are you buying that twin nonsense? He's playing you. If he cared about you, he would've squashed this mix-up a long time ago."

She knew the truth—after seeing the childhood photos of the twins at his mother's house—but the other man's words hit a nerve. Sebastian hadn't wanted to date her because of his professional standards. Yet he let the world believe he was involved with his star actress because being seen with Allora made sense. Just as the cashier said, Allora and Sebastian were a perfect match. She was drop-dead gorgeous movie star and he owned a theater. What could Layla provide? Truly?

Yes, he was her mate; it was destiny and all that crap. But would he be with her if not for centuries-old, match-making meddling? They were already doomed if destiny was the driving force in their relationship; she could barely control her own powers. Besides, it might have been silly, but she wanted more from a life-partner. She wanted...

"Love." Sebastian climbed onto the stage and pulled her away from Alex before she flicked him out of the building. "I love you, Layla. I meant what I said yesterday. I love all of you as you are right now and as you will become. And I'm sorry about Allora. I'll call *Page Seven* and give them a new scoop: Sebastian Tawanti is in love with his favorite actress, mate or not."

Reaching up, she touched one of the curls topping his head. "I love you, too." She watched the glow begin in the back of his pupils as he bent down to join his lips with hers. As she opened her mouth to accept, he hoisted her off the floor and lifted her higher into his embrace.

"That's great. We're all so happy that's cleared up." Jennifer tapped her pencil on her notebook. "Now from the top. Boss, you joining me out here? Or do you plan on making out all day? Let Alex...Where's Alex?"

The couple broke their kiss to glance around the stage.

"The twerp bailed," Layla whispered to the director.

"How dare he ditch my rehearsal! I was supposed to cut this scene anyway..." He smiled and set her down. Stepping away, he addressed his cast and crew. "This play has a number of set-backs. Our main actress has been abducted. We may have just lost Alex. And Layla and I have to leave. Rehearsals are postponed until further notice." He took her hand and led her from the stage, his eyes still glowing.

* * *

Layla pulled the gray t-shirt over Sebastian's head. Sandy brown curls covered his chest and she ran her fingers through it, savoring the contrast of soft hair over hard muscles.

Groaning, he pulled her to him and lifted her off her feet. She wrapped her bare legs around his waist and he eased them both to his bed, bracing his weight with his forearms.

They could hardly keep their clothes on during the cab ride home. Sebastian nibbled her neck and pushed his hands under her blouse. She rubbed the hardness between his legs and only stopped when the driver tsk-tsked loud enough to drown out traffic.

Lying on her back in his rumpled flannel sheets, she looked up at the familiar green glow. "I don't think anyone else sees them glow. You were lit up like Times Square on stage and nobody cared."

"That's probably a good thing." He planted a quick kiss on her lips. "I don't want to end up in a lab either. So don't tell anyone, or I'll let them think you're bat-shit crazy."

She swatted him on the head. "How did you know that was one of my fears?"

"I've heard that term float around your head a few times." Smiling, he tugged at her shirt. "Now off with it."

She would have happily complied, but their position didn't make the removal of clothes easy. Time to test the wind. Looking into her mate's eyes, she concentrated on lifting them one foot off the bed.

He went first. "I would have moved if you asked." He laughed, now horizontally suspended in air.

"Not my intention." She tossed her tank top onto the floor.

He took the opportunity to ease his jeans over his hips, leaving him nude.

She rubbed her fingers along his pelvic bone, leading down to his groin. Circling her hand around, she explored the ridges of his penis, holding the shaft from bottom to jutting top.

Sebastian gasped as she realized she was holding him almost immobile up there. Eyes squeezed shut, he licked his lips slowly and clenched his fists at his sides. Darkened eyes opened. "Let me down, Layla."

She lowered him, opening her legs so she could wrap them around his middle again. His weight resting on top of her, she shifted and felt the full length of his runner's body melding with hers.

As heavenly as it felt having him pressed against her, she longed to ride her mate. A mental image floated from her mind to his, and he flipped her over, lying on his back as he positioned her over his hips.

"As you wish."

On top, she bent her head down to kiss that magnificent chest. With trailing kisses, she traced the line of sandy curls to his erection. It stood proudly at attention, and when she touched it with the tip of her tongue, it bounced. He groaned, taking one of her hands in his own.

Starting from the bottom, she licked her mate's aroused member, sucking and tonguing him until he pulled her up with a gasp.

"Not yet." Positioning her mouth to his, he delivered a mind-shaking kiss.

His arms wrapped around her back, smashing her breasts against his chest as she straddled him. Hands massaged her back, then lower, and one of his digits found its way to her center. Sebastian's tongue caressing hers and his fingers rubbing her most sensitive spot, Layla felt her first orgasm approaching.

She tugged his fingers away just before she came. "Not yet."

He smiled up at her, grasping both of her hips. Of the same mind, she moved her opening over his hardness and slowly impaled herself, stretching to accommodate the intrusion.

Finding their rhythm, she rocked back as he ground forward. She arched her back, and ground onto her mate as the sensations rushed to her brain. Squeezing him with her thighs, she began to peak into orgasm.

He reached up and cupped her face. "Look at me." His green eyes flashed as she came, and he shuddered with her. *I love you so much. Heavens, I'll never get tired of this.* His thoughts rang into her mind.

She threw her head back again as the wave intensified. Riding her mate, she bucked as a second orgasm tore through her.

So perfect. His hands reached up and cupped her breasts, kneading them as she moved. *I need to kiss you again.* He sat up, still rocking his hips, pushing inside her, and pressed his mouth to hers.

She grasped his back and held on, using her legs to pull him closer. Chests pressed together, his shaft directly hit her most sensitive spot as he moved. A cry escaped her lips and she came, convulsing and digging her nails into his back.

He moaned with her, shuddering from her orgasm. *I love you.*

"I love you, too." She panted, still riding the wave.

"Layla, you heard me?"

"Yeah." She smiled, eyes rolling back into her head as she crested again.

This orgasm set off his, and he pushed deeper. She opened her eyes and clutched his back, feeling the clench of her own muscles around an erection that didn't belong to her. Testicles emptying, she suddenly felt the simultaneous caresses of two sets of genitals climaxing, two minds reveling in bliss.

You weren't speaking, were you? she thought to him.

No. He kissed her forehead, her cheeks, her nose, and her lips. *But you can hear me.*

Because we're mated. She didn't know whose thought it was. And she no longer cared.

Chapter Eighteen

Water trickled down Sebastian's back. Steam filled the shower, and the cold black tile beneath his toes provided a cool contrast for the heat pouring off the rest of his body. At the same time, jersey sheets tickled his backside and muscles stretched as his mate entered an impromptu yoga pose on his bed.

How much could she feel from him? He reached down and cupped his ball sack, letting his fingers linger.

Haven't you had enough? Her amused thought broadcast its way into his mind, stronger than ever.

Just checking, he thought back. *I couldn't hear you.*

She pulled her knees up to her chest, twisted them to her left side, and turned her head to the right. *I'm meditating to clear my mind. If I do it right, you won't hear anything from me for a while. …I think I only hear what you send to me.*

Hmm, I'll let you get back to it then. Shower complete, he turned off the water.

Just one before Margie gets home. The deep voice punched in. *Now where did I hide the brownies?*

Sebastian grabbed his head as his neighbor's thoughts rattled around. Okay, he could do this. They knew mating would strengthen their powers. The unwanted thoughts could be tamed with effort. He inhaled and thought of the magic his mate could work with her small hands. The stabbing sensation subsided.

He grabbed his towel and walked into his bedroom. Layla lay in the position he could still feel, eyes closed, breathing deeply.

It stinks in here. I bet TJ didn't change the litterbox. Margie was home. *Why do I have to do everything here?*

This time, the extra voice was little more than pressure. He smiled as he pulled on a t-shirt and left the room. A firewall separated him from his neighbors, but they were less than fifty feet apart. He clapped his hands. How amazing it would be to understand what made people do the things they did, why their faces scrunched into different expressions. His director's brain went wild with the possibilities.

Damn, she's home. Better hide her present.

That ass. Where's the pooper scooper?

He chuckled. Mr. Snugglepants brushed against his leg as he grabbed a sheet of paper from his desk. "What are you thinking, Mister? More food? Catnip?" Hearing nothing from his pet, he decided he probably didn't want to be the next Dr. Doolittle anyway. He jotted a message for Layla and walked out the front door.

No one was around. A jog around the corner changed that.

First, the owner of the taco stand stood wiping outside tables. *If I paid ten dollars an hour, it would cost me two hundred dollars to hire a helper for twenty hours a week. Taxes would be extra. I can't afford that. Maybe I'll pay cash…*

A dark-haired lady pushing an old man in a wheelchair approached. *Ho bisogno habitare qui por due anni. Due anni e posso stare. Voglio stare, si?*

Hmm, Italian. He smiled as he realized he was staring.

Bellisimo! She smiled back and he felt an accompanying wave of sexual interest from the woman.

He gave a quick nod and hurried on; he was a mated man.

They were mated. He wondered how Layla's power had grown. She already stopped an exploding car. What could she do now? Could she start a storm if she sneezed?

Maybe if I buy him flowers. No, men don't like flowers. Think, Gina, think. A middle-aged woman rushed out of Starbucks.

His place was stocked with tea. Layla would appreciate a cup of coffee. He grabbed the door, holding it for the middle-aged woman, and entered.

Venti means large, right?

Don't forget to pick up Mendy.

How many calories are in the whipped cream?

I have got to stop spending so much on coffee.

Maybe I'll go back to school.

Why am I fetching coffee? I have an MBA.

She's kinda cute. Is that a wedding ring?

Fifteen separate psyches crashed into Sebastian at once. He clutched his head. Every thought fought for dominance, poking into his subconscious, stabbing into his mind.

Is that guy okay?

He better not die on my shift.

Cool, I get to call an ambulance!

He dropped to one knee as some of the patrons came closer. The jumble of voices reached a fever pitch, personalities clawing at his brain.

"Are you all right, sir?" A barista laid his hand on Sebastian's shoulder. *It's the theater dude. Would his usual chai tea help?*

Thoughts grew louder as people crowded around him. His head couldn't take the noise. Five more people entered the door behind him.

"Is there a doctor in here?" A woman's voice sounded above them all.

No, but I played one in college. Not funny. Don't say that.

Wish I was. I wouldn't mind giving him mouth to mouth.

Ew. Is he contagious?

Would it be bad if I left? I'm already late.

Sebastian felt something snap in his brain. Everyone screamed while clutching their heads.

Layla's voice broke through the symphony of pain. *Sebastian! What's going on?*

He held onto the feeling of his mate next to him. *It's too much.* He thought to her. *I'm hurting them.*

Picture my eyes. Stare into my eyes.

Closest to him, the barista fell to the floor.

Sebastian closed his eyes and thought of his mate, beautiful, flawed in every perfect way. He imagined her hands pulling him to her and dove into that security.

Build a wall. Close yourself off. Put yourself behind the wall.

Brick by brick, he patched up the hole in his brain that let his pain infect the others.

The barista scrambled backward. *What the fuck was that? He* is *contagious.*

"Is he some kind of terrorist?" An older woman rubbing her temple pointed at Sebastian.

"No, he comes in here all the time."

"He could be a sleeper agent!" *I saw it on TV!*

Layla broke in, a soothing caress. *You have to block them out so you can get out of there. Keep building your wall.*

He imagined Smitty's iron wall with a padlock, himself on one side and the world on the other. Finally, they were all blissfully quiet.

The coffee store's door opened, flying back until its glass shattered. His mate had arrived. He lifted his pounding head and watched her dismiss her destruction as she dashed inside.

"What the fuck was that?" The thought was said aloud. "Who are you people?"

Layla helped him to his feet and he concentrated on keeping his walls up. "We have to get out of here," she whispered in his ear.

"I think it's some kinda dirty bomb," a man shouted out from the back of the store.

Layla held up a hand and a breeze entered. He hoped the patrons would think the wind came from the open door. He and his mate turned to leave.

"Stop! You're not going anywhere!"

Layla put down her hand and glass skittered across the floor.

Focus! He felt her control slipping away, and the breeze growing stronger. Grabbing her hand, he tugged her out of the store.

"I'm calling the police!"

She held his hand. The wind behind them now, they raced out of the store and back to his house. The street was a blur as they moved. Layla was literally as fast as the wind. His five-minute jog took twenty seconds on the return trip.

He sank onto his black leather couch as she closed the door behind them, shattering the small window next to it. Head splitting, he gazed up at Super-Layla. In one of his old t-shirts and rolled up boxers, she looked like she'd just stepped out of a teenage boy's dream. Her freshly washed hair was a tangle of curls, impossibly suspended in a windy halo, floating around her head in a crazy crown. Her messenger bag was slung over her shoulder, completing the urban superhero look.

She stared at him, her face a mask, and he realized he didn't know her thoughts or emotions. He closed himself from her too.

"Don't do it." She sat beside him and placed his head in her lap. "I don't need to be an empath to understand that determined look on your face."

"I can't hear you, Layla."

"You hear me just fine."

"You know what I mean." There was no way he'd give up the connection now.

"Yeah, I do." She climbed into his lap, pressing her forehead to his. "I miss you too, but no one can withstand that kind of torture. I felt the barrage before you shut me out. It'll kill you."

He pulled her small frame to his body, pressing her against him as he tasted her lips. They were linked. He wouldn't risk hurting her by opening himself—and her—to the cacophony of other minds colliding with his own. Not until he mastered the skill.

Standing, he lifted her off the couch. "Okay, let's go."

She slid down his chest, and he had to ignore the sensation of her body rubbing against his as her feet touched the floor. She raised her eyebrows. "I don't think we should leave the house until the 'terror alert' is over."

"We're not. We're going to the basement to teach ourselves how to control these powers. I noticed the wind has gotten away from you." He nodded toward the broken window.

Wincing, she ducked her head, curls falling into her face. "It's worse than before. I don't know my strength anymore. The slightest gesture gets pushed along by this crazy air current... I also broke your dresser." She flopped onto the couch with a pout, looking adorable and sexy with his boxers riding up her thighs.

"You stay there. I'll get rid of tools and anything else we don't need flying at us downstairs." With renewed energy, he walked into the underground basement. Cold and dark, the place was mostly used for storage and the random theatrical set project. Sawdust coated the concrete floor. Now it had the added bonus of being able to cut him off from civilization.

After shoving a rusty saw into a closet, he sat on his old futon and closed his eyes. Right there, in the darkness of his mind's eye stood the iron door blocking out the psyches of the world's inhabitants. First, he mentally tore down the barrier between his mate and himself.

—here, you little furball. I promise I won't blow you down the hall again… Dammit, I can't even pet the cat.

Layla, he thought to her. *Mister has been through enough. Come downstairs.*

Sebastian! Her joy traveled along their connection. *You're back! Just a minute. Ouch…*

He jumped up, reaching the bottom of the stairs as she appeared in the doorway above.

"What happened?" he asked.

She frowned, rubbing her head. "I hopped off the couch and hit the ceiling. What are we going to do? We have to get my prayer sphere back, save Allora, and prevent a windy apocalypse, and we're not fit to leave the house."

"We also have rehearsal tomorrow or we'll both have to find new careers."

"Right, can't forget that. Can your mother help us out?" Down in the basement, she held his hand as she made her way to the futon.

"No. I'm sure she's busy with my brothers and their mates. Besides, we can do this."

She put her head in her hands and groaned.

"We *can*. We figured out the mating, and we can do this, too. Come on." He tickled her side. "Up."

Laughing, she pushed him away.

He loved a strong woman, but as he went sailing through the air, he wished there was a little less oomph behind his mate's slightest exertion.

"Oh no!" She reached out and grabbed the space where he was standing.

He halted in mid-air. From his spot about a foot off the floor, inches from being slammed into the concrete wall, he saw the crease in her forehead, the concentration set in her jaw. This was a good time to practice.

Great, he thought to her. *You stopped the impact. Now let me down.*

She lowered her hands and he dropped to the concrete in a poof of sawdust. "Sorry! That was my version of gentle. Geez, what if you were up high?"

"I wasn't, though." He brushed dust from his face and walked back to the futon. "That's why we're practicing in the basement."

"Maybe if you make your eyes glow, I can focus on them." She reached for his crotch.

"Layla, I can guarantee I won't be in the mood when the evil mist is attacking us. We've got to do this without me having a hard-on."

Snatching her hand away, she stood. "You're right. So what's the plan, director?"

"I'm going to run at you. Don't let me touch you. Start with keeping a buffer around yourself at about two feet."

"You say that like it'll be easy."

"You're an elemental. It should be."

She stuck out her tongue and he almost gave her the advantage of glowing eyes. Dowsing his desire, he prepared to tackle her as if she were one of his brothers. He'd probably be in as much pain when this exercise was over.

"Your shorts are falling down." He used the same trick to distract Trystan.

"What?" As her head went down, he rushed her. Arms up, he was hit by an invisible fist when she realized the ploy.

"Control it!" he called as he was forced backward. "You're leaking energy. Use only enough power to keep me from getting close."

She closed her eyes, her chest expanding as she inhaled.

The wind ceased and he almost fell forward. He rushed her again. *Picture a bubble around your body.* He sent a thought directly into her brain as she concentrated. This time, the impact was more like running into a pillow. He hugged her. *Good job. But you can keep the hard wall for bad guys, okay?*

"Okay." She opened her eyes and smiled. "Your turn. I think we're missing your offensive tactic."

"What offense? Should I think them to death?"

"Yes! When you were in pain, everyone around you felt it. If we learn to focus that, you could be a fierce weapon."

"You've got a scary mind, Layla."

"No, that would be you." She paced the room. "The trick is to hurt the kidnappers without hurting yourself."

"Or anyone else." He pictured the barista clutching his head. This was not a good plan if he risked inflicting pain on more innocent bystanders.

"True." She stopped and touched his arm. "Now try with me."

"I am not sending waves of agony into your head."

"So it's okay for you to get tossed around like a rag doll while training me, but I can't help you?" Her hands went to her hips.

"Yes, that's right." He concentrated on the outline of her thighs through the boxers she wore, allowing himself to guess she wore nothing underneath.

"Why are your eyes glowing? Oh, oh my…" She squeezed her thighs together, biting her lip, and putting her hands on her knees for support. *Did you just send me an orgasm?* She closed her eyes as her mouth dropped open.

If I can send pain, why not pleasure? He walked toward her, pulling her into his arms as she crested the final wave. *Do you trust me?*

"God, yes!" Her face was flushed and she let her full weight rest on his body.

He smiled. How far could he take this mind control thing? Narrowing his eyes, he peered into Layla's. *You never liked your hair.* Drawing on his skill as a director, he was careful with his command, transmitting only the mental image of her chopping off her curls.

His mate suddenly yanked at her beautiful dark tresses, frowning. "Why have I kept this around so long? Got any scissors?" She pushed him away and rummaged through the drawers of his tool chest.

It worked! His Super-sense could kick ass. He delayed the celebration when she pulled out the garden shears.

"Help me, honey." She smiled at him as she angled her head down.

You feel the same as you always did about your hair. Now put the shears away.

Her eyes widened as his hold on her evaporated. "Did you make me want to cut off my hair?"

"Yes..." Perhaps he should have also sent a forgiveness spell. Spell? That was exactly what he did. Whatever he chose to call it, he put his mate under a spell. She wasn't in control of her own actions.

"That is awesome!" She clapped her hands. "Okay, now you have to learn to shut out thoughts. Come on!"

He watched her bound up the stairs. This was the first and last time he'd ever take control away from her. She was right; he did possess a scary mind. But he would use it on whoever tried to harm his mate and other innocent people.

* * *

A few hours later, they figured out his powers. Sebastian didn't think he'd be able to keep a straight face around his neighbors ever again, though. He practiced tuning one out, then the other. Then he made TJ want to wash the dishes and Margie want to wear a negligee. He ignored them both when they decided on their own to have an afternoon quickie.

Layla became a constant companion in his head. Wherever she went in the house, he heard a dim echo of her existence. Now that their connection wasn't all or nothing, he found they were both happiest when he stayed within earshot, but not tuned in to every minute detail.

He peeked down into the basement. His mate stood in the center of a five-foot tall tornado, its diameter spreading from her outstretched arms.

She looked up at him, brows furrowed. *Help me put it out.*

He closed his eyes and felt for their connection. A warm spark flickered in his mind. Using it, he poured love and discipline into his mate. She raised her hands and clapped together, collapsing the air on itself and sending sawdust flying.

She coughed, covered in the dust. "I think we're ready."

Chapter Nineteen

"Eastern Market! Doors opening… on my left!"

Layla hugged her messenger bag to her side as she exited the train. The bag felt empty, containing only her script, spare keys to Tom's bar, cell phone, and a granola bar. The prayer sphere's weight would be welcomed back.

Her watch read 10:02 am. Thursday morning. She should be at rehearsal or opening the Irish pub, or going to an audition—anything but headed home for a change of clothes before battling an ancient Incan cult.

She inhaled as she pushed her way up the Metro station's stairs, careful not to set off any errant breezes. Her power mostly under her command now, it was amazing how quickly this life had become normal. Maybe she could be a competent wind guardian after all.

But she wasn't used to having a mate yet. Sebastian woke her this morning with a dream-worthy bonding session that ended with him staring into her eyes as he whispered, "I love you." He was still inside her, and she came again on the spot, launching them back into bliss.

Their love was no longer a question; and she wondered at the fullness, the completion their connection gave her. The mating bond was like having a constant caress in her mind. Now, walking down the side streets to her house, she closed her eyes and could see a glowing, green gaze, a reminder of his presence.

Her toe hit an uneven bit of concrete and her arms went flailing. In an instant, she was airborne; however, instead of face planting, she hovered about four inches off the ground. Still picturing her mate's glowing eyes, she righted herself and put her feet back on the ground, unscathed.

A quick scan of the other pedestrians proved no one seemed to notice anything out of the ordinary. So just a few steps from her path, she ran up to her front door. The door was scratched all around the lock. *Not again.*

What's wrong? Sebastian's voice rang out in her mind.

She was more panicked than she wanted to admit. Otherwise, her mate wouldn't have tuned in.

Nothing, she thought back. There was no reason to get him worried. *It's nothing. There are scratches on the door's lock. I'm sure they're from the night Anne was taken.*

I'm not convinced. On my way.

You don't have to do that. She couldn't have him dropping everything just because she got the willies. Her key turned the lock. *The door is locked. What kind of intruder locks the door behind him? I'm fine.*

It'll take me twenty minutes to get there. The director was at his theater answering questions from the cast and crew. *Maybe you should call the cops.*

I am not calling the cops. Stop panicking. Layla walked into the living room. Anne had obviously cleaned the place a bit. The couch was righted, and her roommate's ugly plaid blanket was serving as an impromptu slip-cover to hold the stuffing inside. Though not yet on the shelves, the books were in neat stacks. And the glass from the shattered coffee table was swept away.

A pang of guilt hit Layla. She should have been there to help straighten up. Then again, the kitchen was still a mess. Drawers of silverware and oven mitts lay strewn about the floor. There was still plenty of work for Layla to tackle.

Ha! On second thought, come on over. I could use your help cleaning! She reached for her mate and found a closed wall in her mind. He closed himself off to her. *Sebastian!* She mentally yelled.

Right here! You okay?

Why did you—you called the cops, didn't you?

Of course I did. Officer Brull says to leave the house and wait outside.

Layla tossed her bag onto the couch. *Oh for heaven's sake. There's no one here. I'm going to my room. And you're not invited!* Throwing up her own mental wall to block out her overly-protective boyfriend, she jogged up the stairs.

And walked right into a scene from *The Exorcist*. Or maybe it was more like *Single White Female*. Whatever the flick, bad things were happening in her bedroom. Why couldn't she have listened to the empath? Or her own willies?

Hair thrown back into one of her signature messy ponytails, and dressed in an old pair of Layla's flannel pajamas, Allora sat cross-legged on her bed. Rocking back and forth, she held the prayer sphere to her chest while chanting a spell from the play. "Full of light. Full of charm. Full of light. Full of charm…"

"Allora…" Layla approached the actress. "What are you doing?" Maybe there was a logical reason for the missing woman to be wearing her clothes and sleeping in her bed. Please, let there be a logical reason.

Pupils dilated, Allora snapped up her head and spat. "It is not working fast enough! I have tried everything my *abuela* taught me. Potions, spells, chants, everything."

As Layla got closer, she realized the situation was worse than she thought. Surrounded by personal objects from her bedroom—her journal, bits of jewelry, her comb with strands of hair still attached—Allora was in some kind of trance. "What are you trying to do? Are those my dirty socks?"

Allora continued, staring through her. "I mated with one of the cardinals. Trystan fell in love, I know it. I have the prayer sphere and I am in the little bitch's bed. Why can I not access *all* of her energy?" Eyes rolling, she slapped at the mattress.

She was possessed. Layla grabbed the woman's shoulders and shook. "Stop, Allora. We'll get you some help." What could have done this to her?

Turning her glare, the star dropped the prayer sphere into her lap and grabbed Layla's wrists. "You! You think you are the only one with a destiny to fulfill? You are as stupid as he said." A deep guffaw erupted from her lips and she threw her head back to laugh.

"Allora, what the hell is going on?" Layla tried to wrench her wrists away.

Allora smiled as her voice took on a sing-song quality. "Stupid, stupid, stupid girl," she mocked. "You know nothing. We are trapped in these god-forsaken bodies. And you, you go about lifetime after lifetime protecting this world. We will free everyone this time. Not just the people of the Incan empire."

Layla gasped as she connected the dots. "*Free* them? The Incan people didn't disappear, did they? The Supay followers 'freed' their spirits. You murdered an entire civilization!"

"It is time for rebirth! Time for renewal. And yet Ceiba fights us. For millennia, her soul has fought. No more! Human kind must be stopped! You—stupid girl with your destiny—*you* will be stopped!" She squeezed Layla's hands with a strength Layla recognized as her own. Wind blew through the crazed woman.

She squeezed back, and pushing against Allora, picturing glowing, green eyes, she sent her own wind through her fingertips.

Eyes bulging, Allora screamed. "No! It is my power now! The wind belongs to me!" She shoved Layla across the room and leapt to the floor. In bare feet and purple flannel, she almost looked like a little kid. Layla had the absurd desire to pat her on the head and tuck her into bed with a nighttime story.

Maybe you should try that. Sebastian's voice rang out in her mind.

With a sickening thud in her gut, Layla remembered she blocked her mate out just before entering her room. *How did you get back in my mind? Not that I'm not happy, but—*

Allora lifted her hand and sent a gust of air at Layla,

blasting her into the wall. Her vision blurred as her head thumped against the wall.

Focus now. Questions later. Sebastian's voice sounded in her bruised brain.

Allora raised her hands, pushing against the air again, and slamming Layla into the wall a second and third time. "I am so much better than you! You are not fit to be the wind guardian, stupid girl."

Wind pushing against her, she felt her head bounce off the plaster as consciousness began slipping away.

Layla! You are the wind guardian! Claim your power! Follow your gut! her mate screamed into her mind.

But my gut told me to read the woman a bedtime story, she thought. *She's right. I'm not cut out for this.*

You can be whatever you want to be. You're an elemental!

This time, when her head smacked the wall, the last bit of her resistance broke free. She fell deeper into the darkness threatening to overtake her conscious. But there, she found the spark of her bond with Sebastian, and she soaked herself in the love, strength, and endurance the connection provided.

You can do this, Layla. You were born for this. His voice filled her brain, helping to ease the throbbing pain of her skull.

She *could* do this. Sebastian believed in her. A freaking goddess believed in her. She had only to focus and regain a bit of confidence in herself.

She opened her eyes to find Allora pushing the air at her with both arms raised. Clad in Layla's flannel pjs, wearing Layla's earrings and lipstick, the woman was a poseur. She was a child playing dress-up. Layla was the real thing.

She inhaled deeply as the gust pushed at her. "That's *my* wind." Opening her mouth, she swallowed the movie star's attack in one giant gulp. Then her own arms lifted, forcing the gale out and knocking the imposter back onto the bed.

Allora grabbed the prayer sphere, clutching it to her chest. "You can't have it!"

Layla watched the woman defiantly scattering her things as she held onto the clay ball, and understood her vision of Allora as a child. "Allora," she called. "Does your story explain why I'm the wind guardian and you're not?"

Allora turned up her nose. "No, but—"

"I am the wind guardian because *my* soul was chosen to help protect mankind. And even with your fame, your beauty and talent, you had to drape yourself in *me* to get the merest taste of my energy."

"Police!" Officer Brull's voice carried. "Your door is open, we're coming in!"

The wind guardian snapped her fingers and the sphere spun out of Allora's grasp, levitating six inches off the quilt, before shooting across the room into Layla's open hands. "Here's what's going to happen now. You're going to confess your crimes to the detective and get the hell out of my house."

Officer Brull entered the bedroom, pistol raised. "Layla, hand over the prayer sphere." His icy, blue eyes twitched as he pointed his weapon at her head.

"What?" Layla's jaw dropped open as she watched the cop stride over to her, his eyes wide. He seemed to struggle with his weapon, one hand trying to lower it while the other held its aim. The indecision over whether or not to blow her brains out was not comforting. "Why do *you* want the prayer sphere?"

"Alex!" Allora exhaled. "Just in time. You'd better take the sphere. This cop is stronger than you think." She cocked her head and smiled.

Get out of there, Layla! Sebastian warned in her mind. *Officer Brull is no more than a puppet now. I'm almost there.*

"Dammit." Alex walked in behind the officer. "Did you have to say my name?"

"Who cares? You will never possess her love. You cannot have her as a mate. Kill her!"

"Sweet cheeks," he continued. "You know I tried to kill her as soon as we found out who she was. I followed her around town, compelling a chef to decapitate her, and a driver to push her car into a river. I tried to poison her myself, and even forced Smitty to blow up their damn car. We cannot kill the little bitch."

"Somehow, I knew it was you." Layla raised her arms, ready to blow them all against the wall.

"Stop!" Alex held up his hand. "You can make knives miss and cars move. Are you sure you can stop a bullet, though?" He glanced at Officer Brull and the detective put his finger over the trigger. "Are you positive, wind guardian? Or do you have to focus? Will it happen automatically? Or do you need time to picture glowing, green eyes and imagine the director fucking you? You don't know, do you?"

"You're an empath, aren't you?" There was no other way he would instantly know exactly what she was thinking. The awkward, naked feeling she always had around him finally made sense. Instead of the warm openness Sebastian created, Alex made her feel exposed and raw. Ignoring the urge to hide, she started building a wall inside her mind.

A vein in his forehead pulsed as his lip curled up. "Give my friend back the prayer sphere."

She wasn't about to hand over her soul's creation again. Brick by brick, the wall was almost done.

The evil empath attacked without warning. His psyche invaded her subconscious, crashing down her defense. *You can't block me out, Layla. My soul is much older than yours. And I've had more than a day's training.*

"I can't take the sphere by force," he said aloud. "But, I can do something much more fun." Alex crooked his finger and motioned to her. *You're tired. The bed looks comfy.*

Brain itching, Layla joined Allora on her bed.

The corners of Alex's mouth curled up as he sauntered over. *There is nothing you want more than to cuddle up to your play-mommy, and let her place her hands over yours.*

The itching intensified. As Allora moved to hug her from behind, she tried to remember why she shouldn't want to feel the most beautiful woman in the world embracing her. The older woman gripped her hands, and together they held the prayer sphere.

Allora recommenced her chant. "Full of light. Full of charm. Full of light. Full of charm. Full of light…" Her voice carried on.

Layla hyperventilated, her lungs suddenly sucked clear of air. The constant windy feeling was yanked away, replaced by a heavy void. The prayer sphere shined a sickly gray where their hands met. And her fingertips, once alive with the wind, burned. Something wasn't right. She settled in closer to the actress.

You do not want to touch that woman. Remember who you are, wind guardian. Wake. Up. Her mate's voice slammed into her mind, dislodging the tentacles of the evil empath.

Alex roared, grasping at his head.

"Layla!" Sebastian's footsteps sounded on the hardwood as he raced up the stairs.

Alex sneered as he flicked his finger at the motionless police officer. " Goodbye, wind's cardinal."

Officer Brull pointed his gun at the empty doorway, his finger already depressing the trigger as Sebastian barreled into the trap.

"No!" Layla pushed away from the chanting woman, struggling to lift her leaden arms.

Her mate appeared in the doorway and the gun went off.

Would the wind obey? Was she enough? The thoughts rolling through her mind since this mess started evaporated. Without yogic breathing or glowing eyes, the elemental shielded her mate with an air buffer. A fraction of a second later, the bullet bounced off the blockade and ricocheted, nearly hitting Alex as it sunk into the plaster behind him.

Allora stood as she continued her chant. "The power is growing!" she croaked. "Full of light. Full of charm!" Her feet rose off the bed and she held onto the floating sphere. "I can't… what's happening?" Her perfect face stretched out, as if it were an Allora-balloon inflating.

A surge of power expanded Layla's lungs as she

inhaled. Oxygen filled every cell and the very air in the room embraced her. She smiled, understanding the meaning of the word "elemental" for the first time. The wind was a part of her being, part of her soul. There was no commanding it, no controlling the element. She *was* the element.

The ground shifted. As she raised her arms, bangles clanged against her suddenly brown skin, and the prayer sphere glowed. This time, she welcomed the vision from her past life, grateful for the encouragement offered by her former self.

Allora screamed as her nose flared unnaturally, air filling her face. The fingers clutching the prayer sphere began to blister, smoke rising from the contact points as the sphere struggled to free itself from the interloper.

Layla held out her hands to the steaming ball of clay. It leapt from the deranged woman's grasp and hopped across the bed to its rightful owner. The true wind guardian held the sphere to her chest as she leapt to her mate.

He stood immobilized in the air cocoon. Well, that wasn't quite her intention. The thought formed, and he was free, wrapping his muscular arms around her shoulders. Exhaling, she opened her eyes with a smile, safe in the arms of her dream man.

Alex's laughter shattered her euphoria. "That was awesome. Really. I'm glad you've tapped into your power, Layla-love. There's so much more to feed on now." He opened his fists, letting an ooze seep from his fingertips.

"I'll drain you both," other-worldly, his voice carried on from the evil mist.

Sebastian's arms locked around her chest, no longer under his control. As her life force faded, she wondered how she never noticed how Alex reeked of the Filth.

Chapter Twenty

Sebastian struggled against the Filth. One second, he was hugging his mate; the next, he was shoved to the back of his own psyche, a prisoner in his body. This time, the mist invaded his mind before he could even recognize its presence. And now it was inside him, clamping his arms down on Layla, draining her energy.

His body jerked as he battled the thing within. He would not let Alex or this evil mist harm Layla. In his mind, he saw the thing dart toward the spark of his connection with his mate. This was all mental, and he was an empath with a scary mind, as Layla so kindly put it. He imagined choking a shadow, snuffing out the muck, and for an instant, he nearly ejected the Filth from his psyche. It slithered back.

Then the evil empath stepped closer, dropping his psychic shields. At once, the emotional void Sebastian had come to associate with Alex was replaced by a malevolence so strong, he wondered how a single man could contain it. He thought back to the time when he first met the young actor. For one second of that restaurant meeting, Sebastian thought he witnessed something other-worldly about Alex. He glimpsed the ancient evil. If only he heeded that instinct, he wouldn't be the instrument draining power from his mate now. Wickedness poured out of the man, stemming from the invading mist.

Alex's laugh turned into a sneer, the college-boy persona gone. Veins pulsed in his forehead, nostrils flared, and his upper lip curled into a snarl. "You think to throw out my essence?" He focused his glowing, red eyes and sent wave after wave of hatred burning into Sebastian's skull.

Whatever small ground Sebastian gained in pushing back the Filth vanished as his subconscious became inundated by Alex's true nature. He felt himself slipping into an abyss of the cloying mist, shackled by the empath's evil. His traitorous arms squeezed tighter around Layla, sucking the goodness out of her.

He would soon be obliterated, lost in the Filth, but until then, he would fight to help his mate. Drawing on the love still beating in his Filth-encased heart, he concentrated on moving the muscles in his arms. *Let go!* He commanded his limbs. With a mental scream, he wrenched his arms apart and Layla fell to the floor.

"Not yet!" Alex leapt over Allora's twitching form, rushing to the wind guardian.

Layla drew in a ragged breath, her chest heaving. She was still alive.

The spark of their connection glowing again in his mind's eye, Sebastian switched his focus to keep the evil from accessing the only remaining link to his mate. The shadow crept along the edges of the spark, and Sebastian fought back, using his love for Layla to fuel his defense.

"We're not done here!" Alex bent over the wind guardian, reaching his fingers out to her. Stopping short of touching her, he stood to face his fellow empath nose-to-nose. *Pick her up. The draining must continue.*

Sebastian's brain itched and he felt compelled to obey the command. The Filth invaded more of his body, squeezing his lungs, forcing him to breathe when it wanted, and unclenching the fists he readied for Alex. He ignored the intrusion, concentrating on keeping the evil mist away from the connection with his mate. That bond helped him resist the other empath.

The little spark grew into a flame. Her essence pulsed in his psyche, and as she grew stronger, he understood why Alex was so desperate to possess his mate. No doubt Layla was a beautiful, good soul; she was also the source of immense empathic power. With every beat of her heart, every renewing breath she drew, he felt his own being re-energize. She fed his empathy.

Soon, Alex's full emotions, and all of his thoughts were laid bare to Sebastian's growing powers. Fear mingled with the hatred. And the director could hear the elusive actor's thoughts as clearly as any other person. *I must destroy them or we cannot plunge the earth into—* "Enough!" Alex shoved away, and his emotions and thoughts were shielded yet again.

Without Alex's maddening emotions to aid its invasion, the Filth became no more dangerous than the flu to Sebastian's mated psyche. Drawing from the power

Layla offered, he ejected the mist from his body and lifted his mate into his arms just as Alex grabbed the prayer sphere.

"I can't touch the wind guardian," the evil one shrugged down at Allora. "This bonding business has strengthened her more than I imagined. But I'm not done with the clay ball yet. So much destruction, so little time." College boy charm back in place, he began to back out of the room.

Layla's eyes opened. "Give me back my prayer sphere, you perverted, cocky, little twerp before I blow you into the next town." She leaned on her mate, her life force still rebuilding itself.

"Blow me?" The juvenile smirk lit up his features as he kissed the air in her direction. "Would you? Please? Oh, but that's not what you meant, huh? Sweetie, you're still not strong enough to blow me anywhere. Save it." His voice hardened as he narrowed his eyes. "You're going to need that feisty attitude when we're done with this world." He held out his free hand and the Filth consolidated back into a pile of sludge, oozing from his fingers.

We have to stop him. She leaned back into Sebastian's chest, inhaling as she raised her arms.

Alex was right about one thing. Partially drained, Layla wouldn't be strong enough to stir more than a gentle breeze. But together...

Hands around her waist, Sebastian closed his eyes and sought the flame of their connection. He sent everything he had left into his mate. And instead of weakening, he felt their mated bond return the same to him tenfold. The more he sacrificed, the more he gained, until she stood of her own volition and he was fully healed, both bursting with power.

Hair orbiting her head in a floating crown, Super-Layla rose into the air. Wind shot from her fingertips as she directed a gale to hit the evil empath, knocking him off his feet.

Snarling, Alex clutched the sphere to his chest and narrowed his eyes at the woman. Sebastian felt the empath's intrusive mind tearing at their connection at the same moment Layla grabbed her head.

Alex opened his mind to all the souls around them. As dozens of Capitol Hill's personalities crashed into his thoughts, he funneled the pain into Layla and Sebastian. The elemental collapsed into her mate's arms, screaming.

"Stop or you'll kill us all!" Sebastian yelled above the noise in their heads. He pictured the iron wall again, reaching for the essence of his mate, trying to pull her into his protection.

Tears of blood streamed down Alex's ashen cheeks, and he smiled through a grimace. "I've finally found a way to kill the little bitch." He stumbled to the floor, eyelids fluttering. "She would have made the perfect mate. But nooo, couldn't have that, could we? If I can kill just one you—one of Ceiba's elementals—this will be worth it."

More souls joined the dozens already clawing into Sebastian's psyche. He couldn't block them all out, and Alex magnified the agony as he lay writhing on the floor.

Layla lifted her head and reached for her mate's hand. He felt her tug at their connection as she brought her hands in front of her. She knew she had to kill Alex. He felt the realization course through her with a pang of regret, and understood they both pictured defeating a nameless mist when they entered this battle. Neither of them was prepared to end a human life. Sebastian steadied his mate for the inevitable as she crawled to the man radiating death.

She frowned. *I can't do this.*

Alex's blood-filled eyes widened, and he extended his empathic reach, bringing more thoughts, more intrusions, more agony into their brains. All three sank with the onslaught. "Worth it," he whispered.

Sebastian refused to let Layla die with this scum. *There is no choice.* He mentally redirected Alex's assault back at the evil one, redoubling the force of the pain.

Layla inhaled, pulling the oxygen from the air around Alex. The blood-eyed man sputtered, gasping for breath. As he filled his lungs for the last time, he screeched with the symphony of suffering Sebastian poured into him. The black mist rose from his body, flew into the air, and retreated out the open window. Alex sagged, the prayer sphere rolling from his dead hands.

Silence, blessed silence. The voices were gone.

Sebastian moved to his mate, enveloping her in his arms. She pulled the prayer sphere into her lap and they sat, rocking on her bedroom rug.

The sphere lifted into the air, spinning as it glowed.

Epilogue

A year later, Leesburg, Va.

Green silk brushed across Ceiba's ankles as she glided in a waltz with her son. She had already done the mother-son dance with him at his first wedding. This time, however, was infinitely sweeter now that Sebastian had married his true mate.

"You look pleased with yourself." He smiled down at her as he turned them into another twirl on the makeshift dance floor in the sunflower fields of her horse farm.

"I am pleased with my sons. You have all done well for yourselves."

"A professor, an entrepreneur, and a computer programmer. Yeah, my brothers are doing well." The dimple in his right cheek appeared. That little indentation only came out when he was truly happy.

"As usual, you downplay your own efforts. I am proud of you for reasons having nothing to do with your career. Besides, your theatre is a success, and you know it."

He raised his eyebrows. "Mom, I started Armageddon

with my last play. And it didn't even make it to the stage."

"*Ch'inyay!* This is supposed to be a happy day. Stop blaming yourself. The end of this world would have begun with or without you." She stepped away as the song ended, pushing her overly serious son to his gorgeous new wife. "Now, go have some fun with your bride."

She watched her son's guilt dissipate as he took his mate's hands in his and pulled her close. That pair had certainly gotten lucky. While a bit of skill and a lot of destined power helped them defeat the Filth—Malc—*this* time, only happenstance prevented them from going to jail.

An autopsy showed Alex's death was caused by a massive aneurism. When Allora Delaney came to, she could not stop babbling about Incan spells and her ancestors' plan. An especially motivated tabloid reporter dug up her internet history and found the ransom notes she forged. Allora was now undergoing treatment for a mental breakdown. No one believed her claims about an elemental trying to kill her with the wind, and Officer Brull had enough sense to keep his mouth shut.

Of course, Sebastian's theater was at the center of the scandal. A sudden death, an A-list actress' demise, and a script that mysteriously disappeared added up to create the kind of publicity money couldn't buy. Season tickets were sold out for the next three years, and her son was able to break all ties with sleazy producers and other money-lenders. The big downside was the paparazzi snapping photos everywhere the beautiful couple went.

And they weren't the only ones being harassed. Once the tabloids found out Sebastian's twin was the one kissing Allora in that article, they went after him as well. Ceiba saw more than one photo of her boy flipping his middle finger on the cover of a supermarket tabloid. She would have to talk to him about that. But not today.

She made her way to the groomsmen's table where Trystan sat sulking. "This is a wedding, child," she admonished. "Raise your cheer."

The corners of his mouth lifted. Trystan always liked hearing her deliver an American euphemism incorrectly. "You mean, 'cheer up.' This is as high as my cheer goes." He crossed his arms, watching the couple of the night gliding across the dance floor. "I hope you get double prints of these wedding pictures, Mom. Frame a set and put my name on them, 'cause I'm never getting married."

"Trystan, you must find your mate—"

"Mom, I get there's more to the old stories than we thought. I'm not like Benjamin or Roman, I believe you. I believe my twin. But there's no way I can trust a woman again. Not after Allora slept with me and then tried to steal my sister-in-law's spirit or essence or whatever." He reached for the dark beer on the table.

Ceiba pursed her lips and watched the boy. There was no point in arguing. He would find his way when he was ready. He stared at the sky as he sipped his drink.

Suddenly, his eyes went round. "What the hell?"

A fire ball as large as a car went sailing through the clouds, close enough to make its heat felt by all. Guests pointed and screeched. The horses stamped and whinnied as terror of the unnatural event seized them.

Trystan gulped his beer, shaking his head. "I'll see to the animals." Drink still in hand, he made his way from the ceremony down to the stables as Layla and Sebastian tried to calm their friends and family.

Ceiba sighed. Trystan's mate must have given away her prayer sphere already. Gods and goddesses willing, he and the fire guardian would find their way in time. Picking her way through the wreckage, she hid behind the overturned altar, lifted her arms, and sifted her way to London, vanishing in a poof of silk and lilac.

Thank You

Thank you for reading *Layla's Gale, Book 2* of the *Elemental Myths* series. If you enjoyed this novel, please take a moment to leave a review so that others may read it, too.

Thank you so much! I really appreciate it!

XOXO,
Nicole

About the Author

Still amazed to be an adult, Nicole has managed to center her life on raising her two small sons and being true to her family (including husband and friends). She resides in Bellevue, Washington where she runs a marketing agency. Happiest near the water, Nicole spends her free hours plotting her next escape, writing, and staring at the ceiling.

Website
www.NicolePouchet.com

Social Media
Goodreads: https://www.goodreads.com/NPouchet
Twitter: @NPouchet
Facebook: www.Facebook.com/NicolePouchet
Pinterest: http://www.pinterest.com/NPouchet/

Acknowledgements

Many thanks to the Difference Press team for originally bringing this book to the readers' eyes. I love your brain, Angela Lauria!

Thank you to both of this book's editors, The Editor Fairy and Kris Kane.

I'd like to acknowledge Caitlin Alexander and her Master Novel Writing Class at Media Bistro. I'll never forget the supportive, creative writing environment you created or the initial touches you put on this novel to steer it in the right direction.

To Melanie Kidd, thank you for listening and being you.

And last but definitely not least, thank you to my husband and family for allowing me time to write. Yes, that novel is coming along quite nicely.

Books by Nicole Pouchet

Elemental Myths Series:

Ceiba's Grace (Book 1)
Layla's Gale (Book 2)
Annie's Defiance (Book 3)
Cadence's Cauldron (Book 4-coming soon)

Decadent Publishing's _Beyond Fairytales_ Series:

Trapped by a Song